THE CHINA CONSPIRACY

Kick back and enjoy!

P. m. terrell

THE CHINA CONSPIRACY

Published by Drake Valley Press
Clinton, Mississippi, USA 39060
1-866-442-4990
www.drakevalleypress.com

ISBN 0-9728186-2-6 (Hardcover)
ISBN 0-9728186-3-4 (Soft cover)

Library of Congress Cataloging-in-Publication Data applied for

Printed in the United States of America

10 9 8 7 6 5 4 3 2 1

Author's website: www.pmterrell.com

DEDICATION

Dedicated to Donald Terrell, Jr., the kind of son all mothers hope for, and I'm fortunate enough to have.

ACKNOWLEDGEMENTS

This book could not have been possible without a great many people, particularly in the law enforcement community. Special thanks to:

Master Detective Kevin Bacon and Major James Bourque of the Chesterfield, Virginia Police Department;

Rebecca Brown, Editor and Publisher of *RebeccasReads.com* and author of *Standing the Watch: Memories of a home death*;

Don, the best husband a gal could have;

Robert C. Ferland of L. C. Bird Skyhawk Band in Chesterfield, Virginia, for helping Tim come to life;

Officer Mark Kearney of the Waynesboro, Virginia Police Department;

Officer Tom Kifer of the Colonial Heights, Virginia Police Department;

My good friend and thriller expert, Karen Luffred;

My father and head cheerleader, John W. Neelley, Sr.;

My daughter-in-law Stacy Franklin Robinson for her EMA research and expertise;

A CIA operative known simply as "Shadow";

Retired Sergeant Marc Woolverton of the Manassas, Virginia Police Department;

The Virginia Crime Stoppers Association.

CHAPTER 1

—

U
nbelievable," the news anchor announced, shaking his head, "with eighty percent of the returns in, it's safe to say that the Commonwealth of Virginia has just elected its first Independent Governor."

"And what a surprise this is," his co-anchor chirped, a tremor of excitement in her voice. "None of the opinion polls gave any indication that Theodore Stallworth was even a serious contender in this race."

"Obviously, Virginia voters were ready for a dramatic change…"

Bernard Emerson watched the television anchors' bantering, his cheeks flush with a bittersweet mixture of amusement and irritation. Why did they have to make such a big deal over Stallworth's win?

He patted his pockets, quickly locating his cigarettes, but became frustrated searching for his lighter. Finally finding it, his hands shook as he lit his cigarette. It was too damn cold in this room, even with the Swedish fireplace roaring in the center.

He stepped to the window and peered out at the darkening sky. Under any other circumstances, he wouldn't be caught dead at a ski resort. His idea of a vacation was warm water and warmer sand, the kind he had to run across before it burned the soles of his feet. The last thing he'd ever do for recreation is drive up some God-forsaken mountain just for the chance to freeze his buns on a snow-covered slope.

Thank God he was here before the ski season, before the spotty manmade snow was more than an inch deep. Only a few hours from Washington, DC, it felt as though he were on another planet; gone were the crowds, the traffic congestion, and the noise—all the things he loved—and in its place, were thousands of skeletal trees silhouetted against a gloomy sky, interrupted here and there by deserted trails that would undoubtedly be filled with skiers in a few short weeks.

His eyes followed the thick cables that ran from a clearing near the lodge to the top of the closest mountain. The ski lift had been running since he'd arrived almost an hour earlier, the shiny metal on the empty seats glinting in the soft, cloud-enshrouded moonlight.

He finished his smoke and reached for another. His contact should have been here already, and he should have been well on his way back to Washington by now.

He zipped up his jacket, pulling the thin nylon down over his massive belly. Impatiently, he stepped outside and crossed the deck to a platform overlooking the nearest slopes.

He watched as a worker descended on the slow-moving ski lift, his head bowed toward his chest as though he were bracing against the wind, his blue knit cap pulled low on his head, his hands jammed in his pockets. As the man drew nearer, Bernard nervously took another long drag. He had the distinct impression that the rider was watching him. The man remained motionless and although Bernard nodded his head, he didn't return the acknowledgement.

A moment later, he was out of sight behind the refreshment stand. Bernard wandered across the deck to the other side of the lodge. He'd give this guy another five minutes, ten tops, and then he was out of here. Shivering in the cold in the middle of nowhere wasn't part of the bargain.

He felt an anxiety that began in the pit of his stomach and worked its way up to his scalp. It was almost as though there were eyes piercing his shoulder blades, watching his every move, and yet there was nothing but an eerie stillness surrounding him. Even the television was silent.

He flicked the butt off of the deck. He was getting out of here. He whirled around and gasped involuntarily as he came face to face with the man on the lift.

"Where is she?"

Bernard hesitated. The cap was pulled tight over the man's forehead, covering part of his eyebrows, and in the darkness he couldn't quite see his eyes, only a set of dark sockets. "Couldn't make it. She sent me instead."

"I wanted her."

Bernard took a sideways step toward the lodge. "I'll let her know; she can arrange—"

The man blocked his path. "I wanted her, but I'll take you." He motioned for Bernard to step in front. Bernard awkwardly walked to the other side of the lodge, the man only a footstep behind. As they rounded the corner, the stranger pointed with a gloved finger toward the mountaintop. "Up there."

Bernard stopped. "Why?"

In the moonlight, he could see a hint of cold gray eyes and a chiseled jaw. "That's where the money is.

That's what you came for, isn't it?"

Bernard swallowed. "That was the deal. Half up front—"

"And half when the deed is done."

Bernard hesitated. He could see a hint of smoke on the horizon, the telltale sign of a fireplace. He couldn't quite put his finger on it, but something wasn't right.

An empty lift rolled slowly toward them; he knew in another moment it would circle around and begin its ascent. He looked around, but saw no one else.

"Everyone's up there," the man said.

Bernard nodded and stepped to his right as the lift made the circle around the building. After a moment that seemed all too brief, the chair caught him at the knees and he leaned back, settling into the seat. He instinctively reached up to pull the bar down. The man's hand caught him at the wrist, halting him in midair.

"I was just going to lower—"

"It's broken."

Bernard moved his hand slowly down to his side and tried not to think about the chair moving further and further from the ground.

"This your first time here?"

He nodded.

"Not a skier, I take it."

"No."

The man slid his hands into wide hand warmer pockets on the front of his jacket and leaned back while Bernard clutched at the metal arm on the seat. He felt his knuckles growing cold and clammy, as the trees grew smaller. Without wanting to, he found himself gauging the distance to the ground as they climbed ever higher. The top of the mountain seemed a long way off.

"Ever see them make snow before?" the man asked calmly.

"No."

He motioned to a set of machines below.

"They'll have about sixty, seventy inches total on the ground come springtime."

Bernard wished he had the nerve to let go of the lift long enough to light a cigarette.

"You know what that means, don't you, Bernard Gordon Emerson?"

He froze, a cold sweat breaking out across his brow.

"It means they won't find your body until spring."

Bernard jerked his head toward the man, catching a momentary glimpse of his right hand leaving his jacket. Instinctively, he threw his left arm in the air, partially covering his face as if he could ward off some unseen danger. The man's right arm met his, and in the blink of an eye, his steely arm raised Bernard's weaker one, pulling it above his head.

His throat constricted in terror as the man's left hand swung around to his forehead, revealing a twenty-two-caliber revolver. Two explosions erupted from the barrel, and Bernard's head jerked backward.

As if in slow motion, the man reached to the seat beside him and picked up a half-empty box of Camels and flicked them over the side of the lift. "Don't you know smoking is bad for you?"

Then Bernard was tumbling out of the lift like a marionette, his body brutally slamming against the frozen ground. His final gasp was drowned out by the roar of the machines, slowly and systematically covering him with a cloud of manmade snow.

CHAPTER 2

—

Kit Olsen once read that as many as 43,000 vehicles traveled along Washington Boulevard from Interstate 395 every weekday, taking them right past her building. Some would notice the imposing black glass structure, but most would drive past it every day, their attention riveted inward, their minds never even registering the bold blue sign announcing Universal Computer Technologies. But of all those who passed it and countless others who lived within its eye, only a select few would ever know UCT was an outpost for the CIA, while the CIA Headquarters, situated a few short minutes away at Langley, would garner all the attention. A minute number would ever be allowed a glimpse inside, and only a chosen few would know exactly what transpired within its walls.

On the afternoon before Thanksgiving Day, Kit idly thumped her pencil against the top of her desk as she gazed out the window at the cars below. For seventeen years, she'd watched that traffic on Interstate 395, sometimes racing past and sometimes slowed to a crawl. Today it was grid locked, as she imagined every road out of Washington would be. Her own trip home to suburban Springfield wouldn't begin for another hour.

It was times like this that she missed her childhood home in Chesterfield County, a hundred miles south. Traffic jams were a rarity there, and people weren't crowded like sardines in a tin can.

A quick rap at her door jostled her from her thoughts. Without waiting for a response, Joan Newcomb sailed into the room, breezing past Kit's desk and stopping in front of the floor-to-ceiling windows.

"Any word?" Kit asked.

Joan shook her head. "Bernie's been gone almost three weeks. His wife says she hasn't heard from him. He just vanished, leaving her and the kids. No note, nothing."

Joan had never referred to Bernard Emerson by his given name, preferring a nickname no one else used. The air of intimacy wasn't lost on Kit, even though she knew Bernard and Joan were too dramatically different to have ever been romantically linked. "Do you believe her?" Kit asked.

Joan shrugged. "Rush hour's a nightmare, and he's lying on some beach right now getting a suntan."

"How do you know that?"

"He talked about it often enough. It's all he wanted to do when he retired, lie on the beach and soak up rays and alcohol."

"But disappearing isn't retiring."

Joan slammed her fist into the glass so hard Kit feared it might crack. "You don't know enough about the situation."

"You're right; I don't."

Kit had enough experience with her volatile coworker to know when to back off. In fact, there were few that would dare cross Joan. They'd been different people when they were growing up next door to one another. While Joan practiced her cheerleading, Kit studied computer science. But after attending Virginia Commonwealth University together, Joan went to the northeast, where she shed her Southern accent and breeding, while Kit clung stubbornly to her lilting Virginia accent and Southern customs.

When they were reunited seventeen years ago, they'd both joined the inner circle of the CIA in what appeared to be mundane computer positions. Even though Kit could write code Joan couldn't even dream of, she'd stayed put while Joan had swiftly risen up the ladder. Now her UCT business card listed her title as Vice President, a role she played to the hilt.

Not that Kit much minded. She worked with programs so intriguing she thought it was a crying shame she'd never be able to tell another living soul about them.

"You're being reassigned," Joan said.

"I'm in the middle of a project."

"I'll tell Jack to delegate it."

"That doesn't make any sense."

Joan raised her left brow. "I need you on this one. You'll be working with Chen Ling."

"Chen?"

Kit barely heard Joan's response. Chen worked in an area that was off limits to most employees. In a building where security was a fact of life and privacy was an unobtainable dream, Chen's office made the rest of the building seem like the news desk at CNN. It was rumored that employees reporting to his office had to pass through two heavily guarded doors, and their every move was caught on camera, the film stored indefinitely. All computers had removable hard drives, which were checked in and out every time anyone left the room. In an agency that thrived on information, they weren't allowed to have email or access to the Internet. Still, they were an elite group, the envy of every programmer in the agency.

"Report to Customs Monday morning," Joan was saying.

Customs was the nickname they all used when describing the first set of guarded doors, as if once they were passed, entry was gained to another country. Everything brought in was searched and checked at that door. Nothing passed in or out without the guards' knowledge.

Without waiting for a reply, Joan left as quickly as she'd arrived.

On the Monday after Thanksgiving, Kit tried to remain composed, but her rapid breathing and heartbeat were competing for her attention. It had been a long time since she'd experienced such excitement as she felt now.

Passing through Customs would be no walk in the park. She relinquished all her possessions at the first guard post, including, to her great disappointment, a fresh cup of perked coffee. That guard did a cursory inspection that rivaled the attentions of an overly diligent airport screener, before permitting her entry into a holding room she'd heard referred to as "Purgatory."

She remained standing in the windowless, gray room, eerily similar to a bank vault, until another guard motioned her through a separate door and inspected her yet again. This time, she was subjected to imaging equipment that meticulously scanned her entire body. To her amusement, a hairline fracture she'd received while skiing and that had healed imperfectly was even visible.

Then came the retinal scan and the DNA test: a brief second of peering through a camera, followed by a swab of the inside of her cheek. A supercomputer interpreted the results in seconds, comparing it to her personnel records, and she was cleared to continue.

All this technology wasn't new, although it was continuously updated. There'd been some talk in Homeland Security of getting the equipment approved for use in the nation's airports, but that was years away. Even if it passed, the public would never know the technology had been developed by the CIA. For over a decade, a version of it was even in use via satellite, which could not only spot a dog anyplace on earth day or night, but could also view every bone in its body.

Finally, she was directed to the end of the corridor, where she stopped at huge brushed steel doors. As if on cue, a barely audible buzz sounded and the doors parted, sliding into the walls on either side. A slight, dark-haired young man with intense green eyes extended his hand. As she grasped it and stepped forward, he said, "I'm pleased to meet you. I'm Chen Ling."

Before Kit could respond, he started down another hall as the door closed behind them. Cameras mounted near the ceiling emitted a low hum as the cameras rotated, following their movements. At the end of the corridor, Kit and Chen were subjected to a second retinal scan and another set of doors slid open.

The room was circular and the walls a dull gray, like a cross between a dreary day and a farm silo. Two desks were located in the middle, facing each other. Chen approached one, where stacks of computer printouts flanked a desktop computer. He pulled up a chair and motioned for Kit to take the other chair beside him.

Kit was accustomed to receiving fresh stacks of computer printouts on a regular basis. Her job was not to question their origin or the path they'd taken before reaching her desk. It was simply to determine the purpose of the program and to write a report. Sometimes, the report was a single paragraph and the program was a run-of-the-mill set of lines that a teenager could have written. Other times, far less frequently, the reports were long and detailed. Sometimes, she could tell fairly easily that the program had been intercepted, usually from Asia or Russia and occasionally from Israel or the Middle East, but that never made it into her reports. She simply stated the program's purpose, nothing more and nothing less.

This time, however, the code was obviously in a different language.

"I'm fluent in Putonghua and Mandarin," Chen said, as if in answer to her thoughts. "Our assignment is to go through this code as a team, line by line. With me translating the language and you interpreting the code, we can make some sense out of it."

"This question might be as obvious as a headlight," Kit said, "but I understand you're a crack programmer. Why do you need me?"

"I'm fluent in more recent programming languages. This is about twenty years old, but it's still in use."

"Twenty years ago," Kit said, "the Chinese government officially proclaimed the Cultural Revolution a disaster."

"Yes."

"And western programming languages were adopted in the development of some applications," she continued.

"You know your Chinese history."

"Just a little. I also know that the pinyin system distorts a lot of programming terminology…"

"Which is why 'Peking' is a western word for 'Beijing'," he finished.

"I don't know if I'll be able to figure out the pinyin in this code."

"Don't worry about that. I'll translate the text into English, and help with the pinyin system, as well."

"So you get it to the front door, and I take it to the barn, is that it?"

He chuckled. "That's it."

"How old are you?"

He appeared a bit taken aback by this question. "Twenty-six, why?"

"Just curious. This is an uncommon language for someone raised in America. You *were* raised in America?"

He nodded.

"This isn't like taking Spanish in high school."

There was an awkward moment of silence before he said, "My mother is American, my father, Chinese. They fled China during the Cultural Revolution. My father received political asylum here. You'll find I'm fluent in a number of languages."

Kit pulled her chair closer to the printouts. "Well, what are we waiting for? Let's get this show on the road."

CHAPTER 3

≡

Carter Leigh leaned his chair against the wall and cracked his knuckles. The secretary glanced up, her lips curving ever so slightly before returning to her paperwork. Across the room, Carter's cameraman, Bryce, chatted with his girlfriend on his cell phone.

Carter was early, in keeping with his reputation. Governor-elect Stallworth was running late, in keeping with his. It was Stallworth's first in-depth interview after winning the election. The day after his landslide victory, he'd spoken a few carefully constructed statements for the press corps who'd covered his campaign, and then he'd whisked his family off to the Bahamas for two weeks. He'd returned only last night. And Carter Leigh, a reporter for NBC, Channel 4 in Washington, was awarded the coveted honor, over the *Post*, the *New York Times* and *Newsweek*, of interviewing him first.

Carter hadn't time to gloat. Not yet anyway. He was too busy reciting the astronaut's prayer when the door to Stallworth's office opened.

"Carter," Stallworth said, stepping briskly across the room and extending his hand.

"Sir."

Stallworth motioned him into his office. Carter stole a quick glance at Bryce, who quickly ended his conversation and grabbed his equipment.

"How was your trip?" Carter asked as they converged in his office.

"Good. I needed the rest."

"Lighting's good over here," Bryce said, motioning toward a broad window overlooking a wooded knoll.

Carter pulled two chairs in front of the window. Once they were situated, they waited for the signal from Bryce.

Carter opened with his standard spiel, introducing himself and his guest, and then turned to Stallworth for his opening question. It had been a long road. When he'd first received the assignment to accompany Stallworth on the campaign trail, he'd been infuriated. After sixteen years as an NBC reporter, he should have been covering Marc Johnson, a Democrat with thirty years in Virginia politics, or Patrick Wellesly, a newcomer Republican from Vermont who many thought had a good chance of winning. Instead, he was assigned to Theodore Stallworth. Granted, he was a native Virginian, born and raised in McLean, and the multi-millionaire owner of an aerospace company, but he was a political neophyte, a man no one had expected to win.

The early days had been downright depressing. Sometimes there'd been more reporters present than constituents. But to Stallworth's credit, he'd always given a rip-roaring speech, whether he had a hundred onlookers or three. And then something began to happen.

The change had been subtle, at least in the beginning. A couple of dozen people when once there'd been three. Then there'd been fifty, and then a hundred, and by the end of the summer there had been too many to count.

In the weeks after Stallworth announced his decision to run, the polls put him in the single digits, while Johnson and Wellesly ran neck-n-neck. The attack ads were confined to the two major parties, the third opponent going virtually unnoticed until mid-summer. By then he was at 29% in the polls and closing, but no one thought he'd be able to pull it off. No one, perhaps, except Stallworth.

The night before the election, Wellesly had slipped to 20%, largely due to Johnson's vicious attacks on the campaign trail and in the media. Johnson was way out front with 40%, and Stallworth was at 32%. The rest were still undecided.

Still, Carter and the rest of the press were resigned to a victory speech by Johnson, probably early in the evening, followed by the standard conciliatory speeches by Wellesly and Stallworth. Carter made plans for a late dinner with an old friend. It would be over by ten o'clock, at the latest.

No one was more shocked when the early figures came back with Stallworth out front. Not by a slim margin, but running away with the election. It was Johnson who was caught off guard, Johnson's victory party that was smashed to pieces by the realization that he'd been whipped soundly at the polls.

And it was Stallworth who stood at the podium at precisely 11:15 to give his victory speech.

He'd been the only one to take his victory in stride, not appearing to be surprised at all that he'd garnered 47% of the vote to Johnson's 36% and Wellesly's 17%. In fact, Stallworth acted as if he'd always known he would win, that there had never been a doubt in his mind, even when there'd been many in everyone else's.

Now Carter went through the normal routine of questions on how Stallworth proposed to balance the budget, his plans for the elderly, how he intended to improve the schools, and his position on crime. And Stallworth answered each question without skipping a beat, without batting an eye. He was so uncontroversial that the interview was in jeopardy of being downright boring.

"What happens after the governorship?" Carter asked as they began to wind down.

Stallworth chuckled. "I don't know. I'm not looking beyond the next four years at the moment."

"You're aware this election has received national attention," Carter prodded. "There are those who think you're headed to the White House."

There was a spark of interest in Stallworth's eyes, a gleam Carter had seen too many times before in politicians too ambitious to stop with local politics. A gleam he knew was too subtle for the camera to catch. He needed a statement, a sound bite for tonight's evening news.

But Stallworth wasn't going to be trapped into a statement before he was ready, and the interview ended as it had begun, on a polite and lackluster note. As Carter gathered his notes and Bryce packed his equipment, he felt a pang of disappointment. He found himself wishing that the next reporter, and the one after that, wouldn't glean anything else out of him. Nothing earth shattering, anyway.

"Don't look so down," Stallworth said, resting his hand on his shoulder. "When I'm ready to drop a bombshell on the public, you'll be the first reporter I'll call."

"I'll hold you to that." When Stallworth didn't respond, Carter continued, "Sure you don't want to comment on any national news? The rising gas prices, high unemployment rate, rising tensions with Russia, kids starving in China—"

"What about kids starving in China?" he snapped.

Carter took a step back, stunned by the tension in his voice. "What about it?"

"Who's fault do you think that is?"

The room fell deadly silent. Carter could sense Bryce frozen in place, his camera already turned off and secured. He could feel Bryce's indecision as he weighed whether to grab his camera, open the lens, and point it at Stallworth before it was too late.

"Who's fault do *you* think it is?" Carter asked quietly.

Stallworth marched to the door as if he hadn't heard him, opened it, and turned to shake his hand. The anxiety was gone and in its place was the politician from the campaign trail, the face fixed into a warm smile, a smile that, until now, had always seemed sincere.

"What the hell happened back there?" Carter said as he stepped into the bright sunlight.

"You obviously hit a hot button," Bryce said, while they exchanged questioning glances.

"Yeah." Carter hesitated only a moment before stepping onto the sidewalk. "You can bet I'll try that again."

"Do it when the cameras are rolling next time, okay?"

"Right." They reached the van and Carter settled into the front seat while he waited for Bryce to secure his equipment in the back. "Why would starving kids in China make him act like that?" he mused.

"You saying something up there?"

"Forget it," he replied. But even as the words rolled off his tongue, he knew he couldn't forget it. Not if he wanted that sound bite.

CHAPTER 4

四

Kit closed the agency-issued laptop case, and set it on the floor in front of her desk as she struggled with the anger welling up inside her. It had been two weeks since she'd started working with Chen, and Jack still hadn't reassigned her other duties or extended the deadlines, as Joan had promised. Her inbox had long since overflowed with all the new projects that continued to pour in.

No wonder she was dreaming about computer code.

Not to mention the guilt she was feeling. Oh, Frank could cook as well as she, and he was so married to his job that she didn't think he'd noticed that she hadn't been around much lately. No, it was Tim she was concerned about. Not that he'd given her anything to worry about. He was a good kid, ideal really, not into drugs or drinking, and very conscientious about his grades. He deserved better than to have two absentee parents.

She glanced at her watch. Tim would be at a high school football game now, and would probably grab a hot dog and soda there. She consoled herself with the knowledge that she'd get home long before he did.

She was jamming paperwork into her briefcase when there was a quick rap at the door.

"Glad I caught you," Joan said.

Kit glanced up long enough to catch a glimpse of her friend breezing into the room, her laptop case weighing down her shoulder.

"I need you to do a quick program for me," Joan said, sitting in the chair across from Kit's desk, her laptop and briefcase hitting the floor with a simultaneous thick thud.

Kit placed her hands on her hips. "You've got to be kidding."

"It'll only take you a couple of hours."

"Get real. When was the last time you saw a program take 'only a couple of hours'?"

"What's wrong with you?" Joan asked, absent-mindedly wrapping her fingers through the chunky silver bracelet that never left her wrist, a medical bracelet that served as a constant reminder of her diabetes.

Kit watched her for a few seconds and then finished shoving paperwork into her briefcase. "I'm overworked as it is," she complained. "You said when I started working with Chen, my other work would be reassigned."

"And it will."

"When? After it's done?"

"Next week. I promise. I'll talk to Jack." Joan tossed a stack of papers onto Kit's desk. "Take a look at this. Let me know tomorrow how much time it'll take."

Kit skimmed the material. "There are a hundred programmers here. Why are you giving this to me?"

"You're the best." Joan stood up and buttoned her coat. "How's your project going with Chen?"

"Slowly. I can't make heads or tails out of the programming code."

"You will."

"Yeah? Well, at this point, I haven't the faintest idea what it's supposed to be doing."

Joan grabbed her laptop and briefcase. "Let's get a drink."

"Can't."

"Why not?"

"I've got to get home."

Joan shrugged, and when she spoke, she sounded uncharacteristically resigned. "See you tomorrow then."

"You bet."

She waited until Joan's footsteps had faded down the hallway before reaching for her coat. Joan had been a good friend over the years, but right now Kit's nerves were on edge. She'd taken on too much work. Or maybe she wasn't up to the challenge of deciphering this Chinese code.

Or maybe she did need a drink.

She hesitated. They used to be so close. They'd shared everything in college—clothes, food, even secrets. But in the past year, they'd drifted apart, their personal conversations becoming scarce, as work-related issues took over. They'd gone from two good friends to a manager and a subordinate.

She struggled to close her briefcase, cramming the few papers inside that seemed determined to poke haphazardly out of the top. If she hurried, maybe she could catch up with Joan and go for that drink after all. She'd call Frank from her cell phone, and she'd still be home before Tim.

She slung the laptop strap over her shoulder and took off down the hall.

The hallways were eerily silent, the lobby empty. It felt like only a moment ago when the halls had been filled with voices and idle chatter; now they seemed like long, narrow passages to a tomb.

She glanced toward the end of the hall. The night guard was sitting at the door to Customs, warily watching her. She wondered briefly if Chen were still hard at work. It seemed as if he was always there, always bent over mountainous piles of code.

The elevator doors opened and she stepped inside, impatiently pushing the button for the garage. Joan's little red convertible would be at the far end of the garage, in its usual reserved spot. She'd have to drive past the elevator door on her way out. Now that Kit had made up her mind to join her, she hoped she wasn't too late.

The elevator door opened, and she stepped out. At the far end of the garage, she spotted Joan's convertible. Joan was only a few steps away from the driver's door, her slender shoulders drooping with the weight of her laptop and briefcase.

Kit called out to her, and Joan turned in her direction.

At that moment, Kit heard car tires squealing as they rounded the sharp turns, and she caught a glimpse of a huge black vehicle hurtling toward Joan. "Watch out!" Kit yelled, terrified that the fast-moving SUV would mow her friend down.

Joan turned as the vehicle came at her, the brakes screeching to a halt as it neared her. Just as Kit thought she was out of danger, the back doors flung open and two men jumped out. Joan stood completely motionless as they rushed her. Only after they seized her and began dragging her to the vehicle did she begin to scream. One man threw a scarf over her head, wrapping it around her mouth as if to gag her. Her head jerked back as he quickly tied it.

The other man took hold of her legs, lifting her unceremoniously off the ground. As she began to fall, the first man grabbed her flailing arms, pulling them against her back. She writhed against them, the scarf muffling her screams. The laptop and briefcase crashed to the hard concrete floor.

Kit rushed toward them, screaming. They ignored her as they threw Joan into the back seat of the vehicle. One man snatched the laptop case and tossed it in, followed by the briefcase. Within seconds, both men were in the vehicle and it was speeding away.

As they rounded the corner near the elevator doors, Kit caught a glimpse of sandy hair under a blue knit cap, the features of a man bent over the seat, as he raised his hand in a fist. As the vehicle raced past her, the fist came down violently toward the seat. "Fight back!" Kit cried out. *"Fight back!"*

Kit rushed after the vehicle as it headed for the exit ramp. Another man with heavy black brows and thick, wavy hair stared at her through the back window. His eyes were hard and cold, the image searing into her brain.

A moment later, they were gone.

The abduction couldn't have taken more than twenty seconds. Kit peered through the garage at the red convertible. Nothing remained where her friend had been only a moment ago.

She heard the bell as the elevator doors opened behind her. She rushed past the startled faces of her coworkers, lunging for the doors before they closed. She managed to jump in, and frantically pushed the button. As the elevator whisked her upward, she pulled the cellular phone from her purse and dialed CIA security.

CHAPTER 5

五

Kit sighed. "I already told the police at my office," she said in exasperation, "I don't know of anyone who'd want to hurt Joan."

Detective Munski hesitated, his pen held a few inches above his notebook. "I know what you told them. Now I need you to tell me."

"Tell you what?"

"What about money?"

"What about it?"

"Could they have taken her for ransom?"

Kit was silent. She'd lived in the same house for more than a decade, but for some reason, everything in the room felt foreign to her now, as if she were out of place. Across the room, Frank leaned against the fireplace mantle, his narrowed eyes drifting slowly between his wife and the detective. "I suppose it's possible."

"Who would they contact?"

"I don't know," she answered. "She wasn't married, wasn't dating… not that I know of, anyway."

"Family?"

"Only child. Her father died a few years back, mother's in a nursing home. Alzheimer's. They couldn't get anything out of Joan's mom if they tried. She doesn't know half the time that Joan even exists."

"The nursing home?"

"Tipton," she replied as he jotted it down, "near Bailey's Crossroads."

"We'll pay her a visit." The detective closed his notebook and reached in his pocket. Pulling out a business card, he handed it to Kit. "Call me if you think of anything else."

She nodded.

He rose and crossed to the doorway. "And you say this was a black Chevrolet Suburban—"

"Part of the tag was 'RRJ'; I didn't catch the numbers. Thing is, with all the security at our building, I can't imagine how they got in there…"

"We'll check it out. In the meantime, you'll come down to the station and look at mug shots," he stated as if he were issuing a directive. "Arlington station on Courthouse Road. You know where it is?"

She nodded.

"I'll be expecting you."

"I'll see you out," Frank volunteered, following the detective into the entranceway. Kit heard their muffled voices as though they were a million miles away. Or maybe it was just that *she* felt a million miles away, disconnected from everything around her.

"It's my fault," she said when Frank returned.

"How do you figure that?"

"I should have gone with her. If I'd been there—"

"You *were* there," he answered, sitting on the sofa beside her and wrapping his arm around her shoulders. "If you'd been any closer, you might have been taken, too—or worse."

"I don't think they wanted me."

He leaned away from her and peered at her curiously. "Are you disappointed?"

"Don't be silly. But I'm right puzzled. I'm a witness. I got a good look at them both. Why would they leave somebody behind who could identify them?"

The telephone rang and Frank hurried down the hall toward the kitchen. She vaguely heard him answer the phone as she made her way into the front hall. She was slipping on her coat when he returned.

"Where are you going?" he asked.

"Police station. The faster I identify these goons, the better off we'll all be."

"What about Tim? He'll be home soon."

"I'll call Lisa next door, and ask her to keep an eye out for him."

"Well, I can't go with you," he said apologetically. "That was my office; I've got to go in."

"Now?"

"I'll meet up with you at the police station. I won't be long. You can get there on your own, can't you?"

"Of course I can. It's just—"

"Then I'll see you there." He gently but firmly pushed her toward the door. He gave her a small peck on the forehead as he handed her the car keys. "I'll be right behind you, I promise."

A brief moment later, she was standing on the front porch, staring at the closed door. She shivered in the cold night air, drew her coat closer to her neck, and started slowly toward the minivan.

As she walked down the sidewalk that wound its way from the front porch to the driveway, a light colored vehicle drove slowly by the house, and she found herself moving faster, her heart beginning to pound in her chest.

By the time she reached the driveway, she was almost running.

"Damn you, Frank," she muttered as she jumped in and slammed the door shut. As if things weren't bad enough, it was beginning to rain. "It's always work. Even at a time like this."

They had just turned on to Nebraska Avenue when the call came in. Carter could see his office building as he answered it, the letters "WRC-TV" illuminated on the side of the building like a beacon pulling them home. "Yeah," he said, writing down an address. "Yeah, I've got it. We're on it."

Bryce groaned. "I can't do this," he said. "Tasha's waiting for me, we've got to pick out the china tonight."

"What are you talking about?"

"The wedding, you know, we're registering at Macy's."

"What do you care what the china looks like? You can eat off anything."

"She's expecting me, you know how women are. I stand her up, and she won't let me forget it. Give me a break, man."

"Yeah, yeah," Carter replied, glancing at his watch. "Drop me off at the police station. I won't need you, anyway. I'll get a quote for the eleven o'clock news, and we can get Munski on camera in the morning."

"What's up?"

"Abduction in Arlington."

Bryce made a u-turn in the middle of the street and headed south toward Arlington. It was raining in torrents as they turned onto Courthouse Road. Carter stared out the window, watching every vehicle and studying every person entering and exiting the police station.

There was a story on every corner… the wino being taken in by the beat cop, the domestic dispute erupting on the front steps, the punk with pink hair and black leather climbing into the back seat of Dad's station wagon. Too many stories and not enough time.

Bryce slammed on his brakes. "Watch it, idiot!" he yelled as the door to a late model blue Volvo opened into traffic. The driver climbed out, too involved in a heated conversation on his cell phone to have even noticed them. "Jerk," Bryce muttered as he pulled up to the front steps.

Carter threw the door open and hopped out. "See ya tomorrow. Give my best to Tasha."

He watched as Bryce continued down the street, the white vehicle with the call letters emblazoned on the side garnering attention from passersby. Crowds always formed when the press came calling. He started up the steps, glancing to his right. The man was standing outside his Volvo now, still talking on his cell phone, his tan trench coat getting soaked by the rain, his face contorted into rage. He seemed oblivious to everything else around him.

A moment later, Carter was through the door and looking for Munski.

In her naiveté, Kit thought they would have narrowed down the suspects into a few mug shots; she'd spend all of fifteen minutes looking at them, pick out the two guys she'd seen, and Frank would be there to escort her home.

She glanced at her watch. Where was he? It had been over an hour, and there'd been no word from him. He didn't even answer his cell phone. And identifying those guys was laughable—there were more books here than she could count, each one filled with at least a hundred photos.

She glanced at her watch, and then called Lisa's house. Tim was there, watching television and complaining because he couldn't go home. After talking to him briefly, Kit acquiesced, but cautioned him to keep the door locked and the phone close by. "Sixteen going on thirty," she mumbled as she hung up the phone.

The door behind her opened. "How's it going?"

"It's not 'going' at all, but I am," she answered as Detective Munski wandered into the room. "This is downright ridiculous. I could spend the rest of my life going through pictures."

"We'll get them down to a few dozen."

She slammed the book closed and stood up. "Well, you just call me when you do."

"Listen, Mrs. Olsen," he said, his eyes wandering away from her face, "there's a reporter in the lobby. I can't keep you from talking to him, but I'm going to ask you not to."

She pulled on her coat. "That shouldn't be difficult."

"It's only one reporter; no one else has picked up on the story yet. I gave him a little something to satisfy him, not much, and you can tell him you have no comment. Fair enough?"

"Sure." She grabbed her purse. "My husband ever make it in?"

"Haven't seen him."

"Well, that's just peachy." She made her way to the door. She was suddenly very tired.

As she walked into the lobby, a man stood and made his way toward her, his eyes locked on hers as if willing her to look at him. Truth is, he wasn't right hard to look at. He stood out from the rest of the crowd. Maybe it was his height, just a bit taller than the people around him, or the way he carried himself with such confidence, or maybe it was the intensity of his dark eyes, boring into her as if she were the only person on earth.

"Kit Olsen?" he asked as he drew near.

"Yes."

"Carter Leigh. I'm with WRC-TV."

Kit glanced behind her as Detective Munski disappeared around a corner.

"You were the only witness?" Carter was saying.

"I don't know."

"You're the only one who's come forward."

Kit started to the door.

"Joan Newcomb was a friend of yours?" he continued, following her onto the front steps.

"Look, I don't have any information," she answered. Before he could reply, her cell phone rang. She turned away, grateful at last that Frank was calling.

"Honey, I'm sorry, I'm tied up here," Frank said as she answered. He seemed a bit on edge, his voice irritated.

"What's going on?"

"Big proposal due tomorrow. I thought it was finished, but we forgot something."

"Can't somebody else handle it?"

"Afraid not. Listen, sweetie, you can get home by yourself, can't you?"

"Of course I can."

"How did things go? Were you able to identify them?"

"Nope. They have hundreds of pictures here; everybody looks alike."

"Don't wait up for me. I'll be late."

"Sure."

They said their good-byes and Kit returned her phone to her purse.

"Weren't able to identify them?"

The voice startled her. "Listen—"

"Carter. Carter Leigh."

Kit pulled her hood over her head and started down the steps. "I can't give you any information."

"There were two of them, weren't there?"

She reached her car door, slid inside, and put her key in the ignition. "I can't tell you; Detective Munski asked me not to comment."

"He always does that. He knows you will, anyway."

Kit turned the key in the ignition. Instead of the minivan starting, she was met with a dull silence. She exhaled sharply.

"Car won't start?"

"Oh, it'll start. I just enjoy sitting here."

"Can I help?"

"Yes. You can leave me alone."

"You have AAA or anything?"

Kit climbed out of the driver's seat. "Look, Mr. Leigh—"

"Carter."

"Mr. Leigh, I'm standing in front of a police station. I have a cell phone. My husband and assistance is a phone call or a few steps away. I really don't need your help."

"Then let me buy you a drink."

"What?"

"You'll have to wait for a tow truck or your husband to get here. There's a place around the corner, open all night, we can have a cup of coffee or a drink where it's nice and warm, while you wait."

Kit hit the lock button and slammed the door shut. "Look, Mr. Leigh, I've had a very tough day. No offense, but the last thing on earth I want to do right now is spend my evening with a reporter."

CHAPTER 6

六

Kit almost knocked over her drink when the cell
phone rang before realizing it wasn't her phone,
but Carter's, ringing. Annoyed, she took another
sip of her coffee and wondered where Frank could be.
She'd tried calling his cell phone and his office repeatedly.
Tim hadn't heard from him as of an hour ago, when he
was getting ready for bed. Now, as the clock inched
toward midnight, she was bone tired and just wanted to
go home and get a good night's sleep. After she made
Frank acutely aware of her dissatisfaction, that is.

Carter hung up the phone. "My ride's here."

"Congratulations."

"Let me drive you home."

"No, thanks."

"I'm going your way."

Kit hesitated. He hadn't said anything even mildly
flirtatious... hadn't even probed that much into Joan's
disappearance. Instead, they'd spent a rather pleasant
two hours talking about local politics and DC in general.

"I'll have you home in half an hour," he coaxed.

He helped her with her coat and tossed a few bills on the counter. The bartender nodded but appeared too preoccupied with other patrons to pay much attention to them as they left.

"Where do you live?" Carter asked as they turned onto Interstate 395.

"Springfield. How did you know you were going my way, if you didn't know where I lived?"

"I didn't."

Despite her weariness, she smiled.

"So, where did you say your husband works?"

"Tyson's Corner."

"What kind of business is he in?"

"Insurance," Kit said. "He's the marketing director for an insurance agency. Look, no offense, but I really don't want to talk about my husband's job right now."

He shrugged. "You've got to be worried about your friend."

"Yeah." She wondered for the umpteenth time if she were dead or alive. No, she couldn't afford to think that way. If they'd wanted to kill her, they could have done that at the garage.

"Munski seems to think it was a professional job."

"Oh? Funny, he didn't mention that to me."

"Munski and I go way back." He looked at her out of the corner of his eye. "He's my sister's ex-husband."

"Well, that's convenient. You get a lot of stories this way?"

"A few."

Kit eyed him curiously. "Why would anyone want to take her?"

"I was hoping you could tell me."

"I wish I knew."

"You two were best friends?" he asked casually.

"At one time. We grew up in the same neighborhood, went to school together. We even shared a dorm room at college."

"But you're not best friends now?"

Kit sighed. "Our lives took different paths..."

"Yet you two worked together all these years."

"Not really. I mean, we worked for the same company. But we were usually on different projects."

"She was vp at your company?"

"That's right."

"She make a lot of money?"

"How would I know?"

Carter's eyes remained fixed on the road. "What other motive would there be for grabbing her?"

"Take the Franconia exit," Kit directed, changing the subject.

The subject was dropped as he navigated through the empty, silent streets toward Kit's home.

A few minutes later, they pulled in front of her house as a dark blue Volvo at the end of the driveway shut off its lights. Carter pulled up slowly behind it.

"Thank God," Kit said with a sigh of relief. "It's Frank."

They watched as a man stepped out of the car and stared at their vehicle, his eyes narrowed with a look of contempt.

"You said he worked at Tyson's?" Carter asked.

Kit started to climb out of the car and then stopped when she noticed Carter's expression. His brows were furrowed, and his lips were somewhat pursed. "What is it?" she asked.

"Nothing. I just thought I saw him tonight."

"You must be mistaken," she answered.

"Yeah. I guess so."

"Anyway, thanks for the ride," she said as she climbed out. She was too focused on Frank to notice Carter backing down the driveway. When she reached her husband and turned around, he was gone.

"I told you, my cell phone battery died," Frank said as he hung up his tie.

"I tried your office, there was no answer there, either," Kit grumbled as she climbed into bed.

"I was in the conference room. What's with the third degree? You pick that up from Detective Munster?"

"Munski." Kit pulled the covers up to her shoulders, and rolled onto her side. "I was stranded, Frank."

"Stranded at a police station. You were safe. Why didn't you call a cab?"

"I was trying to call you."

He strode across the bedroom floor toward the bathroom. He was a large man, over six feet with a barrel chest and arms a weight lifter would envy. "Were you at the police station all that time? Or out with your reporter friend?"

"He isn't my friend. He was asking questions about Joan; he was nice enough to drive me home."

"So why weren't you home two hours ago?"

Kit didn't answer. Frank let out an expletive and left the room.

The red light on the telephone was blinking, and she reached for the phone and scrolled through the caller id. Four calls from her, spaced about twenty minutes apart. And another call, from Frank's office, that came in just after Detective Munski left.

She cleared the calls, hung up the phone, and rolled back over. In less than six hours, she'd be expected at work. She hoped sleep would come quickly.

CHAPTER 7

七

Carter made sure his earpiece was in securely, and
waited for the signal that he was on the air. He
was standing where Joan had been abducted
twelve hours earlier. Just outside was Interstate 395,
already clogged with commuters on their way into DC.
Inside, the garage was eerily silent as though it were an
entire world away. He'd had a hard time getting past
security to do this segment, and as he waited for phone
calls to be made and permission granted, his curiosity
mounted and he found himself wondering how anyone
could have made it past this checkpoint and back out
again, especially if Joan were struggling in the back seat
of the vehicle. But his repeated questions went
unanswered by the security guards, who only eyed him
and his cameraman with suspicion—suspicion, Carter
thought, that obviously was one day too late.

He took a long sideways glance at two guards that
were watching them now. The sun had yet to rise, even
though the cold gray concrete blocked any entrance of
daylight. The fluorescent bulbs overhead barely
illuminated more than a few car lengths away.

Bryce switched on the camera lights, and Carter squinted in the glare.

"Light picks up the police tape," Bryce said admiringly.

Carter heard the voice in his ear, counting down the seconds. Then came Dina's voice. "Carter Leigh is at the scene now with a full report... Carter?"

"Thanks, Dina." He walked dramatically to the police tape that stretched from one cement post to another. "This is where it all happened yesterday evening, as employees of UCT left work..." He crossed to the spot where Joan's car had been parked before the police towed it as evidence. He tried to impart an air of mystery and suspense around the empty space, then walked back to the approximate location where Kit would have stood while her coworker was abducted. While he talked, he heard the familiar call in his earpiece counting down the time. He stopped a few seconds shy and waited for Dina to ask him prearranged questions, designed to look as though they were offered casually and he wasn't anticipating them. As usual, he had a ready answer.

"So there was only one eyewitness? Was he or she able to identify the men who took Ms. Newcomb?"

Carter glanced down at his notes. "Kit Olsen, one of Ms. Newcomb's coworkers, was the only witness. She was unable to identify the assailants."

"Do the police have any leads?"

"No leads and no suspects so far."

"Alright. Thank you, Carter."

The camera lights switched off and Bryce began to disassemble his equipment. Carter looked at the blank piece of paper he held in front of him. It hadn't been necessary to write down Kit's name. He remembered it all too well. He couldn't get her name or her image out of his mind all night.

Dark hair, enormous liquid brown eyes. So petite that he found himself wanting to shield her, protect her. He shook his head as if the movement could clear his mind. He had a lot of work to do.

The room was quiet, the constant hum of the ventilation system reassuring. Kit fought to stay awake as she hunched over the computer code. She'd been staring at it for hours, trying to make sense of it.

"What do you think?" Chen asked.

"It's mathematics," she said.

When he didn't respond, she continued, "A counting program of some sort. The user makes an entry, and the program counts it."

"It can't be that simple."

"It is. That's what makes it so frustrating. I've tried turning the code every which way, trying to come at it from a different angle, but it all leads right back to a simple counting program."

"What's it counting?"

"Data entry. I told you, every time the user makes an entry, the program counts it. I enter one word, it counts it. I enter another word, it adds the count to the first word. I enter sixteen words, the program tells me I have sixteen data entry lines." Kit rubbed her chin thoughtfully. "I'm telling you, the U.S. has nothing to fear from the Chinese."

"Why do you say that?" Chen asked, his voice barely above a whisper.

"They can't even add straight. Every so often, the program drops some numbers."

"What do you mean?"

"I wrote a small routine that would perform data entry for me," Kit explained, bringing up her code. "If

I set it to make one thousand entries, the Chinese system tells me I've made 996."

"How do you know your program actually made a thousand?"

"Watch this." Kit entered a few keystrokes. "I've turned on the entries, so my system would show me the count while it's entering the data. Watch the numbers."

They sat in silence as her program looped through one entry at a time while displaying a running total. When at last they had reached a thousand, Chen responded, "So?"

"So look at the Chinese program. It counted 996."

Chen looked obediently at the monitor, but Kit could tell he was somewhat disappointed—and decidedly unimpressed.

"Look, Chen, I think this one is a waste of time."

"Keep working at it."

"Keep working at what? I told you what it does."

"Find the flaw in the program."

Kit groaned. On the desk in her office was a pile that was growing taller by the minute, and she couldn't do a thing about it until she was released from this assignment. About the last thing she needed to do was debug another country's code. And this room was stifling. Radios weren't allowed; they had no Internet access. She didn't have a clue what was going on outside that door. She was dying to know if anyone had any news about Joan.

"I'm taking a break," she announced, exiting the programs. She shut down the PC, removed the hard drive, and under the watchful eye of the guard, dutifully returned it to the safe. Breaks were usually more trouble than they were worth; it took a full ten minutes just to get cleared to leave the room and go through security, but today she needed a break. Badly.

CHAPTER 8

K it propped her feet on the corner of her desk and stared out the window at the interstate below. It was barely a week before Christmas, and there'd been no news about Joan, no ransom call, and still no leads. The only thing that had changed was the arrival of a media circus on her street, thanks to Carter Leigh's announcement of her name on the nightly news. All the shades in her house remained drawn and all the curtains closed. They'd become prisoners in their own home.

Carter had telephoned every day, leaving messages at both her office and home. Kit hadn't returned any of his calls. He was obviously digging for a bigger story, and all of her instincts told her not to oblige. By now she'd heard her eyewitness report told so many times and with so many variations that she almost wished she hadn't been there.

She sighed. Reporters weren't the only ones asking questions. It was unprecedented for the police to show up at UCT. Yet they'd been there twice, questioning Joan and Bernard's relationship, obviously trying to make a connection between their disappearances. Kit heard through the office grapevine that some employees were using the opportunity to paint a love relationship between Joan and Bernard, as though it were fact and not rumor, and Jack apparently wasn't doing anything to stop it.

She'd been to the police station twice more, looking at photographs, but none of them even came close to the men she'd seen.

The telephone rang, jolting her from her thoughts.

"Mom," Tim said, "I'm at Jason's house. I'm spending the night."

"You are, are you? Who okayed this decision?"

She heard a heavy exhale on the end of the line, the kind of sound that was usually reserved for Frank and always accompanied by rolling eyes and a look that meant the other person was just plain ignorant. Sometimes, she wondered if Tim's sudden independence wasn't payback for her own feisty teenage years.

"It's okay with Jason's mom."

"Gee, Son, I missed the memo where you'd been transferred to Jason's mom's department."

"Mom," Tim groaned.

Kit thought of asking to speak to Jason's mother, but held her tongue. The media frenzy had been hardest on Tim. He'd been captured on camera once, shown on the nightly news, and his classmates teased him mercilessly about it. Truth was, she completely understood if he wanted to get away for a while. It was the real reason she was still sitting in her office instead of halfway home.

"Mom?"

"Yes?"

"Can I go skiing with Jason tomorrow?"

"Who else is going?"

"Charlotte's driving; she's taking a bunch of us."

"Charlotte?"

"Mom, she's nineteen. She's in college."

"Who else is going?"

Kit listened while Tim rattled off the names of people she didn't know, and after a few hesitant moments, relented. She hadn't known Jason's parents that long, had never spent any length of time with them socially, but they seemed nice enough. Their oldest daughter, Charlotte, was in her second year at American University, had aspirations of becoming a lawyer, and Jason, like Tim, was consistently on the honor roll.

As she hung up the phone, she consoled herself with the thought that the ski resort was only a few hours away, safely nestled in the Blue Ridge Mountains, and it was better than Tim hanging around some street corner.

That also meant, for better or worse, she would be alone for the better part of the weekend. Frank had flown out this morning to a conference on the west coast, and wouldn't be back until Tuesday.

She studied the stack of paperwork on her desk. Jack had never reassigned her other projects, as she'd known from the beginning he wouldn't, and she was slipping further behind with every passing day.

Her laptop was still at home, still sitting in the corner of the living room where she'd hastily dumped it two weeks ago, the night Joan disappeared. It was enough to try and concentrate while at work; it was too much to ask for her to do it at home as well.

There were strict rules prohibiting programming code from being removed from the office. But with the weekend looming before her, there was no way she would spend it sitting in this office. Besides, if Chen knew she were here, he might recruit her to continue work on his dead-end project, an assignment she was growing to dread about as much as she'd despised cleaning the henhouse when she was growing up.

She sifted through the work and pulled out those assignments she thought she could make some headway on. Several of the programs had already been started, were on her laptop, and might only require a few hours to complete. No one would be the wiser. It certainly wouldn't be the first time in her career she'd had to do this. Besides, everybody did it at one time or another; they had to, with the workloads they carried.

She'd return on Monday with the work completed, and at least she'd be able to feel like she was making progress.

Carter hung up his cell phone while the bartender poured another scotch. It was only eight o'clock, and he'd already lost count of how many drinks he'd had.

"Not there, huh?" Bryce said, eyeing him curiously.

"Got her voice mail."

"Why do you keep calling her? You know she can't add anything to the story."

"Yeah," Carter said, taking a deep drink. "I know."

"Then why—?"

"I told you, I know."

"You like her, don't you?"

"You're full of it."

"Carter, she's a married woman. Back off. Don't do this again."

"Stay out of it."

They sat for a while in silence, Bryce shaking his head and Carter pretending not to notice. Then Carter whispered conspiratorially, "I've been thinking about Stallworth."

"What about?"

"His trigger. It's starving children."

"You're crazy," Bryce answered.

"I'm serious. I've gone over and over everything. I asked Stallworth if he wanted to make a comment on anything, and the one he picked up on was children starving in China."

"Why would that set him off?"

"Let's ask him."

"Yeah, right."

Carter started to stand, then caught the bar as he lost his equilibrium. "No, I'm serious now."

"What are you gonna do, march up to his house and ask him?"

"We'll set up another interview."

"On what pretext?"

"I don't know; we'll pick a subject."

They fell silent. Bryce accepted another glass of Coke, and Carter nursed his drink. "History will be made when he takes office," Carter said.

"Yeah, every network including our own has been all over that story for weeks," Bryce said. "Every political pundit that ever existed has been making predictions on how an Independent Governor will have an affect on legislation. He's aligned with Democrats on some issues, Republicans on others…"

"There's got to be something that hasn't been covered yet."

"Why not just call him up and ask him what he'd like to talk about?"

"And get an hour about his pet projects, no thanks. I'm a serious reporter, not a public relations firm."

"How about doing a piece on dark horse candidates and how governors have dealt with their respective legislatures—successfully or otherwise?"

Both their pagers sounded, and they scrambled to catch the number. "Great," Bryce said. "We've got an assignment, and you're drunk."

"I'm not drunk," Carter said, coming unsteadily to his feet. "You get the camera on me, and no one will ever know I've had a few."

"You'll have to do something with your breath," Bryce said as he placed some money on the bar, "or nobody'll let you near them."

"I've got it," Carter said as they walked outside, "something nobody else has talked to him about."

"Yeah?"

"A sister state."

"A *what*?"

"You know how all these cities are finding a 'sister city' in another state or country?"

"You're gonna have to come up with something better'n that."

"No, I'm serious. There's more than a dozen cities in Virginia who have sister cities already."

Bryce eyed him skeptically. "Like?"

"Like Alexandria and Dundee, Scotland, or Arlington and Aachen, Germany, or—"

"Okay, okay, I get the point."

"We'll ask for an interview to discuss his plans for international commerce, setting up an alliance with another country or province—"

"Like the governor who sent a bunch of bureaucrats to Russia—"

"And during the interview, I'll slip in some questions about starving children. You catch it on camera, and we'll have a sound bite."

"I hope we get more than a sound bite."

"We will," Carter answered as they reached their vehicle. "We will."

CHAPTER 9

九

Kit had just set the laptop case on the dining room table beside a fresh cup of hot apple cider and a warm croissant when she heard a soft knock at the back door. It was a little after eight on Saturday morning. The sun was streaming through the glass on the back door, sending fingers of sunshine across the pale yellow kitchen walls and into the dining room. She spotted the shadow of someone's head, and hoped it wasn't a nosy reporter. Making her way back through the kitchen, she was relieved when she opened the door to her neighbor's smiling face.

She gestured her in.

"Mmmm, what's that smell?" Lisa asked.

"Cinnamon sticks. Care for some hot apple cider? It's homemade."

"Hey, if it came from your Mom's house, definitely."

"You bet. Grab a croissant, too, and come on in."

Kit moved into the dining room. After a moment, Lisa joined her, her hands filled with a steaming cup of cider and a croissant piled high with chunky strawberry preserves.

"Frank's on another business trip?"

"Of course."

"He's traveling a lot these days."

"Tell me about it," Kit answered, and then hoped her response didn't sound too sarcastic. She glanced up quickly, but Lisa appeared not to have noticed.

"Where's Tim?"

"He's with Jason. They're going skiing."

"Where?"

"Ski Top Mountain."

"Out past Staunton? You know they're predicting a record snowfall there today." Lisa took a bite of her croissant. "It's supposed to hit here by evening."

Kit stuck her finger in her cider and stirred it around, an action that Frank always hated. She licked her finger. "I hope he doesn't get stranded."

"I see the media's gone," Lisa said abruptly.

"They must've left during the night. Been called to some bigger story someplace else, I reckon."

"No news about Joan?"

Kit shook her head. She'd known Lisa for ten years; their children had grown up together. Lisa had seen Joan a few times when Kit had given dinner parties, but they'd never been close. Lisa always considered Joan too abrupt and self-involved. And Joan thought of Lisa as nothing more than a soccer mom, whose most meaningful conversation was the current price of hamburger. "I'm afraid she's going to become another statistic, just another missing person on some police report somewhere."

"The police don't have any leads?"

"Not that I know of. And as much as I try to make sense of what happened, I just can't."

"You two were always close."

"We go way back." She gently extricated her hand from Lisa's grasp and busied herself with drizzling honey on top of the strawberry-laden croissant.

They chatted for a few more minutes, filling the time and the air with small talk, even after Kit pulled out her briefcase and spread its contents across the dining room table, arranging the paperwork by project. She selected the project she'd work on first, and then opened her laptop case.

She was always precise about how she packed her computer. The mouse was always in a specific pocket, the power cord in another. The diskettes, pens, and even her business cards were arranged neatly in their own designated spots.

When she opened the case, she gasped.

"What's wrong?" Lisa asked, coming to stand beside her.

"This is a mess," Kit said, staring at the disarray. The mouse and power cord were tossed in, their cables intertwining. Her business cards and her pens were gone.

Lisa laughed. "You ought to see mine."

Kit didn't answer for a long moment, remembering the last time she'd seen its contents. "I was carrying this when Joan disappeared. Maybe I dropped the case when all the commotion started," she said, more to herself than to Lisa.

"Or maybe you were in a hurry last time you used it. It's no big deal, right? Everything is there?"

"Except my business cards."

"So you think someone stole all your business cards and left the laptop?"

Kit chuckled. "Yeah, I hear identity theft is on the rise."

Still, she felt uneasy as she untangled the cables. She powered it on and waited for the network logon to pop up, barely hearing Lisa's cheerful banter. Since she wasn't connected to the office network, she cancelled the password prompt that displayed, and waited for the Windows logon to appear.

It never asked her for her Windows password, which struck her as odd. It was agency policy to have all laptops password protected; the penalty for forgetting this detail was dismissal.

When the Windows desktop was finally displayed, Kit's heart felt like it was in a vise. "As much as I'd rather sit here and visit with you," she said, hoping her voice didn't reveal her anxiety, "I have a lot of work to do. I hope you understand."

"Sure," Lisa answered. "Anyway, I just popped in to see if you'd pick up my newspaper for me tomorrow. We're going to visit David's parents."

"Be glad to."

"We're only going to be gone overnight," she continued as she finished her food and carried her plate to the kitchen. "They live in North Carolina. At least we're headed away from the storm." Lisa gave Kit a quick hug. "Hang in there, gal."

"I will. I always do."

Kit closed the door and locked it as Lisa left, then quietly lowered the shade. Her heart was pounding as she rushed back to the dining room.

Her Windows desktop was always organized, the icons arranged in a logical order, the customized toolbar displayed at the top of the screen. The background was a placid blue, the font easily readable.

This desktop was a mess.

The icons were scattered with apparently no logical order, the toolbar was gone, and the background was a pale yellow.

This wasn't her laptop.

She sat heavily in her chair, stunned. If this wasn't hers, who did it belong to? And where was hers?

She frantically thought back to the last time she'd used it, the day that Joan disappeared. The day that Joan stopped in her office and asked her to join her for a drink. The day she set down her laptop just before Joan entered with hers.

They had switched computers.

She felt a sudden chill in the room. That meant when Joan was abducted, the laptop case the men threw into the vehicle after her, wasn't Joan's but hers. The projects she was working on, all of the sensitive information, was in someone else's hands. How would she explain this? How would she ever explain that it took her weeks to notice her laptop was missing?

She was horrified. The paperwork she'd have to complete, the security she'd breached… She saw her career flashing before her, years of hard work and competence, erased in a single crazy second. She fought to calm herself down, to think.

Her laptop was password protected. As a career programmer, she knew that any password could be broken. But that was assuming they wanted to break it.

It was more likely that they didn't even know what they had; that they'd tossed the laptop. Then why hadn't they left it at the scene? And with the police combing the city, why hadn't it turned up?

And she had Joan's computer.

It was as if a switch had been flipped inside her as her fingers flew across the keyboard. A moment later, she'd logged into Joan's email and was rummaging through them.

There was nothing out of the ordinary. There were only the standard emails she'd expect to see on anyone's computer—the jokes that made their way around the world in mere minutes, the emails to coworkers regarding the latest deadlines… but no emails to close friends, no clues to her disappearance.

She scrolled back in time, to the weeks and then the months before Joan was abducted. There was a long list of emails between her and Bernard, especially between mid-summer and fall. She scanned the contents. They were working on several top-secret projects together, combining their expertise, as she was doing with Chen now. There were emails from Joan expressing increasing frustration as she hurried Bernard through projects he was lagging behind in, and replies from him explaining the complexity of those programs and begging for more time.

There was a deadline back in October that they had to meet, a deadline that couldn't be pushed back, that accounted for a large number of emails. But try as she did, Kit couldn't gather enough detail to understand what the project was about or who else may have been assigned to it.

She paused at one email, sent from Joan to Bernard in late October:

Toy wants the program delivered to the gristmill Saturday night 11 p.m.

Who was Toy? What were they doing delivering a program at eleven o'clock on a Saturday night?

And what and where was the gristmill?

The doorbell rang, and she jumped. She closed the lid on the laptop, stuffed it back into the case, and slid it behind the couch as she made her way to the front door. The doorbell rang again, and then a third time before she reached it.

"Who is it?" she called through the door.

"Detective Munski. I'd like to speak with you."

She slid the chain from the door and unlocked the deadbolt. She motioned the detective into the house.

It might have been her imagination, but she thought he was peering too closely at everything, as though he were searching for something.

"Please, have a seat," she said, gesturing toward one of the chairs. She sat on the couch across from him.

"I'm going to come straight to the point, Mrs. Olsen," he said. His blue eyes were piercing in their intensity.

"You found Joan?"

"No."

"Then you know something?"

"You could say that."

She waited for him to continue, but he appeared to be waiting for her response. She became acutely aware of Joan's laptop behind her. "Is she still alive?"

"I think you're the best one to tell us that."

"What are you talking about?"

"Mrs. Olsen, we believe Ms. Newcomb and Mr. Emerson were having an affair."

"That's impossible!"

He continued as if he hadn't heard her. "In fact, all of our evidence points to them leaving voluntarily, perhaps to be reunited."

"What are you saying? I saw—"

"Yes, I know. In fact, Mrs. Olsen, you're the only one who 'saw' anything."

"What are you insinuating?"

"I'm not insinuating anything. I'm accusing you of fabricating Ms. Newcomb's disappearance."

Kit's jaw dropped. "Why on earth would I do a fool thing like that?"

"Why don't you tell me?"

She stared at the detective, too stunned to speak.

"We found their bank account, Mrs. Olsen. We know large sums of money were wired into it before either disappeared. We also know large amounts were wired out, to a bank in Stockholm. We know they were meeting outside of business hours, fabricating business trips when they were together right here in Virginia."

"But, why? Why would they do that?"

"Some of your coworkers were more forthcoming than you with information about their affair. Everything points to two people who wanted to run away together."

"Joan was taken against her will—"

"Was she? Or did you concoct the story to cover for your friends?"

"Are you accusing me of lying? Of making a false police report?"

"That's exactly what I'm accusing you of."

"Am I under arrest?"

"Not at the present."

"Then get out of my house."

Detective Munski rose. "You have 48 hours," he said slowly. "48 hours to tell me exactly what happened. Or I'm booking you as an accessory."

"Accessory to what?"

He crossed the living room and turned at the door. "48 hours, Mrs. Olsen."

With that, he was gone, the front door closing softly behind him.

CHAPTER 10

✝

Kit listened to the telephone ringing, her apprehension mounting. It was almost seven o'clock, and she'd been trying to reach Frank for hours. Each time she dialed his cell phone, she received a recording that his telephone was out of range. Frantic, she'd scoured the house, searching for information on the conference he was attending. At last, she found a brochure and called the Los Angeles hotel.

"May I help you?" came a friendly voice.

"Yes, Frank Olsen's room, please."

There was a slight pause. "I'm sorry, we don't have anyone here by that name."

"He checked in last night."

"How do you spell the name?"

Kit complied and waited through another long silence while she paced the living room floor.

"I'm sorry, ma'am, we don't have a guest here by that name," the woman said. "Could it be under another name?"

"No. No, I'm sure it wouldn't be. Do you have a contact for the American Insurance Conference?"

"The what?"

"The American Insurance Conference." She looked at the colorful brochure she'd been clutching in her hand. "It's being held at your hotel today through Monday."

"Hold on please."

A long moment passed before a man with a heavy accent answered the telephone.

"Is this someone with the American Insurance Conference?" Kit asked.

"No, I'm sorry, but that conference was cancelled."

"Cancelled! When?"

"Several weeks ago."

"Why? Was it scheduled someplace else?" Kit plopped onto the living room couch, and watched tiredly as the brochure fluttered to the floor.

"I don't think so. They didn't have enough interest in it; that's why they cancelled."

"I see. Thank you." She had just hung up the telephone when it rang.

"Mom?" came a hesitant voice.

"Tim, where are you?"

"At Ski Top Mountain. Mom, we're stuck," he whined.

"Stop whining. I hate it when you whine. What do you mean you're stuck?"

"Charlotte can't get her car out of the parking lot. There's too much snow."

"Jesus. Isn't there someone there who can help you?"

"Even if we found somebody, they'd just get us out of the parking lot. They couldn't get us home." After a moment, he continued, "Mom, can you come get us?"

Kit peered out the window. There was at least six inches of snow on the ground now, and more predicted. Her minivan was rear-wheel drive, as slippery on ice as butter on a hot plate. "What's the weather like there?"

"About two feet of snow. It's a blizzard. We can't even ski in this."

"I'll come after you. Give me directions." She grabbed a pen and started writing. After Tim and his friends gave her directions that sounded pretty unreliable, she said, "Stay put. They have a lodge there, don't they? I'll find you there. I'll be a few hours."

As she rushed around, gathering her coat, purse, and snow boots, she couldn't help but wonder if she'd even make it. It had to be at least three hours from their home in good weather; with blizzard conditions, she could be all night getting there.

She made it to the vehicle in five minutes' time, and settled into the front seat. She placed the key in the ignition and turned. Nothing. No noise, not even the battery trying to start. Just dead air.

I don't believe this, she thought. What next?

She climbed out and glanced around the cul-de-sac, trying to decide whose door she should approach and ask for help, when a white Ford Expedition pulled in front of the house.

The door opened, and Carter Leigh stepped out. "Going someplace?" he called.

"What are you doing here?" Kit said as he approached.

"You haven't returned any of my calls. I figured you must not be getting my messages."

"I've told you everything I know."

"I don't think so." He stopped a few feet from her, his hands thrust into the pockets of a heavy wool coat. A tweed English walking hat cast his eyes in shadow.

"What do you want from me?" she said, exasperated.

"Just to talk. Off the record."

"Oh, I believe that." She glanced at his vehicle. "Is that four wheel drive?"

"Yeah."

"Take me to Ski Top Mountain, and we'll talk on the way."

"There're travel advisories out for that area. They're being hit hard."

"My son is stranded. I've got to get to him."

"You've got a deal," he answered without hesitation.

Kit grabbed her purse. When she turned back, Carter was already at his vehicle, opening the passenger door for her. The snow was turning to sleet as her feet slid and slipped down the driveway. Something deep inside her was crying out for her to stay at home and not to venture into the storm, but like a kid on a waterslide, she felt propelled forward and out of control.

It was after 11:00 when traffic slowed to a stop on Interstate 81. It had been maddeningly slow going for most of the way, but now they were at a standstill as the minutes ticked by, the only sound the repetitive *thump, thump* of the windshield wipers. They appeared to be fighting a losing battle as the ice formed into thick clumps on the wipers, rapidly restricting their view.

Finally, the traffic began crawling forward. Eventually, they were able to make out the blue lights of patrol cars up ahead. As they approached the next exit, an officer directed them to turn.

Carter pulled the vehicle alongside the officer. "What's going on?"

As the officer leaned toward the window, Kit caught a glimpse of ice crystals on his hat, and when he spoke, his words were clouded in a cold mist. "We're closing this stretch of the Interstate. Conditions are too bad."

Carter nodded wordlessly, and took the exit.

"Do you know where you're going?" Kit asked.

"I'll figure it out," he answered. "I've been through here before."

They soon found themselves driving through Staunton's historic downtown, and there was no doubt in Kit's mind that Carter was in fresh territory. The cars that had surrounded them when they left the Interstate were nowhere in sight. The streets were still and empty, the town eerily quiet. It reminded Kit of an old western movie with a lone horseman riding into a near-deserted town; only instead of tumbleweeds in a dry dusty wind, there were small mountains of drifting snow, the only sound the whistling of a nor'easter whipping around the buildings. Even a strip of local restaurants were closed, their signs darkened, the doors closed tight against the weather. A stoplight transformed a swath of pristine snow to green, then yellow, before turning to a fire engine red.

They came to a stop at the empty intersection, and Kit glanced at the building on the corner. "The Book Stack" was printed in neat letters across the glass, and the carefully arranged displays seemed to beckon. A cat sat attentively as if mesmerized with the snowflakes. A soft golden inner glow appeared to announce that the shop was warm. Kit longed to be inside, away from the cold, the ice, and the snow.

For several hours, Carter and Kit made small talk, comparing childhoods, schools and college years, jobs and marriage and responsibilities. Kit kept her cell phone in her lap, her mind periodically wandering, wondering if Frank had called her at home and trying not to question why he hadn't tried her cell phone. Several times, she thought of calling him but stopped short of dialing the number, not really wanting to know if he were still unavailable. The cancelled conference weighed heavily on her mind, and she couldn't help but wonder and worry about his whereabouts.

Carter remained conspicuously silent about Joan and Detective Munski. Now that they were so close, Kit was anxious to get the real conversation out of the way, out of earshot of her son and his friends.

"I know why you came over tonight," she said.

"You do?" Carter's eyes didn't waver from the street.

"Detective Munski got there before you."

"Did he have any news?" he asked casually.

"You know he did."

"I know that, huh?"

Kit studied his face, strong and angular, his narrowed eyes now focused on the road as the traffic light turned green. "He thinks I'm lying."

Carter jerked his head toward her. "Why does he think that?"

"You don't have to pretend not to know anything."

"I don't know anything."

There was silence as their vehicle gained traction and cleared the intersection. "He thinks Joan and Bernard were lovers," Kit said, "that they ran away together. That I made up the story about Joan's abduction."

"Do you think they were lovers?"

"Am I going to see this on the morning news?"

He paused as if he were weighing his options. "No, it's off the record."

"All of it?"

He peered at her. "If that's what you want."

They were through the town and beginning a steep ascent into the mountains. Kit was silent. Carter hunched forward as if by doing so, he could see the narrow, winding road better. On their left was the sheer face of the mountain, and too close to Kit's right was a vertical drop into oblivion. With the snow obscuring their way, it was impossible to tell where the road ended and the shoulder began.

They rounded a corner and the darkened sky gave way to the bright glow of headlights from two snowplows inching their way toward them. Carter slowed as they approached the nearest one, and rolled down his window.

"Hope you're not going far," the driver of the snowplow called out, huddling into his thick turtleneck as the snow swirled between them.

"How far's the road cleared?" Carter asked.

The driver chuckled hoarsely. "As soon as we plow, it's covered up again."

"Think we can make it to Ski Top Mountain?"

He studied the Expedition. "I'd turn back if I was you."

Carter nodded wordlessly and rolled up the window. Then he pulled the Ford as far to the right as he dared, while the snowplows crept past him.

"I give you my word," he said when they were again surrounded by darkness.

"On what?"

"I won't use what you tell me on the news."

"How do I know your word is any good?" she said, half teasing.

He looked at her with a dead serious expression. "My word is all I have. Without it, I have no sources and no stories."

"What do you want to know?"

"For starters, why does Munski think you're lying?"

"I told you. He thinks Joan left on her own, to be with Bernard, and that I'm covering for them."

"Would you do that?"

"Of course not. Even if they did run away together, which I absolutely do not believe for one second, I would never lie for anybody."

"How can you be so sure they didn't run away together?"

"You'd have to know them," Kit said, trying not to think how close the Ford must be to the edge of the road.

"Tell me."

"They were opposites."

"Opposites attract," he quipped, then added, "or so the saying goes."

"Not these two. Bernard was a chain smoker; Joan thought he was a walking ashtray. He lived on junk food; she was a natural food fanatic. She was ambitious; he didn't seem to care if he ever moved up."

"Oh?"

"He was like a turtle. He'd get there someday, but you'd just want to pick him up and carry him along, he was so slow. It used to really get on Joan's nerves."

"Was he good at what he did?"

"One of the best programmers we had. Maybe that's why he was so slow; he paid attention to every little detail. Things others wouldn't even think of."

"Like?"

"Can't give you specifics. All our projects are confidential."

A sign for the ski resort loomed ahead, and Carter slowed and leaned forward, searching for the road to turn onto. The snow was so deep it was impossible to see where the grass ended and the road began.

Once he made the turn, she continued, "Anyway, Detective Munski told me I had 48 hours to tell him the 'truth'." She glanced at her watch. "I guess it's closer to 34 now."

"Did you tell him the truth?"

"Yes. I told you I wouldn't lie."

"Then don't sweat it."

"That's easy for you to say." Kit leaned against the back of the seat and closed her eyes.

"Listen, I've known Munski for twenty years."

"Yes, you told me. He's your brother-in-law?"

"Was." He glanced at her. "My sister divorced him. Anyway, I've known him since college days. I've seen him close a lot of cases. And I've seen him leave a lot unsolved."

"What are you saying?"

"Munski closes the cases that he can, right away. Usually within the first couple of days. When he can't, he's got to move on. He gets too many cases to linger on one for any length of time."

"What does that have to do with me?"

"Everything. He wants you to confess to lying, tell him they ran away together, and both cases are closed."

"You're kidding." She peeked at him then closed her eyes again.

"I've seen it work before. Trust me, when the time passes and he hasn't heard from you, the case will be quietly transferred to another box on his desk."

"And what box is that?"

"The one he's not currently working on."

"But what about Joan?"

"Do you know how many women are reported missing every year? About fifteen thousand. That's *women*. That doesn't account for men, or children. Do you know how many the local police departments are equipped to handle?" He continued without waiting for a response. "Next to none."

"You sound pretty jaded."

He continued as if he hadn't heard her. "Your friend isn't a Kennedy, or a Gates or a DuPont. Her picture will be filed away in a computer system somewhere, and maybe—ten to one odds—her remains will be found before you grow old. She's already gotten more publicity than most do."

"Why do you think that?"

"Because you're a witness. Most abductions happen without witnesses, leaving everyone to speculate whether they left on their own. And in that case, there's not a whole lot the police can do."

A siren pierced the silence, and Kit turned to stare out the back window. "Police," she said. "Two cars."

Carter slowed to a stop as close to the edge of the road as he dared. They both watched the flashing blue lights lumbering toward them, the sirens growing louder as they approached.

"What the—?" Carter said as they passed by them, the chains on their tires crunching through the snow. Then he threw the vehicle into gear and took off behind them.

"What are you doing?"

"Following them!"

Kit was thankful that the Ford Crown Victorias were slower in the deepening snow, but even so, as Carter took the turns, the back tires felt as though they were coming dangerously close to the edge. She held tight to the grab handle as they were overcome by the snowstorm, the flashing blue lights in front of them the only bit of color she could see through the white blanket that fell all around them.

CHAPTER 11

✝—

Kit heard Tim calling her as soon as she'd stepped out of the vehicle. She was vaguely aware of Carter rushing across the parking lot to the police cruisers as she scoured the crowd. She breathed a sigh of relief when her eyes landed on his bright orange ski jacket as he separated from the onlookers and rushed toward her. She hugged him, and though he pulled away from her and cut his eyes over to his friend, she knew he was glad to see her.

"What's going on?" she asked, nodding toward the cruisers.

"Two snowmobiles crashed," he said in the same tone of voice he used to describe a great football game. "They couldn't see 'cause of the snow—"

Kit glanced toward the police. Carter appeared to be alternating between speaking to one of the officers and talking on his cell phone. "Let's get inside," she said, starting toward the lodge.

"They're in there now, on stretchers, waiting for the ambulance to get here," Tim said breathlessly.

"How many were hurt?"

"Three, I think."

They reached the main entrance just as Kit realized how shaky her knees were. The first room she entered was packed with people trying to make the most of being stranded. She wandered into a second and then a third room, finally locating an empty table. She'd sat down before she realized that Tim was still talking.

"—just happened, not ten minutes before you got here. Whose car is that, anyway?"

"A friend's," Kit said tiredly.

"What's he doing talking to the police?"

"He's a reporter."

"God, Mom, you didn't bring a reporter with you! We're gonna be on the news again!"

"Stop being so melodramatic, Tim, please." Her eyes wandered to a television set that was attracting a crowd in the corner. A "late-breaking news" banner appeared across the screen before cutting to a news anchor. Someone turned up the volume, and Kit watched the unfolding story along with the rest of the crowd, which was now hushed, listening intently.

"Carter Leigh is there at Ski Top Mountain, reporting in by phone. Carter, can you hear me?"

"Yes, Dina, we have the exclusive report on three people seriously injured in a snowmobile accident that occurred just minutes ago. The ambulance is trying to make its way through this blinding snowstorm. Will it get here in time? What caused this accident? Could it have been avoided? We're working on answering those very questions now…"

Tim gaped at Kit. "And you call *me* melodramatic?"

"Where's everybody else?" she asked, changing the subject.

"Everybody, who?"

"Tim, who did you come up here with?"

"Oh, everybody else got a ride except me and Jason."

"Where is Charlotte?"

"She left with some guy."

"She left with 'some guy'?" Kit asked, her anger rising. "And she left you two here to fend for yourselves?"

"She knew you were coming, Mom. Don't get spastic."

"What if I hadn't been able to get here? What if I'd been stranded somewhere between here and home? I can't believe she left two kids here by themselves!"

"Mo-o-om," Tim said, rolling his eyes and turning ten shades of red. "We're not kids anymore."

"Oh, yeah, I forgot. You're adults," Kit said heatedly, rising from her seat. "Get Jason. We're leaving *now*."

"You're not going anywhere." She turned on her heels and came face to face with Carter.

"The road's shut down," Carter said. "It'll probably open soon, but right now we can't go anywhere."

"I don't believe this," Kit sputtered. "Young man, you are *never* coming up here with Charlotte ever, ever again. Do you hear me?"

"Why? It's not my fault!"

"You are grounded *forever*."

Tim slouched in his seat and mumbled under his breath. Kit rolled her eyes as she caught the words "Charlotte" and "victim".

"Let's get something to drink," Carter said, motioning for a harried waitress. "Something to warm your insides, calm you down."

A few minutes later, despite herself, she began to relax. Maybe it was the drink, or maybe the fact that it was now after midnight, or maybe even the hot sandwich she'd downed without a second thought. Or maybe it was just that she was tired.

The conversation between Carter, Tim, and Jason sounded far away, their voices low and monotonous. Her heavy eyes followed Carter as he rose from the table, but it didn't quite register what he leaned down and said to her. A moment later, she was staring at his empty chair and wondering where he'd gone.

She pulled her cell phone from her purse and tried Frank's number again, but she received a recording informing her the phone was out of range. She never had a chance to leave him a message. And now she had no idea where he was, and he wouldn't have a clue how to reach her or Tim.

A rumor swept through the room that volunteers were needed to retrieve the snowmobiles. One of the injured was a diabetic, and they needed people to search for medicine that was presumably lost at the crash site.

"Can we go, Mom?"

Tim's voice sounded faint and faraway.

She cupped her head in her hands, fighting a sleepiness that made her feel as though she'd been drugged. "Go where?"

"To search for the medicine," came his distant voice.

"No, stay here," she answered, closing her eyes.

"Kit? Kit?"

She felt as though she were moving through a haze. She felt two strong hands on her arms, gently shaking her. "Kit, wake up!"

"Frank?" She tried to force her eyes open, to shake the sleepiness from her brain.

"No, it's Carter."

Her eyes shot open and she bolted up, starting out of her chair. Carter's hands gently pushed her back. "Where's Tim?" he asked hoarsely.

She glanced around. The room was still, filled with people asleep with their heads buried in their arms, sprawled across the tables; a few were sitting propped against the walls, their chests rising and falling rhythmically. There was a hum of voices from a distant corner of the room, whispering words that sounded as faint as the wind on a calm, clear night.

"What's happening?" she asked.

"The road's still closed. Most people are asleep."

"What time is it?"

"Almost three o'clock." Carter bent down in front of Kit's chair, grasping both her hands in his. "Kit, do you know where Tim is?"

She looked around the table. "He was right here. He was here with Jason."

"How long ago?"

"I—I don't know. I must have fallen asleep." She stared into his eyes, his heavy brows furrowed and eyes veiled. "What's wrong? What's happened?"

"The security guards found someone on one of the trails."

"Tim—?"

"No, it's definitely not Tim."

"Someone from the accident?" She was fully awake now as a strange prickling sensation crept up her spine.

"No." He pulled a chair close to hers. "Be quiet. They don't want to start a panic."

"Who?"

"Security. They were looking for the officers who were here earlier." He took a slow breath, and glanced around the room. "Listen, Kit, they found a man near the accident scene. He'd been shot twice in the head."

Kit gasped.

"The only reason they found him under all that snow is they were searching—"

"Yes, yes, I know. Is—is there a killer here?"

"Probably not. He looks like he's been dead for months. But I'd feel better knowing where Tim is."

She stood up. "I told him to stay right here."

He grasped her arm. "Was there any reason for him to go outside?"

"I—I don't know." She grabbed her coat. "We have to look for him!"

"The visibility's bad out there. He could be an arm's length away, and you might not see him."

She pushed past him. "I have to look!"

"Kit—" he pleaded, following her down the hall toward the back doors.

The doors flew open with a strong gust of wind, swirling the snow through the hall, the biting, raw air catching her off guard. Carter quickly reached her and wrapped his arms around her, pulling her back as security guards carried in a stretcher draped in a blue blanket.

"Don't look," he said, pulling her back.

"Don't be ridiculous," she said. "In case you haven't noticed, I'm not that delicate."

The men labored past her, the weight of the stretcher appearing heavy and cumbersome as though the person they carried was grossly overweight. And frozen solid, Kit thought. They stopped at one of the interior doors and whispered about the best place to keep him until the ambulances could arrive. As she watched, the blanket slipped from one end, showing a frozen shock of familiar gray and brown hair.

She pushed Carter's hands off of her. In seconds, she was at the stretcher, reaching out and yanking the blanket back. The face underneath stared back at her with frozen blue-green eyes, widened as though filled with terror, the mouth contorted in agony.

"Oh, my God!" she gasped. "Oh, my God!"

CHAPTER 12

十二

Kit stood at the window, her eyes following the snow as it drifted downward, but her mind was a thousand miles away. She was mentally retracing her steps, trying to imagine someplace she hadn't checked for Tim yet, someplace he could still be, safe and sound, but no matter how she tried to direct her thoughts elsewhere, Bernard's frozen face kept popping up in her mind's eye.

She and Carter had checked every one of the resort's half dozen buildings, every room and every corner, at least twice. They'd awakened every teenage kid and questioned them thoroughly, looking for someone—anyone—who could have seen the missing boys.

They'd even ventured from the buildings past the police tape marking the location where Bernard's body had been found, venturing as far as they dared in the blinding snow, their calls lost in the squalls that haunted the resort.

It was as if they'd simply vanished.

Now she stood in the security office watching the snow removal equipment below. They'd been working for more than an hour, clearing an area large enough for a helicopter to land.

Behind her, the police officers and the resort's security team were in a heated debate. The officers were clearly upset that the body had been moved and the crime scene tampered with, while the security guards struggled to justify their actions. Then the conversation turned to the accident victims, who were still waiting for help to arrive. To Kit's chagrin, the missing teenagers didn't even enter into their discussion.

A helicopter would be the only hope of getting the injured to a hospital, as they'd received no assurances when the mountain roads would be cleared and reopened. She watched the snow swirling back onto the pavement as soon as the plows passed through. The wind was too strong, the snow falling too rapidly.

There was a blast of noise from the radio. "We have white-out conditions," came a crackling voice.

"Here, too," the security officer responded, with one eye on the window.

"Weather report doesn't look good," came the response. "It could be several hours before we can launch a helicopter."

There was silence in the room as the men looked at one another, the words that were left unsaid hanging in the air like a balloon waiting to burst. Finally, an officer responded, "We understand. Keep us informed."

Kit strained to see beyond the plows, searching for a glimpse of a bright orange ski jacket and two teenage boys who were going to be in a mountain of trouble. *If* they were okay, that is. Right now, she'd feel a load lifted off her if they simply showed up unharmed.

She felt Carter's hand on her arm, quietly squeezing it as if to reassure her that he was there.

"Where could they have gone?" she asked for the umpteenth time.

The officer joined them at the window. "They'll show up," he said calmly.

"I don't think you understand the gravity of this situation," Kit spat.

He cut his eyes toward her. "I know you're upset, Mrs. Olsen, and if I were in your shoes, I would be, too. But you see those kids over there?" He pointed to a group of teenagers in brightly colored outfits, throwing snowballs. "We've asked everybody to stay inside, and look at them. One of them'll get hurt, and come crying to us for help. We've got our hands full enough as it is."

She caught a glimpse of Carter as he shot a thinly veiled look of annoyance at the policeman. Carter had not been patient while Officer Brinley had questioned her about Bernard and her relationship to him. Apparently, Joan's disappearance had made headlines around these parts, but Bernard's had not been a high profile case.

One of the security guards called to Officer Brinley, and he excused himself. As they watched him leave the office, Carter said, "You haven't tried calling Frank."

It sounded strange to hear Frank's name rolling off his tongue so easily. "I don't know where he is."

"Didn't you say—?"

"He's supposed to be at a convention, but he wasn't there. Fact is, it was cancelled."

Carter's brows were furrowed. "Come with me."

Kit cupped her hands around the Styrofoam and allowed the warmth to creep into her freezing fingers. She had just finished explaining to Carter how she'd tried repeatedly to reach Frank and the conversation with the hotel convention clerk, and was waiting for his response. She was fighting an increasing maelstrom of emotions, from anger with Frank to anger and fear for Tim and Jason's safety, to a growing terror at learning that Bernard had been murdered. She was also trying vainly to suppress the feeling that Joan was dead, too.

"You remember the night we met?" Carter asked.

"At the police station," she answered. "The night Joan disappeared."

"You told me your husband was working in Tyson's Corner."

"Yes, his office is there."

Carter hesitated. Kit found herself caught between wanting to know what he knew and the overwhelming need to protect herself from the knowledge.

After a moment, he looked up, as though he were focusing on an object located on the side of the mountain. "I saw him that night."

"How could you—?"

"He wasn't in Tyson's Corner. He was in Arlington."

"You're mistaken."

"No. I'm not." He looked back at her, as though trying to gauge her reaction. "He was outside the police station when I got there."

She paused. "Maybe he was coming to meet me, and got called back in."

"Maybe," Carter said quietly.

As the clock hands crept toward midday, people began to show signs of irritation. Kit sat at the bar, her back against the wall where she would have a clear view of the room. Nursing a hot cup of buttered rum, she tried to ignore the fight between two kids, apparently brothers, at the opposite end of the room, and the arguments breaking out between parents and their children.

Her outer calm masked her inner turmoil. She wanted to jump up and start screaming, demanding that everyone look for her son. She wanted to wring Tim's neck like a turkey at Thanksgiving and make sure he never disobeyed her again. And she wanted to be home in her own bed, sleeping away the rest of the weekend while Tim was safe and sound in the next room.

She pulled the cell phone from her purse and dialed her home number.

The answering machine clicked on after four rings. She keyed in her access code. The outgoing message abruptly stopped, replaced by the familiar voice on her answering machine indicating she had two messages.

Both were from Frank. He'd called Saturday night at nine o'clock, saying that it was six in California and his conferences were finished for the day. He was in his room, changing clothes, before going out for dinner with a group of conference attendees.

He called again just half an hour ago, letting her know he was on his way to breakfast and then another full day of meetings. His cell phone was turned off, he said, because of bad reception, so he would try her again that evening.

She saved both messages and then returned to her drink. He hadn't questioned why she wasn't at home on a Saturday night or early Sunday morning, hadn't seemed worried about her in the least. He didn't leave a phone number where he could be reached. He was in California, attending the conference.

Her thoughts were interrupted as Carter pulled up a chair next to her and ordered coffee with a shot of whiskey.

"We have some folks that are bad off," he said in a low voice.

She waited for him to continue.

He glanced around him, as if determining who was within earshot. "One of the injured might not make it," he whispered.

"What's happening?" she said, studying his concerned expression.

"Nothing's happening, that's the problem. If they don't get a helicopter or ambulance here soon…" His voice trailed off. The bartender set the coffee and whiskey on the counter. Carter poured the whiskey into the cup and stirred it.

"Is there a doctor here?" Kit asked.

"A nurse. She's got her hands full; she's in over her head. They need a surgeon." He motioned for the bartender. "Can you turn on that TV set? Turn it to NBC."

The bartender complied, and within a few minutes a banner ran across the bottom of the screen. The snow was expected to stop by noon, but the storm had left its mark. The Washington Metropolitan Area was immobilized. Even police cruisers couldn't get through the snow, and they were calling for people with four-wheel-drive vehicles to transport doctors and nurses to the hospitals.

"We'll be lucky if they have these roads cleared today," Carter said. He squeezed Kit's shoulder. "When this storm is over, we'll have better visibility. We'll get a search party together."

"Could he have been in an avalanche? Do you think he's buried in snow?" she said, her voice rising.

"No," he answered quickly. "Conditions aren't right for an avalanche. More likely, he and Jason wandered outside and couldn't find their way back to the lodge.

They're probably hunkered down somewhere, waiting out the storm."

Kit tried not to think of them trying to keep warm while the blizzard raged around them. "Tim's smarter than that. He grew up hunting and fishing around my folks' house. He could always find his way home, no matter what."

"How many blizzards has he been in?" Carter asked. When Kit didn't respond, he said, "Let's go to the security office. I have an idea."

The security office was bustling with activity. The phones were ringing constantly. From what Kit overheard, there were calls from the media wanting statements regarding Bernard's body and the injured skiers, calls from as far away as New York and Chicago. There were other calls from people with family members here, demanding to know when they would be allowed to leave. In between, the security personnel checked the weather reports and surrounding police departments in an effort to determine when the roads would be passable and emergency vehicles could get through.

Carter found Officer Brinley talking to the radio dispatcher.

"Will the helicopter be able to get in here?" he asked.

"We're trying now," the dispatcher answered. "It's clear in Charleston; they're waiting for conditions to improve here."

"When it comes in," Carter asked, "can we have it circle the lodge and look for Tim and Jason?"

"I understand your concern for your son," the officer said, "but we have a man dying here, unless we can get him to a hospital. I'm not going to divert his only hope to look for two kids who're out there snowboarding."

"They're not snowboarding," Kit said hotly. "They're missing. They could be freezing to death out there."

"What about the state police?" Carter asked.

"What about them?" Officer Brinley said.

"They have aircraft. Can't one of them search the area?"

Brinley sighed. "When the weather clears," he said with resignation. "We'll request it. But you've got to understand, we have a lot going on here, and I can't guarantee anything."

An hour later, Carter and Kit had gone through each building yet again, checking each face, and asking questions of each group. No one had seen the two boys.

The weather cleared, bringing with it a bright sunshine that threatened to melt the snow with its intensity. Almost immediately, groups of people began venturing outside.

Kit and Carter wandered to the back of the lodge and watched the people hitting the slopes as though nothing out of the ordinary had happened.

Carter dialed his office from his cell phone and spoke for a moment in hushed tones. When he hung up, his expression was serious. "It's going to take hours for them to clear the roads up here," he said.

"I'm sorry I got you into this," Kit said.

"Don't be silly. As long as no other reporters get through, I've got an exclusive here—Emerson being found, a skiing accident, two lost boys—"

"How will we ever find them in this crowd?" Kit groaned, raising her hand over her eyes to protect them from the blinding sun. There were too many people up there now with bright orange ski jackets, too many who looked just like Tim.

"Look at the bright side," Carter said. "If they're out there, one of those skiers is likely to run across them. They can't have gone too far, not with the storm as bad as it was, or the weather as cold—"

"I know."

They were interrupted by the distant sound of a helicopter. Kit shielded her eyes and watched as it appeared over the mountains, a mere speck on the horizon that grew steadily until it was almost upon them.

They'd been too busy to notice the activity in the clearing below. The maintenance men had returned and cleared an area that was still white from blowing snow. Now they watched as they set out flashing strobe lights along the perimeter.

The helicopter grew larger until it was directly overhead, the roar of the engines and the whirring of the blades almost deafening as it circled the makeshift landing site before making a running landing.

As the helicopter neared the ground, the snow was swirled upwards for yards in every direction, until Kit could barely make out the uniforms of the maintenance crew. It wasn't until the whining of the blades began to diminish that they knew it had touched ground.

Before the snow could settle back to the ground, the side door opened and the pilot climbed out. He walked around to the back and opened clamshell doors. Another man climbed out, and then reached back in to pull a collapsed stretcher from the helicopter with the help of a shadowy figure still inside. Once it was firmly on the ground, they raised it to a height above their knees.

A woman climbed out behind the stretcher. Together, they moved deliberately toward the building with the stretcher between them.

"I'm going to talk to the pilot," Carter said.

Kit's telephone rang, startling them both.

Carter hesitated.

"It might be Tim," she said, mirroring the look in his eyes. Then she frowned. "Caller ID is blocked."

Carter took a step toward her.

"Hello?" she said.

The voice was unfamiliar, with a hint of an accent in its calm, deep tone. "You have something that belongs to me."

"Excuse me?" she said. Carter raised an eyebrow, and she tilted the phone so he could hear.

"Kit Olsen?"

"Yes."

"You have twelve hours to get it."

"Get what?"

"You know what I want."

"But—"

"I'll call you at your house at precisely midnight. Be there."

"I can't—I'm—"

"Mom?"

Kit's knees buckled beneath her, and Carter surged forward to catch her. "Tim?"

"I should have gone skiing in Copperhead County."

"Are you okay?"

She was interrupted by a calm voice. "Be home at midnight. I'll have instructions for you. Don't contact the police, don't tell anyone at all, or your son won't see another dawn."

Then the line went dead.

CHAPTER 13

十三

The cold wind bit at Kit's hands, her fingertips numb from the flesh-freezing snow she brushed off the Expedition. Her gloves were wet and hardened with ice crystals, rendering them useless.

"Get in!" Carter ordered as he wrestled with removing icicles from the wiper blades.

Kit labored from the hood to the passenger door, her feet sinking into the hip-high snow as though it were quicksand. She'd just opened the door when she heard a voice behind her.

"Where do you think you're going?"

She turned as Officer Brinley and another officer trudged toward them. She'd last spotted them at the site where they'd found Bernard's body, an image that made her nauseous.

"We're leaving," Carter answered.

"I wouldn't advise that, if I were you."

Carter popped the windshield wiper back onto the glass. "We've got an emergency. We don't have time to argue about this."

The other officer, a younger man with the smooth skin of one just reaching manhood, stepped forward. "The roads aren't passable. You'd be committing suicide."

"I'll take that chance," Carter answered, opening his door.

Kit took the cue to climb in, closing the passenger door behind her. The two officers appeared to take scant notice of her as their attention was riveted on Carter.

"I have a dead body in there," Brinley said, his brows furrowed as he jabbed his finger at the ski lodge. "And I have a lot more questions for your lady friend here."

Carter climbed in, his face reddened with anger. "So get a warrant. You have her address."

Kit felt her blood pounding in her temples. She could barely see Brinley's figure through the window as Carter slammed the door shut in his face, throwing the gear into reverse.

The tires spun on the snow before the four-wheel drive kicked in. The Expedition slid backwards. Then Carter angrily stomped on the brake and threw it into drive. Officer Brinley was now on Kit's side. He leaned toward her window and shouted, "What about your son? What kind of a mother would run off and leave her son missing—?"

Kit grabbed for the door handle. "You son of a—"

Carter grabbed her arm and pulled her away from the door as the Expedition moved toward the entrance. "Whoa, there," he chuckled as they left the officers behind to brush the splattered snow and ice from their uniforms.

"How dare he say that to me," she sputtered. "If he only knew—"

"If he only knew, your chances of getting Tim back would be nil."

As they pulled onto the road, reality hit her full force. It was completely covered with virgin white snow, the trees on the sides of the mountain so heavily laden with the thick stuff they appeared to be an extension of the road itself. Now as Carter took the curves, she found herself holding her breath and praying that they wouldn't slide off the narrow shoulder and plunge down the mountainside.

"Relax," Carter said. "I know what I'm doing."

"You can't see any better than I can," she answered. "How do you even know we're on the road?"

"Because if we weren't, we'd be dead."

Kit grabbed the handle above the door. "Oh, God."

"Just call me 'Carter'," he said.

The vehicle careened around the corners, the tires slicing through the snow as if it were whipped cream. More than once, the pine needles and branches of majestic trees brushed against the windshield.

"I don't feel right about this," Kit said.

"I told you, I know what I'm doing."

"It's not your driving," she snapped as she felt the vehicle's backend sink into the soft shoulder, "although it could use some improvement. It's just… I feel like we're moving further and further away from Tim."

He didn't answer, and Kit continued, "There aren't any other tire marks in the snow. Look at this," she gestured to the road in front of them, "nobody's driven here. They've got to have Tim back at the resort. They've got to."

Carter took his time before answering. "They wouldn't risk trying to get him into a car in the parking lot. Tim would know he was being kidnapped, and would try to get attention."

"They took Joan before she knew what was happening."

"Chances are," Carter continued, "they lured the kids away from the lodge, then took them somewhere on the mountain, someplace they could reach by foot."

She stared out the window, looking below them at the scattered wisps of smoke from faraway homes tucked in the valley below.

"With all the skiers out there, it would've been impossible to follow any footprints," he added as if trying to dissuade an argument before it began.

"We're moving away from them," she repeated with a sinking heart.

"They want something from you," Carter said as they slid past a stop sign and lurched onto an adjoining road. "Do you know what they want?"

"I haven't the foggiest."

"Whoever called had to know that you didn't have it with you. He knew it was at your house, or near your house." It felt as though the high bumper on the Expedition was cutting through the snow as if it were a snowplow, but Carter seemed not to notice as he added, "You've got to go home to get it."

"I don't know what I could possibly have…" her voice faded.

"Think, Kit," Carter insisted, his hands clenching the steering wheel tighter. "It's got to have something to do with Joan and Bernard."

"But Tim never had anything to do with Joan and Bernard. Why take him?"

"Because they need you."

"I don't follow—"

"You have something they want, something you can't get if they kidnap *you*. They've got to ensure that you cooperate, that you get them what they need."

"And what better way to do that, than to take my child?"

"Now you're catching on. We've got to figure out what it is they want."

"I just keep hearing Tim's voice," she said softly, "he sounded so small and lost. His words just didn't make sense."

"People say weird things when they're under stress."

"I hope he doesn't get them upset," Kit continued. "I should have told him to do whatever they tell him. I should have told him I loved him…" She gulped back tears.

"Don't do that to yourself. Just focus on the present. We're going to get whatever it is they want, and we're going to exchange it for Tim and his friend."

"How would I even know when I had it?" Kit wondered aloud, as she stared out the window at the cold, gray sky. She thought of Joan's office, probably locked and the paperwork dispersed throughout the office, of Bernard's projects, all reassigned… and of the laptop with the emails that might hold a clue.

They would call at midnight, and Frank wouldn't be there. Frank, who was always off on a business trip, always putting his career ahead of his family. And now their son was gone, missing like Joan, and she could only hope and pray that he didn't end up like Bernard.

Frank wouldn't be there, but Carter would be.

She glanced at him out of the corner of her eye. He was so close, she could easily reach over and touch him. His eyes were narrowed, focused on the road in front of him, his large hands gripping the wheel so tightly that she could see the knuckles protruding under his leather gloves. His dark hair was tousled, and for the first time she noticed a few streaks of gray at the temples. His forehead was lined, as was the outer edges of his eyelids, lined as if he were used to squinting, used to driving into the sun—

The vehicle swerved around a corner, and she saw his eyes widen, his hands grip the wheel even tighter. She swung around and stared through the windshield as a racked buck darted directly into their path.

"Watch out!" he yelled as the vehicle spun wildly in the road. The bumper caught the deer squarely in the chest, hurling him into the windshield. Kit screamed as the antlers ripped through the glass, her arms instinctively covering her head as shards of glass pounded her. In the next instant, the deer was gone and in its place was a gaping hole. The trees spun around them.

She heard a crunch. In her panic, she imagined the vehicle striking the deer again, and then they slowed, the trees coming to a stop, their huge branches low with the weight of the snow.

"Don't move," Carter whispered.

Kit fought the scream that rose in her throat. Keeping as still as possible, she turned her eyes from Carter to the side window. Her side of the vehicle hovered off the road, off the mountain, and above the sheer drop below.

"Are you okay?" he whispered.

"I think so. Are you?"

"I've been better."

It felt as if every second was the last one of her life.

Carter reached for her hand, whispering for her to inch her way slowly toward him. Carefully, she unbuckled the seatbelt, her hand guiding it back to the doorframe. Holding her breath, as if the movement of her lungs could send them tumbling over the precipice, she maneuvered to Carter's side of the vehicle. It felt like an eternity before he had the door opened, and they slithered into the snow.

Beyond them in a pool of blood lay the still buck, its unblinking eyes fixed on the sky.

"What do we do now?" Kit asked shakily, awed by the vast ruggedness surrounding them.

Carter pulled himself to his feet and helped Kit up. He slid, more than walked, from the front end of the Expedition to the back.

Minutes crept by. A cold northern wind howled through the trees, picking up the snow as if a giant hand was scooping it up and tossing it about, encircling them with the biting wet flakes.

"I haven't seen a house for miles," Carter said, echoing Kit's thoughts.

She raised her arm to the wind to protect her eyes, and peered around her as he walked down the road and rounded a bend. A few minutes later, he was back, shaking his head.

"We can't just stay here like this," she said.

"We can't pull this vehicle back to the road with our bare hands, and I don't see anything resembling shelter." He pulled his cell phone from his belt clip.

"What are you doing?" she asked.

"Calling for help. What did you think I was doing?" He walked back to the vehicle and surveyed the damage. A short while later, he pressed the *Off* button and retracted the antenna.

"What's happening?" Kit asked.

"Nothing. Not a damn thing."

"Didn't—?"

"State Police are overwhelmed. They aren't promising when they'll be able to respond."

She crossed the road and surveyed the sheer face of the mountain. "We've got to get out of the wind, or we're going to freeze to death."

Carter juggled his phone for a few seconds, deep in thought. Then he joined Kit as she walked along the side of the mountain. A few minutes later, they found an overhanging piece of cliff that would protect them from the blinding wind.

They used their feet to brush away the snow. The crevice was barely large enough for the two of them. Then they crawled inside and drew their knees to their chins.

Kit blew on her gloved hands and covered her face, trying to warm her nose and cheeks. She brushed shards of glass out of her hair. Her lips felt like they were going to peel off.

She felt Carter's arm reach tentatively around her.

"I'm not coming on to you," Carter said before she could speak. "We'll fare better if we keep each other warm."

She nodded and cuddled against him, and tried not to think about the long way home and the telephone call that would be waiting for her there.

The sun was low in the sky when they heard the crunch of tires approaching. Stiff from huddling in the crevice, they slipped and slid into the center of the road. Carter waved his arms as the vehicle approached.

It was a quarter ton pickup, the red paint dulled with age, the front fender rusted with long ago accidents that creased the metal into grimace flanking a weather-beaten winch. The truck slowed to a stop.

Carter ran to the passenger door and opened it. "We had an accident up the road."

"Hop in," the man answered, his face partially hidden by the brim of his cap.

Kit climbed in first, followed by Carter. He'd barely gotten the door closed before the truck began to move.

"You're a godsend, buddy," Carter said. He briefly explained what had happened. The man nodded a couple of times but remained silent. He kept both hands firmly on the steering wheel. As Kit stared at his gloved knuckles, she thought it was odd somehow, a man driving a beat up old pickup wearing expensive leather gloves.

Carter nervously pulled out a pack of cigarettes. "You mind?" he asked.

"Rather you didn't," the man answered, without removing his eyes from the road. "Don't you know smoking is bad for you?"

Carter glanced at Kit. Without a word, he returned the pack to his pocket.

They were back at the Expedition almost immediately.

A few moments later, blocks secured the pickup and the winch's hook was in place. Carter climbed into the driver's seat, and Kit watched silently as Carter slipped the vehicle into neutral and gave a nod.

"Watch yourself," the man said to Kit.

She glanced toward him and found herself staring into the coldest gray eyes she'd ever seen. They were so light they looked like glass, and as the man stared back at her, she felt his eyes boring straight through her. She stifled a sudden urge to run, to pull Carter out of the vehicle before this man plunged him to his death—

"You might want to stand over there," the man said quietly, nodding his head to the opposite side of the road, "out of harm's way."

She nodded, her mouth dry. Somehow she managed to move her legs, to make her way to the side of the road. When she'd stopped and turned back, she found Carter staring at her across the road with a quizzical expression.

She shook her head silently. It was her imagination, after all.

A moment later, the vehicle had all four wheels on the road, and Carter was climbing out of the driver's seat, wiping the perspiration off his forehead. The man joined him as he disengaged the hook.

Carter pulled his wallet out. "I don't know how to thank you," he said, pulling out a few bills.

The man waved them away. "No need for that." He retracted the cable, and before Carter or Kit could say another word, he was back in the truck and driving away.

Kit shivered as the taillights, one broken and shining white, the other a dull red from winter grime, disappeared around the next bend in the road.

"Come on," Carter said, wrapping his arm around her shoulder, "you're freezing."

"It's not that," Kit murmured. But Carter appeared not to have heard her as he swept the glass off the seat out into the road.

CHAPTER 14
十四

It was two minutes past midnight when they pulled into her driveway after making their way to Interstate 81 toward Strasburg, then to I-66 to the Washington Beltway, the wind whipping them through the gaping hole in the windshield. Once they reached the DC area, a thick layer of sand and salt replaced the pristine snow. But when they took the exit to Springfield, they found themselves again in a winter wonderland.

The lights were still on from when Kit had rushed from the house after Tim's call, only 30 hours ago.

As they made their way up the slippery walkway to the front door, they heard the telephone ringing.

Kit shakily unlocked the door. They almost fell over each other as they hurried inside.

Kit reached the telephone first, her fingers closing around the receiver as she fell to the floor. "Hello? Hello?"

A calm voice answered. "You're late. You think we're playing games here?"

"No. No," she said breathlessly. "The roads—"

"Your son's life depends on how well you follow instructions. Understand?"

Carter was on the floor now, his ear pressed close to the receiver.

"Yes."

"You have some software that belongs to me."

"Software?" She glanced at Carter, who was staring at her with furrowed brows.

"A set of programs. Written partially in English, the rest in Chinese."

Her heart was beating so loudly, she was sure he could hear it over the phone. "Yes."

"Get it."

"What do I—?"

"At precisely eleven o'clock tomorrow night, be at First Virginia Bank on Route 1 in Alexandria. Go to the night deposit box. Behind the envelopes, you'll find instructions."

She swallowed hard.

There was another soft beep, and he continued, "Come alone. If you call the police, if you tell anyone, your son is dead."

Before she could answer, he'd disconnected. Slowly, she returned the handset to the cradle.

UCT was impenetrable. She would never make it past Customs, never be able to smuggle a disk out without it being detected.

She leaned against the couch. Joan had given her that assignment; it was one Bernard was supposed to have worked on. Had he worked on it at all? What connection could Joan and Bernard have had with a program written in Mandarin?

"Mind filling me in?" Carter said gently.

She shook her head slowly. "He wants a program."

"That much I heard."

"I don't know how I can get it."

"You know what he's talking about?"

She stared across the floor at him as if seeing him for the first time. "Yes."

"What does this program do?"

"It counts."

"*It counts?*"

She shook her head as if trying to free herself from an internal spider web that had taken control of her and wouldn't let her go. "It doesn't make sense."

Carter's voice returned to its normal timber. "Bernard is murdered, Joan is missing, Tim and Jason have been kidnapped—over a program that *counts?*"

The thought was so ludicrous that Kit burst into nervous laughter, and then quickly became subdued as the gravity of their situation sunk in.

"It doesn't matter what it does," she said. "All that matters is, I've got to get it. Some way, somehow, I have to steal that program."

"Where is it?"

"In my office."

Carter jumped up, and reached his hand down to Kit. "What are we waiting for?"

She grabbed his hand and pulled herself to her feet. "You don't understand."

"Then enlighten me."

"It's not that simple. I can't just waltz into my office, retrieve the program, and waltz back out."

"It's the middle of the night. If we go now—"

"Carter," Kit said, grasping his hands and squeezing them tight, "I appreciate what you're trying to do. But my office is guarded around the clock."

"But you work there; surely you can get past security…"

"Yes, I can get past security going into the building. And I can get back out. But what I'm trying to tell you is, I can't take the program with me. The office where that program's kept is under such tight security that there's just no way I can smuggle it out."

They fell silent. Kit knew that Carter was out of his league now, and there was only so much she could tell him without risking her job—and her life. If her life wasn't already ruined by the disappearance of her laptop, that is.

"Wait a minute," Kit said. "I've been working on that program for weeks now. I can rewrite it."

"Do you remember that much of it?"

"I remember enough. There's just one minor detail…"

"What?"

"I can't translate it into Mandarin. I need Chen for that."

"Chen?"

"Chen Ling, a coworker."

"Can we trust him?"

"We're going to have to. More importantly, he's going to have to trust us."

The elevator doors opened smoothly, the chime reverberating through the empty lobby. Kit cautiously peeked her head out before stepping into the lobby.

Barely an hour ago, Carter jump-started her minivan. She'd followed him to a body shop in Arlington, where he'd left the Expedition for an appraisal, dropping the keys in the night drop-off slot. Then she'd driven him to his apartment building. It was strange, seeing where he lived; for some reason, it made her breath catch in her throat, almost as if she were crossing a threshold of some sort. Now her minivan was downstairs in the garage, and she was certain the battery would be deader than road kill when she returned.

Now that she was at Customs, it felt like the entry to Fort Knox. When she finally passed through, she found Chen at his desk, as though it were noon and not the middle of the night.

"What are you doing here?" he asked.

"I could say the same to you," Kit answered. Her palms were drenched with sweat as she pulled her chair beside him.

"Chen, I swear to God, everything I told you is true," Kit whispered a few minutes later. "They know we have their program, and they want it back. There's at least two lives at stake here, maybe more…"

"There's just a couple of problems with this whole thing," he said, leaning back in his chair and propping his feet on his desk.

"What's that?" she asked.

"First, how do you know which program they want?"

"It's the Chinese program—"

"*Which one?*"

"Which one?" Kit repeated.

"Kit, you're working on one program. That doesn't mean that's all there is. We've been working on Chinese code for decades."

She felt her heart sink. "Of course."

"And we didn't take their programs—any of them."

"What do you mean?"

"They're copies. They're not the originals."

"So?"

"So, why would they come to us, and want a copy of it? Why not go to their own government, their own military or intelligence?"

"Unless," she said, hunching forward, "these are renegades, people working outside normal channels."

Chen shrugged. "Possibly."

Kit sighed loudly. "I just want to write a program similar to the one I've been working on. But I need you to translate it."

"Are you crazy?" Chen asked.

"Maybe. Probably."

"And you don't think they're smart enough to know whether it's the program they want?"

"Chen, who knew what I was working on?"

"What do you mean?"

"Who knew? You and I were working on this counting program together, just the two of us in this office. How would these guys know to come after me, instead of anybody else in this company?"

He hesitated. "I can't tell you."

"Chen, my son's life depends on it."

"Your son's life depends on you delivering some code. How we got it doesn't matter."

There was a moment of silence. Then Kit said, "Will you help me?"

Chen surveyed Kit for what felt like the longest moment of her life. Then finally, he answered, "Yes."

Kit stood up. "Let's get out of here."

"Why? I thought you wanted—"

"That's why we've got to get out of here. It's too risky to write it here. I have a PC at home."

"I'll meet you there," Chen said.

"Oh, no, you won't," Kit said. "I'm not letting you out of my sight. Not until this program is finished."

CHAPTER 15

十五

Kit watched the water drip through the automatic coffee maker. She could hear Chen and Carter talking in the next room, but their voices were too low to make out the words.

Not that she cared much about their conversation. It was barely eight o'clock Monday morning, and none of them had slept. Chen had jump-started her car and followed her home, and now that the minivan was parked in the driveway, that's where it would have to stay.

They'd gotten home around two. She'd spent several hours writing a program to count user entries, much as the Chinese program had done. Only hers, she thought smugly, didn't have that crazy bug in it that dropped entries. It counted up to four users simultaneously, the limit set by the original program, and each user's entries were counted independently of the others.

Now Chen was translating the program into Mandarin. It was a tricky process, because the statements couldn't be translated exactly. It needed to be converted into a computer language that would be understood and processed correctly by whatever computers the Chinese used, something Chen was more versed in than she was.

A short while ago, Carter had arrived at the house via taxi, and had been on the telephone ever since, trying to find out when his company vehicle would be ready. He mentioned in passing that his own car, a vintage 1964½ Mustang, couldn't handle an inch of snow, much less the avalanche of this weekend. He appeared worried about the damage to the Expedition and the furor it would cause—but not half as concerned as he was about getting it back.

She poured herself a cup of strong black coffee, and quietly closed the door between the kitchen and the dining room. Carter and Chen appeared not to notice.

She picked up the cordless phone. She was relieved that Carter was finally finished with his calls, so she could dial Frank's office.

The main receptionist, Dorothy Bethel, answered on the fourth ring. Kit formed a quick mental image of the woman she'd met at the company's summer picnic: fifties, maybe sixties, heavyset, graying hair pulled into a loose bun. Piercing blue eyes, a soft, wrinkled smile. Her grandchildren had accompanied her to the picnic.

"Dorothy, this is Kit Olsen." She thought she heard a slight gasp on the other end of the phone, but she couldn't be sure. "Are you there?"

"Yes, Mrs. Olsen," came the reply. Her voice was softer, seemed a little further away.

"Dorothy, where is my husband?"

"He isn't here."

"*Where is he?*"

There was a slight pause. "He's been out of town, at a convention, I think…" her voice faded.

"Where is Miranda?"

"Miranda?"

"Frank's secretary, Miranda Wade."

Now there was a longer pause. The talking in the next room had stopped, and the silence was suffocating. "Dorothy," Kit repeated, holding onto the counter with one hand, as if it would help to stabilize her, "where are they?"

"I'm sorry, Mrs. Olsen, I really can't tell you."

"You can't tell me, or you won't tell me?" she snapped. She felt the door behind her open, but she didn't turn around.

"I really don't want to be a part of this…" Dorothy's voice faded again.

"Listen to me. I have a family emergency. I've been trying to reach Frank all weekend, and I can't. I know there's no convention. I've spoken to the hotel. I have to reach Frank, and something tells me, you know where he is." Dorothy didn't respond, and Kit continued, "It's an emergency with our child. For God's sake, if you know where he is, you'd better tell me."

"Paradise Island, Bahamas," she answered softly. "They're both there. They're at the Paradise Island Casino and Resort."

"What are they doing there?"

"I told you, I don't want to—"

"What are they doing there?"

"They're having an affair. I don't like this, Mrs. Olsen, and I told them both before they left. It's not fair…"

Dazed, Kit clicked off the phone and stared through the kitchen window. Although her eyes were riveted on her snow-covered herb garden, her mind wasn't registering anything beyond Dorothy's words.

"Something wrong?" came Carter's soft voice.

She didn't turn around.

He walked up behind her and placed his hand on her shoulder. "Are you okay?"

"No, I'm not okay. My whole life is falling apart. My son's been kidnapped. We're putting together some bizarre hodgepodge of a program to try to get him back… and now I find that my husband's been having an affair with his secretary!" She laughed, but it sounded angry and forced. "His *secretary*! The woman's been in my house so many times, I can't even count them. She's eaten at my table, she's—she's—"

"Okay, okay," Carter said, pulling her around to face him. "Calm down. Everything's gonna be okay."

"How can you say that?" Then without waiting for his answer, she continued, "Almost twenty years, we've been married, and I've not once—not once— thought of any man but him. Now the worst thing that could happen to us, our child's been kidnapped, for God's sake, and he's at some island resort, frolicking with his *secretary*!"

"Listen to me," Carter said, pulling her face up to his, so his deep brown eyes met hers, "you're a strong woman. You've got to be strong now, more than ever. Maybe you can't depend on Frank right now, but you can depend on me. I'm here, aren't I? And I won't leave until we get your son back."

A lone tear trickled down her cheek, and she furiously wiped it away. "I don't know why you're doing this—"

"Don't worry about whys right now—"

"—but I swear to God, I'll make it up to you someday, somehow."

"Don't even think about that now," Carter said. "Just do me a favor, okay? As hard as it is, don't think about Frank and what he's doing. Not now. You'll have time for that later."

"I've got to call him."

"No, you don't."

"Yes, *I do*. Whatever he's doing to our marriage, one thing hasn't changed: Tim is his son, too. And he needs to know what's going on."

Carter let out a long sigh. Kit leaned her head against his chest. She could hear his heart beating so strongly. His chest was hard beneath his shirt, his arms muscular and protective. If she could just close her eyes and pretend that none of this was happening…

She felt his chin rest against the top of her head.

She'd have to call Frank and let him know what was going on. And she should call the police. They were experienced with this kind of thing.

And she'd just have to hope that the program Chen was translating would fool them long enough to make the exchange. Once she had her son back, once he was out of danger, then she would deal with the fragments of her marriage. Then she would sort everything out.

There was a quick rap on the back door, and she felt Carter turn slightly. She peered over his shoulder. The window blind over the door was pulled up, and on the other side stood Lisa, with an incredulous look on her face.

"I'm sorry, Lisa, I forgot to pick up your paper," Kit said for the umpteenth time.

"That's okay," she repeated. "We'll find it when David clears the snow from the driveway."

Kit stood awkwardly, not quite knowing what to say next. Carter stood near the kitchen table, obviously no closer to leaving the room than either Kit or Lisa were. Finally, she walked toward the back door and opened it. "I hate to be rude, Lisa, but if you don't mind…"

Her neighbor stood for a moment as if undecided whether to take the hint or stick around.

"I think she's trying to tell you," Carter said softly, "that we'd like to be alone."

Lisa didn't respond, but stood there as if she were weighing the situation, while Kit awkwardly held the door open for her to leave. Finally, Lisa walked outside. Once on the back stoop, she turned to say something, but Kit had already closed the door behind her. As Lisa stood gaping through the window, the blind was drawn and the door locked.

Kit pulled the laptop case from behind the couch, and took some time going through it. She was looking for clues: a stray note, a suspicious name, or a piece of equipment or supply that didn't fit… but found nothing. It was just a mass of tangled cords and equipment that appeared to be tossed in, as if Joan had been in a big hurry when she had last packed it.

Her mind wandered to the last time she'd seen Joan. Nothing had seemed out of the ordinary when she stopped in Kit's office. And if she was in a hurry or apprehensive about something, why had she asked Kit if she'd wanted to go for a drink?

Unless she was planning to tell her something, something she couldn't discuss in the office.

Kit steepled her fingers while she stared at the case contents. No, there'd been no indication that she'd wanted anything more than to relax over a drink with an old friend. Nothing at all.

She set the laptop on the dining room table, plugged in the mouse and the power cord, and powered it up.

Chen and Carter had been gone for almost an hour, and the house was hauntingly quiet. Chen had finished translating the program and had copied it onto a CD for her to deliver tonight. She glanced across the table at it, and wondered how the kidnappers would know if it was the program they wanted. She hoped they wouldn't have their own laptop present, and planned on going through it, line by line, while she waited. God help her.

She hesitated. How did she know if Chen had translated it exactly as he should have?

Of all the people who should have been approached regarding a Chinese program, it should have been him. So why hadn't he? Or had he been approached already? Could he be a spy?

The Windows desktop appeared, and Kit quickly logged onto Joan's email account. She sorted the list every way she knew how—by date, by sender, by subject—looking for clues.

Everyone at UCT received background checks at least twice a year. They had to be approved for every individual project they worked on. They had to report any contact they'd ever had with a foreign national, and had to get their vacation plans and trips cleared whenever they went out of the country. Certainly, Chen with his background and his knowledge would be watched. For all she knew, she was being watched even closer since she'd started working with him. They didn't let just anyone past Customs.

She went back to the email that mentioned meeting Toy at the gristmill, and pondered over its meaning. What could Joan and Bernard have been working on?

She went into the directories and studied the project names. Joan, like her, had also copied programs onto her laptop, programs that shouldn't have left the agency offices. There was a program designed to track accounts held by the CIA—off-shore accounts comprised of money seized in covert operations, money the American public would never know anything about. Could the Chinese want that program?

She flipped through it. It was just a shell, a program with no data. It was worthless without the data.

Another program was just the beginnings of an application designed to break codes, looping through millions of combinations until it was able to translate coded text intercepted by intelligence sources. But it was in the preliminary phases, and didn't have enough in it to be of any value.

A third program was the election program they'd designed last year, to computerize election returns so the problem of dimpled and pregnant chads that so haunted the 2000 presidential election would never happen again. Nothing secretive about that, except that the American public thought it had been developed by a private company. She'd always thought it interesting that the CIA, normally focused on foreign affairs, would even have had a hand in it's development.

The grandfather clock in the hallway began to chime. Twelve noon. Eleven more hours until she would deliver the program, and God willing, get her son back.

Chen was driving Carter to his office, and then he was going in to work as well. She was off the hook, at least for today, since the federal government was officially shut down due to the snow. Chen, of course, would be expected to show up regardless...

They'd had a debate before they'd left, on whether to call the police. Kit had been emotional, Carter logical. She wanted to call them; he was adamantly opposed. In the end, he'd made her promise not to make any phone calls. She'd reluctantly agreed, only because she was tired and wanted everyone to go away and leave her alone with her thoughts. Once they were gone, she would make up her own mind.

She glanced into the living room at the telephone.

Why hadn't Jason's mother called?

The last his mother had heard from Jason, his sister had left the ski resort without him, and they were waiting for Kit to pick them up. Since then, there'd been news reports about people stranded at Ski Top Mountain, an accident on the slopes, Bernard's dead body had been found, and neither Tim nor Jason had returned home.

Wasn't it kind of odd that his mother wasn't on the telephone, frantically calling Kit's house to find out where everyone was?

Or had they gone to the resort themselves, to try and get their son?

Could they be dealing with the kidnappers themselves?

Kit tapped her fingers on the table. What would she tell them? That their son was missing, that she hoped she could make a switch with the kidnappers tonight? That would bring at least one, maybe two, more people into the mix. No, she shouldn't try to call them.

On the other hand… maybe she should call them. Maybe Jason's mother was just as worried as Kit would be, if she hadn't heard from Tim. Fact was, if she hadn't heard from Tim in forty-eight hours, she'd be parked at the police department, demanding action. She'd be fit to be tied.

She should call them.

And tell them what?

She pushed the laptop back, walked into the living room, and picked up the phone. She'd just have to wing it.

The phone was answered on the second ring.

"Stephen?" Kit asked. It didn't sound quite like Jason's father, but—

"No, this is Jason."

"*Jason?*"

"Mrs. Olsen?"

"What are you doing home?" she asked, her heart beating so loudly that she was sure he could hear it over the phone.

"They closed school today, didn't you hear?"

"How did you get home?"

"Get home from where?"

God, she hated talking to teenagers. "From Ski Top Mountain, where do you think?"

"When you and Tim left—"

"*When me and Tim left?*"

"When you and Tim left," he repeated in a voice that betrayed his impatience, "one of the security guards offered to take me home."

"One of the guards at Ski Top Mountain?"

"Yeah."

"When? When did he take you home?"

"I don't know. Sunday morning, sometime."

"What time Sunday morning?"

"I don't know, I wasn't checking my watch," he said in a voice that Kit was all too familiar with. She could picture Jason rolling his eyes on the other end of the line, as she knew Tim did all too often.

"Jason, listen to me. Who told you that Tim and I had left?"

"The security guard."

"A security guard, in uniform?"

"Yeah."

"How did you and Tim get separated?"

"We went out looking for those skimobiles that crashed into each other, you know."

"No, I don't know. I told you both to stay with me."

"Yeah, but they asked us to help."

"Who asked you to help?"

"The security guards. Geez, Mrs. Olsen, don't you think you should be asking Tim all this?"

Kit hesitated. If she went on much longer, he'd know that Tim wasn't with her—

"I don't want to get Tim in any trouble," he was saying. "It's no big deal. We found the skimobiles, I was talking to one of the guys there, and all the sudden, Tim was gone. Then one of the guards told me you two had left, and he offered to drive me home."

Kit was quiet, and Jason asked in a small voice, "Tim's not in any trouble, is he? I mean, we were only gone a few minutes—"

"Yes, he's in trouble," Kit answered, squeezing back the tears that threatened to engulf her, "he's going to be grounded for a few days. Don't bother calling him. He'll call you, when he can."

After some curt good-byes, Jason hung up. Kit remained in the living room, clutching the phone, not even hearing the dial tone that droned on against her ear.

CHAPTER 16

十六

It was after ten o'clock when Kit locked the front door and pulled it closed. It was unusually cold for December, the temperature already plunging below freezing. A full moon had already risen and was so intense that the snow reflected its brightness, illuminating the front lawn almost like afternoon.

She began to slip on the ice-covered cement. Instantly Carter's firm arms grabbed her and kept her from falling. He kept his arm protectively around her as they made their way down the sidewalk. He was so firm footed his shoes must have been made from tire treads, while she continued to slide along.

Once she was seated, Kit watched silently as Carter closed the door behind her. She noted that the windshield had been replaced, but the damage to the front fender had not been touched. She decided against asking him about it. A flash of light caught her eye, and she turned in the direction of her neighbor's house. Lisa had the curtains pulled back in an upstairs bedroom, and was watching them. As Kit's eyes met hers, Lisa dropped the curtain.

Carter and Kit were silent as they headed east toward Route 1, each engrossed in their own thoughts. Kit still hadn't heard from Frank. Not a single phone call. She wondered if he'd spoken to his office, and if he was aware that his affair was out in the open.

She glanced at Carter. And now here she was, going to meet her son's kidnappers with a man she barely knew.

He must have felt her looking at him; he half-smiled and grasped her hand.

"It's going to be alright," he said softly.

With her other hand, she tightly held the compact disk that would be the key to her son's freedom. "I know," she answered with more conviction than she felt.

Route 1 was known as Jefferson Davis Highway along this stretch, and was normally covered with bumper-to-bumper traffic at just about any time. But tonight it was deserted, except for the occasional police cruiser and snowplows. Kit thought it looked surreal.

They drove past Beacon Mall, it's neon lights bright against the snow, the parking lot empty. Even the Krispy Kreme was closed, the "hot donuts now" sign dark.

They reached First Virginia Bank, and Carter paused while he shifted the vehicle into four-wheel drive. Their parking lot hadn't been cleared; it looked as if more than two feet of snow had fallen. Their eyes met. Both of them had noticed it: tire tracks leading from the street through the lot and past the night deposit box.

Across the street, a police car was stopped beneath a light, the officer watching the road crews. He turned his head in their direction. They stared at each other for a brief moment. The officer adjusted his glasses and peered at them with more than a little curiosity.

"We're not doing anything wrong," Carter said, his lips barely moving. He stepped cautiously on the gas. They felt the snow crunching under their weight. They circled the front of the bank and turned toward the night deposit box.

Kit glanced in her side mirror. The police car was still sitting there, but she couldn't see the officer clearly. Was he still watching them?

Carter turned on the interior light.

"What are you doing?"

He stopped at the night deposit box. "Open your purse, act like you're getting something out," he said.

Kit complied, her hands clammy as she rifled through her purse, while he reached through the window to the stash of envelopes. She watched him out of the corner of her eye as he reached toward the back and pulled out an envelope—and a neatly folded note.

He handed them to her; the note slipped into her lap as she slid the envelope across her purse and held it up to lick it. Then she closed it and handed it back to him. He opened the drawer and deposited the empty envelope, pushed the drawer back into place, and started out of the lot.

Her fingers shook as she opened the note.

"Don't hold it up," he said. "The cop's still watching."

"Head south," Kit said.

As they moved away from the officer, she read out loud, "Turn left at Roy Rogers. Go one quarter of a mile. Stop at the parking lot. Get out and walk to the building. Come alone. Leave the reporter behind."

Roy Rogers was a fast-food restaurant less than three minutes away, the kind of place Kit had taken Tim when he was younger, but for some reason she couldn't remember now, they hadn't been to in years.

Carter made the left turn, and promptly pulled into a gasoline station.

"What are you doing?" Kit asked.

"Getting a cup of coffee. Or appearing to."

Kit nodded.

"Get out, come around to the driver's side."

"I can slide over—"

"Do what I tell you."

She got out and half-walked, half-slid to the driver's side, where Carter was waiting with the door open for her. She climbed inside and adjusted the seat.

"I'll give you ten minutes. Then I'm coming after you." He closed the door before she could reply.

Without looking back, he walked to the door of the station's convenience store, which was open but deserted, and stepped inside. Through the window, she could see him approaching the counter, his shoulders squared.

She put the vehicle in gear and turned onto Mount Vernon Memorial Highway.

She glanced at the odometer. "One quarter mile," she half-whispered.

She'd been down this street before, especially when family and friends came to visit. At one end was Mount Vernon, the plantation home of George Washington; at the opposite end was Woodlawn Plantation, the home he'd given his daughter when she married. They were roughly three miles apart. They had once been part of Washington's plantation, divided into a handful of farms, but were now littered with subdivisions and the urban growth of the DC area.

It seemed as if she'd never reach the quarter mile point, and she was beginning to wonder how Carter would ever get to her through the snow and the slick streets. She doubted if he would hear her screams for help, if she needed him. She was on her own.

Her mouth was dry, her lips parched. For all she knew, she was driving straight into their hands. She might be joining Tim, Joan—and Bernard.

She glanced at the compact disk, now lying on the front seat. What am I doing? But in the next instance, she knew: she would do whatever it took to get Tim back, even if it meant going into a lion's den.

There was a street light at the quarter mile mark, and a small turnaround where a plow might have stopped on a break. She pulled off the road and turned off the engine.

There wasn't another vehicle in sight.

On the other side of the road was a solitary building. From the light cast by the moon through the naked trees, it appeared to be of brown brick, a chimney rising high at one end but with no comforting smoke to indicate a fire within. In fact, it appeared deserted.

Kit hesitated. What if this were the wrong place? What if the kidnappers were waiting somewhere else, and she was here, waiting for them?

She looked at the odometer again. One quarter mile, exactly.

She peered down the street in both directions. There was nothing even remotely close.

Grasping the disk, she opened the door.

The street had been cleared but with the plummeting temperatures, the thin layer of slush left behind had turned to a slick layer of ice. Halfway across the street, she began to slide. She jerked backward, then forward in an effort to keep from falling, her movements catapulting her across the road. She slammed against a wooden sign, dropping the disk into the snow.

Frantically, she knelt down, her gloved hands searching for the all-important disk. At last, she felt it against her fingertips, and pulled it out, wiping it dry against her coat.

Slowly, she used the sign to pull herself up. Her coat had brushed off part of the snow that had accumulated on the face of the sign. Roiling clouds obscured the moon for a brief moment; then with a flash of light, it emerged and illuminated the sign: George Washington's Gristmill.

She felt her face freeze in fear and trepidation. So this was the gristmill, undoubtedly the same place Joan and Bernard met Toy at precisely this same hour, a lifetime ago.

She peered through the darkness at the building. Now it had a haunted quality, the darkened windows were sunken eyes, the smokeless chimney sinister against the sky.

She trudged through the snow to the door. A new padlock was in place.

As she stood there, holding the padlock, she felt the hairs on the back of her neck bristle, as if something was behind her, breathing down her neck. Her heart was pounding so hard her chest hurt.

Slowly, she turned around.

"Kathryn Olsen?"

The voice came from a short distance away. The only time she could recall being referred to by her first name was as a child, when she'd committed some unpardonable sin that her parents were sure would land her at the gates of hell.

The trees cast long silhouettes across the ground, reaching like tentacles from the edge of the woods to her feet. Something moved quietly in the shadows—a figure, tall, with broad shoulders. He wore a wide-brimmed hat, dark gray. His raised coat collar obscured his neck. The gloom cast by the collar, the hat, and the trees shrouded his face in darkness.

"Yes," she said, her voice sounding stronger than she felt. "I'm Kathryn Olsen."

When he reached her, he calmly pulled the padlock from her with a leather-gloved hand. With one swift movement, it was opened. "Were you followed?"

"No."

"Are you sure?"

"We were careful. No one knows I'm here."

He opened the door and motioned her inside.

It took a moment for her eyes to become accustomed to the black interior. The walls were brick or stone, she couldn't tell which in the dark—and they seemed to close in on her, causing her to shiver as much from fear as from cold.

The door closed behind her. She turned as the man switched on a flashlight and fumbled at the door. He was locking them in.

She wanted to brush past him, to begin screaming and try to make her escape while she still could, but she stopped herself with every ounce of willpower. No one would hear her screams. She had no bargaining power. She still gripped the disk tightly in one hand; in the next instance, he could shoot her and he would have the program and she would be dead. And there would be no one left to rescue Tim and Joan—if they were both still alive.

Her heart was pounding so loudly that she was certain the man could hear it. Her breathing was labored, the cold causing her short puffs of air to enshroud her in a thickening fog.

He turned around and cast a light onto wooden steps. "Follow me."

She glanced at the door. The padlock was in place on this side now. That meant he held the key.

He climbed a few steps and stopped, not bothering to turn around. His coat looked more like a cape from behind.

Kit took a deep breath and made her way to the staircase. He waited until she began to climb the stairs before he continued, the darkness of the wood and stone seeming to swallow them up as they ascended.

They were standing on the third floor. As cold as it was, he opened a window, fastening it in place with a wooden peg. When he turned toward her, she caught a glimpse of a squared jaw and hawk-like nose. His eyes were still obscured by the brim of the hat; she wasn't sure if she wanted to see them anyway.

He turned off the flashlight.

"What do you have for me?" he asked.

She held out the disk.

"What is it?" he asked, his hands firmly planted in his coat pockets.

"It's the program, the one you wanted."

"How do you know it's the right one?"

She swallowed. "It's the Chinese code."

"How did you get it?"

"Never mind that. I got it. That's all that matters. Now where's my son?"

He chuckled. "Hold it up, so I can see it."

She held it in front of the window. The light cast by the moon reflected off the gold cover.

He reached toward the disk, seemed to pause just short of touching it, and then with a slight chuckle, took it from her.

"Has anyone missed your laptop?" he asked.

She hesitated. "No."

"No one has questioned you about it?"

"When do I get it back?"

"It has some very valuable information on it. Information we can use. Information the CIA would be hard-pressed to explain, if they find out we have it."

"Keep it," she said abruptly. "Just let my son go."

"Don't you care what happened to your friends Joan and Bernard?"

The wind had picked up, causing the room to suck in the chilly air like a person inhales when frightened. Kit shivered uncontrollably. With the window open, she could throw herself through it. The snow would break her fall, and if he didn't have friends waiting outside—

"They double-crossed us," the man answered evenly. "Don't play games with us. You'll have a better chance of staying alive."

"I don't know what you're talking about."

He placed the disk into a pocket on the inside of his coat. Kit noticed his weathered brown leather gloves. He had long fingers. He had no hint of an accent. He was an American, not Asian. What could he possibly want with Chinese code?

She watched as he calmly loosened the wooden pegs and closed the window. The darkness closed in around her like a casket slamming shut. She struggled to adjust to the darkness.

She could hear him, hear the brush of metal against metal. She was a fool to come here. She could never have bargained for Tim's life; she was at their mercy. And now they had separated her from her only ally, who was probably drinking a hot cup of coffee a quarter of a mile away.

She lunged through the darkness. She had to get out of here, to get away from this monster before he killed her. Her shoes slid across the wooden floor, now damp with melting snow from their clothes. In one moment, she was sliding across the floor and in the next, she was airborne, her feet frantically trying to find solid ground, her arms flailing as she plummeted down the stairs.

She landed on the next floor with a solid thud, the breath knocked out of her.

She heard a chuckle above her. She hastily came to her feet, one forearm protecting her eyes from the light he shone in her face, her other arm groping for anything that could be of use.

"Don't be an idiot," the man said as he deliberately descended the stairs.

Her hand closed around a metal pole of some sort, and she ripped it away from the wall as he neared her. "Get away from me," she snarled.

He stopped. In the darkness, he appeared to be assessing her weapon.

The flashlight was no longer pointed into her face. She studied him as she stood there, the metal pole pointed toward him as if to impale him if he stepped toward her. He held the flashlight in one hand. His other hand was calmly resting in his pocket. How would she know if he were going for a gun? He could shoot her right through his coat, and she'd be dead before she could react.

"You're not going to kill me to get back the disk, are you?" he said calmly.

She didn't answer.

"You did make a backup, didn't you?"

She remained silent. This wasn't what she'd expected. But then, she hadn't thought far enough ahead to know what to expect.

She hoped in the minutes that had ticked by, that Carter had been able to make his way toward her, that he'd spotted the Expedition parked across the street and was able to follow her footprints through the snow to the building. Maybe he was waiting just outside the door, waiting to clobber this guy when he opened the door, to whisk her away to safety—

Or maybe he was still drinking a cup of coffee and waiting for her return.

Maybe her fate was in her own hands.

"Where's my son?" she asked in a firm voice.

"You'll never know, if you attack me with that thing," the man said. "Now will you?"

She noticed for the first time that he was shuffling his feet, inch by painstaking inch, moving toward her without raising his feet, quietly and methodically coming closer without a sudden lunge or rapid movement, but in another instant he would be upon her.

She jabbed the pole in his direction. His right hand was outside of his pocket now, his left still holding the flashlight. She felt a cold sweat trickling down the back of her neck. If she jabbed again, she'd better be prepared to penetrate right through his body, or he'd be likely to grab the pole and yank it away from her—and use it on her.

"Where's my son?" she repeated.

"He's waiting for you," the man answered calmly. She wished she could see his eyes, but they remained in shadow.

"Where?"

"In front of the main gate at Mount Vernon."

"If he's not there, I swear to God I'm coming after you," she hissed with more conviction than she felt.

"You'll never know if you don't let me open that door, now will you?" he answered.

She hesitated. He was right. She was standing between him and the door, and the door was padlocked. And he held the key.

Then the flashlight was turned off and they were encased in blackness.

CHAPTER 17

十七

Her bare foot jammed the gas pedal to the floor. Both hands gripped the steering wheel so tight her knuckles looked as if all the blood had been drained from her body.

Somewhere between the building and the road was her shoe, sucked into the snow as she ran. And in the road was the mate, hurled with such a force that the heel appeared embedded in the ice where it fell, slung off as she raced to the vehicle.

Behind her was Carter, perhaps making his way toward her—or maybe standing in the gas station's convenience store, nervously cooling his heels, waiting for her return.

She wouldn't stop to find out.

The odometer clicked off the miles as Carter, the gas station, and the gristmill disappeared behind her.

And in front of her lay a white wonderland, a frozen landscape of trees bowing toward the ground under the weight of the snow, the car headlights illuminating flashes of outstretched branches reaching toward the car as if to ensnare her within their grasp.

And on the front seat lay the metal pole, a three-foot-long fireplace poker, a blackened piece of iron with an accumulation of soot at one end, the pointed end paired with a protruding fishhook that only moments before, she'd been ready to pierce through a man's body.

She glanced into the rearview mirror. He was nowhere in sight. There was nothing behind her except the red reflection of taillights on the icy road and haunting trees stooping toward the freshly fallen snow, left in the darkness as she sped away.

When the flashlight was turned off, she instinctively bolted from where she'd been standing, convinced the next thing she'd feel was a bullet penetrating her body. But the room was silent, stiflingly silent; she couldn't even hear the sound of the man's breath or his footsteps on the wood, just her own heart pounding in her chest. And the next thing she knew, the door was banging open and shut, the padlock hanging precariously from the hasp, the glistening snow beckoning her out of the darkness.

So she ran. She ran like she'd never run before. She ran without breathing, without feeling the cold, without feeling the wet snow against her feet and legs. She ran without hesitation, ran as though every step could be her last, ran with the single solitary thought of reaching the safety of the vehicle—

She ran without so much as a glance behind her.

Even when she tumbled into the Expedition, started it, and raced into the road, she didn't look back at the gristmill, the stream, the woods, or the sign in front of the building, a sign that would be etched into her memory forever. Not until she was a mile away did she glance in the rear-view mirror to ensure that she was alone.

About three miles from the gristmill, the road curved slightly as she approached Mount Vernon. Reluctantly, she came to a stop.

She sat for a moment, her foot trembling on the brake pedal, her breath so heavy that the windshield was encased in a layer of fog.

She switched off the headlights.

The road was ghostly now, the only illumination from dim streetlamps leading to the parking lots and the main entrance of Mount Vernon.

Had he sent her on a wild goose chase? Would his cohort be waiting for her, waiting to finish her off as she drove around the bend?

Her palms were sweating, the steering wheel slick. She reached for her purse, and pulled out her cell phone. Should she call Carter now? What could he do, now that she had driven three more miles away from him?

Or should she call the police, and tell them everything?

She was wasting time.

Slowly, she eased the vehicle forward, remaining close to the edge of the road, staying in the shadows.

The sound of the tires crunching on the snow was deafening. It was impossible to sneak up on them. If they were there waiting for her, she was heralding her arrival like thunder in a storm.

She rounded the corner. Before her lay a wide sidewalk, a gathering place for tourists entering and leaving Mount Vernon. A place she'd spent more than one lazy Sunday afternoon, eating ice cream from the shop or resting her feet. There were park benches scattered around the circle, benches that normally were filled to overflowing with guests but were now vacant and laden with snow.

Except for one.

On one bench sat a lone figure, hunched over as if
to fend off the cold, a bright orange jacket and black ski
pants the only bit of color in the white wonderland.
The hood was pulled over his head, obscuring his face.

It could be a trap.

She could drive directly to the bench, stop on the
street right in front of it, and find out too late that it
wasn't Tim. She could be there like a sitting duck while
a hand came from the jacket pocket, pointed a gun
directly at her, and fired.

But she had to try.

Her foot felt like a slab of ice against the gas pedal,
the grooves biting into her skin. As she approached, the
hood rose a little and turned in her direction. Then the
hands slipped swiftly out of the pockets. Huge, blackened
hands.

She stopped and stared at the figure, tried to see it
clearly through the fogged windshield. Then finally:
black mittens. They were black mittens.

Could she see his face?

She struggled to see him, to identify him, afraid to
continue driving toward him but afraid not to attempt
it. Cautiously, she peered around him. Was he alone?

She glanced across the street toward the parking lots.
The roads were almost pristine, as if the road crews hadn't
reached this far.

The figure rose, one of the hands grasping the back
of the bench in what appeared to be an attempt to steady
himself. He looked as if he were staring at her, unsure
of what to do perhaps, or waiting for her to come closer.

She inched forward.

The wind was picking up, whistling past the vehicle,
causing the trees to sway violently, the snow flying off
their branches like whitecaps on ocean waves. Only these
whitecaps obscured her vision, made her lose sight of

the lone figure… he was there again, still standing in the same position, still watching her.

The wind whipped against him, pulling the hood off his head. As he reached up to grasp it and pull it back on, she recognized the dark brown shock of hair and her mouth went dry. She slammed her foot on the gas, raced toward him, and abruptly stopped in front of him.

As she threw the door open for him, she could tell by the look in his eyes that he had only just that moment recognized her. Without saying a word, he jumped into the front seat, slammed the door shut, and leaned against the back of the seat as if the weight of the world was falling from his shoulders.

She shoved her foot to the floor and made an abrupt u-turn in the middle of the street, riding over the curb in the process and coming back down on Mount Vernon Highway headed back the way she came.

He was whimpering in the front seat like a puppy left alone, his gloved hands covering his face, his back to her, looking small and frail.

She reached over to him, pulled the hood off his head, and ran her fingers through his damp hair. "It's okay," she said through her own tears. "You're safe now."

He didn't respond, and she wondered how safe they really were. Even as she continued reassuring him, she knew they would either have to drive right past the gristmill to get back to Carter, or spend the better part of an hour going around it.

She grabbed the phone and dialed Carter's number.

He answered on the first ring.

"Where the hell are you?" he demanded, his voice a mix of worry and anger.

"I'm coming back down Mount Vernon Highway," she said, her voice amazingly clear for the way she felt. "Where are you?"

"I'm at the gristmill—"

"Jesus."

"I see you—"

"Are you alone?"

"Of course I'm alone—"

"Are you sure?" she said.

"What the hell happened?"

"Are you sure?" she repeated.

"Yes, I'm sure!"

She saw him ahead, near the middle of the street, one arm raised in a wave, the other holding the phone against his ear.

When the car came to a stop, she was inches from him. He started to say something, perhaps yell something, and then he saw Tim in the front seat.

Kit's frantic glances around her appeared to unnerve him, and he raced to the back door. She hit the *unlock* button and he tumbled inside. Before he'd closed the door behind him, they were off.

They didn't stop until they'd reached Fort Belvoir four miles south on Route 1. The entrance was closed, an iron gate pulled tight across the roadway, barricades erected on either side.

They rolled to a stop, and Kit slipped the gearshift into park.

Carter didn't ask questions. He climbed over the seat, forcing Kit into the middle. As they took off with Carter at the wheel, Kit wrapped her arms around Tim and comforted him as he sobbed.

CHAPTER 18

十八

Kit felt the knot in her stomach long before they turned into her neighborhood. It was coupled with a feeling of impending doom, like watching a tornado form on the horizon. It was deathly quiet in the vehicle as she struggled with her emotions.

It was more than Tim pulling away from her. It was more than seeing his sobs turn to a cold, emotionless stare, more than the icy wall he was erecting around him. And it was more than her fear and anger toward the man at the gristmill. And more than wondering what would happen when they realized the program was not the one they wanted.

No, this feeling of an approaching disaster was about returning home… and about Frank.

When Carter pulled up in front of the house, she wasn't surprised to see Frank's Volvo in the driveway, parked behind her minivan. And maybe she should have been surprised at how the house appeared to be lit up as if fully occupied, but she wasn't.

She was trying to keep her heart from jumping into her throat when the Expedition rolled to a stop. Carter still had his hand on the gearshift when Tim flung the door open and bolted out of the vehicle. Before Kit could say anything, he was gone—his shoulders stooped as though he could make himself invisible as he hurried across the walkway to the unlocked door.

Kit watched until the door slammed shut behind him before turning to Carter.

He placed his fingers to her lips as if to silence her before she began. She searched his eyes, but they appeared veiled, his thick lashes shielding them from scrutiny.

She reached for his hand and pulled it away from her mouth. But as it fell to his lap, she didn't let go. "You can't come in."

"I know."

"I—"

"Just remember one thing for me, okay?" He leaned toward her and placed his other hand on her shoulder, giving it a slight squeeze as she stared into his eyes. "You've got options."

Kit swallowed. "Yes. I know."

"You have my number."

"Yes."

"Call me."

"I will."

Carter looked beyond her at the house. Reluctantly, she followed his gaze. The door was opening. The light was on in the front hallway. Frank's hulking figure stood in the doorway, a sinister silhouette that stretched from one side of the doorframe to the other.

"I have to go."

Carter nodded and released his grip on her shoulder. Her hand slipped away from his as she slid across the seat to the door. Once out, she turned back to him.

"Thank you. I won't forget what you've done for me—and Tim."

He nodded silently.

Kit closed the door. She stood in the stillness of the night and watched as Carter drove off. Every fiber in her body was screaming for her to race after him, but she didn't. She just stood there until the taillights had disappeared around a distant curve.

It hit her all of a sudden that her shoes were gone. She looked down at her feet, planted in two feet of snow, and marveled that she hadn't really noticed their absence before now. She shivered, but whether it was due to the cold, biting wind or her own growing apprehension, she couldn't tell. Finally, reluctantly, she trudged through the snow to the house and Frank's waiting figure.

She was bone tired, as if she'd used every ounce of energy, every bit of strength. And now that she was there, it was all she could do to keep from sinking to her knees.

She didn't look at Frank. She felt rather than saw him stepping aside as she passed by him, the tension so thick it threatened to engulf her. Instinct told her his face was red, his hands clenched in big, beefy fists. She could feel his breathing, hot and labored, as she entered the house.

Despite herself, she jumped when the door was slammed behind her.

She felt as if she'd been up for three days straight. It was her gut more than her brain that made her realize that she had a lot to say to Frank. But now was not the time. She'd been living from one moment to the next, and hadn't had a chance to think ahead to what she would do.

Now that Tim was safe and they were home, she wanted nothing more than to lock Frank out of the bedroom and crawl into bed. Tomorrow she would think everything through—Tim's ordeal, Frank's deceit… her own budding feelings for Carter.

She'd taken only a few steps into the house before she stopped short. They were not alone. She peered into the partially lit living room. From a darkened corner, she detected the light from a cigarette. Silently, she stepped inside.

The cigarette was abruptly snuffed out and the figure rose.

"Lisa," Kit said in astonishment.

"I've got to get home," she said as she grabbed her coat from the back of the sofa. "David's going to wonder what happened to me."

"What are you doing here?" Kit asked.

"I'll let myself out, Frank," she said as if she hadn't heard her.

Kit watched as she nonchalantly strolled through the dining room and into the kitchen, as if she'd just stopped by to borrow a cup of sugar. A moment later, the outside door opened and closed.

"Don't you dare—don't you even dare accuse me of cheating on you," Frank thundered. "I've been gone what, two days? Three days? It didn't take you long to pull up your skirt to that reporter!"

"I didn't do anything with that reporter," Kit said, "and you know it."

"I know it, huh? I know it?" He paced the room, and then stopped in front of her. He was so tall and his shoulders so broad that he cast a shadow across her face. "You didn't even try to hide it! Our neighbors even saw his car parked here all night! You were necking with him in front of Lisa—"

"No, I wasn't."

"You're saying Lisa's a liar? And you expect me to believe that?"

"I don't care what you believe."

"Well, you'd better. Because when you try to shove it up my nose that I've been having an affair, you'd better be prepared to have it shoved up yours. You're nothing but a slut."

Frank was a full eight inches taller than Kit, maybe more, and at least sixty pounds heavier. But now, as Kit squared her shoulders and straightened her backbone, her knuckles clenched and ready to pound him, it didn't seem to her that he was all that much bigger. She would whip his ass and take names, if it came to it.

"You don't even care to hear the truth," she said through clenched teeth.

He crossed his arms in front of him. "Try me."

She took a deep breath. Her words came out rushed, as though she was trying to get everything out before he could stop her. "Two days ago, Tim went skiing with Jason. They called and said they were stranded at the ski resort, and they asked me to come and get them."

"And you did," he finished. "You showed up with that reporter, and you two left with Tim."

"No, I didn't—"

"Spare me the lies, Kit. I've already talked to Jason and his mother. You'll be lucky if Tim's ever welcome at their house again, after you left Jason by himself—"

"I didn't leave Jason. And I didn't take Tim. Tim was kidnapped."

Frank snorted. "Yeah, sure. Whatever you say."

"I'm telling you, Tim was kidnapped."

"Show me the police report."

"I can't."

"Then I'll call Detective Munster—"

"Munski—"

"He'll get it for me."

Frank crossed the room and picked up the phone, but before he could dial, Kit was there with her finger on the cradle switch.

"There is no police report," she said.

"What a surprise." He slung the phone down. "Let's see now, he was kidnapped, the police weren't notified, your boyfriend helped you get him back, and now he's sleeping peacefully."

"He's not my boyfriend, and I doubt if Tim's asleep."

"Then let's just ask him what happened!"

"You don't have to," Tim answered from the doorway.

"How much have you heard?" Kit asked, coming to the door. Frank was right on her heels.

"You know, Mom, it doesn't matter how much I heard. Nothing matters. I just want you two to shut up and leave me out of this—"

Out of the corner of her eye, Kit saw Frank's arm recoil as if in slow motion, his powerful hand balled into a gigantic fist. She lunged for her son at exactly the same moment as Frank's muscular arm swung toward them, and just as Tim jumped back and out of the line of fire. Her husband's fist landed on the back of her head with a gigantic crack, and she plunged forward, her feet slipping out from under her as her head bounced off the doorframe.

The hallway swam around her, the air rippling like an ocean current. Tim's figure was tilted like an angled camera lens, and then he was gone. Somewhere in the darkness she heard a muffled noise, a door slamming...

When her eyes began to focus again, she was alone. She started to stand when she noticed the gaping hole in the bedroom door and saw the blood smeared across the white paint. She reached as if on automatic pilot to the back of her head. A huge welt was already beginning to surface. When she pulled her hand away, her palm was soaked with blood.

She grabbed the doorknob, pulled herself up and steadied herself. Frank was across the room, standing over the bed, pulling his clothes out of his suitcase as if there was nothing out of the ordinary.

She crossed the room in two seconds flat, grabbed his clothes out of his hands, and tossed them back in.

"What do you think you're doing?" he shouted.

"Don't bother unpacking," she said. "You're not staying."

"The hell I'm not—"

She brushed past him to the nightstand. With a speed that astonished her, she opened the top drawer and pulled out a Glock that Frank had purchased for her as protection while he was away on business. When she turned back to Frank, she had it clenched with both hands and leveled at his expansive chest.

"What are you doing?"

"Get out of here. And don't you dare come back."

"You can't keep me out of my own house," he said, taking a step toward her.

"One more step, and I'll empty this thing," she said, cocking the hammer. "It'll be self defense."

"You gonna use Tim as your star witness?" he said cockily.

"I don't have to. Your DNA is all over my head." She glanced at his knuckle. "You've even got my blood on your hand."

He looked down, startled. "It'll wash off—"

"Clean the door, too, while you're at it. You know as well as I do, you can't get it all."

"Kit," Frank said, his voice soft and smooth, "we're both tired. Let's kiss and make up, and everything'll be all right. I'll help you get cleaned up. You know I didn't mean to hit you—"

"Everything *will* be all right. But not with you here."

"Where do you expect me to go?"

"There's got to be a bed waiting for you somewhere," she said calmly.

"Fine. I know another woman who'd be glad to have me tonight." He returned to the bed and slammed his suitcase shut. "I'll be back in the morning."

"No, you won't. I'm changing the locks, and I'm getting a restraining order. And I swear to God, if you ever come back here, I'll shoot you dead."

"You can't keep me out of my own house—"

"Try me."

"Kit, all my clothes are here. Everything I own—"

"In less than twenty-four hours, everything will be packed and sitting at your office door."

"So you can run off with him? The reporter?"

"So you can run off with *her*, the *secretary*." She motioned toward the door. "Now get the hell out of here."

CHAPTER 19

十九

Bryce replayed a tape of Saturday's late night news broadcast. "You're just full of surprises," he said. A file photo of Carter appeared in the corner with a shot of Dina at the news desk, asking questions about the people stranded at Ski Top Mountain and the discovery of Bernard Emerson's body. On the tape, Carter's voice was scratchy, patched in via cell phone.

"What do you mean?" Carter said, propping his feet up on his desk and clasping his hands over his waist. He knew he'd been uncharacteristically quiet today. He'd been accused too many times of being a shoot-from-the-hip kind of guy, a man who'd talk first and think later, but today was different. Today, he felt introspective, which didn't come easy or often. And he knew if he didn't snap out of it soon, Bryce would figure something was up.

"I have so many questions, I don't know where to begin," Bryce was saying.

"Like…?"

"Like, how did you wind up at Ski Top Mountain to begin with?"

Carter shrugged.

"You don't ski," Bryce said.

"Nice observation."

"So, you just decided to take a leisurely drive in the middle of the worst storm to hit DC in a decade, and just happened to wind up at a ski resort, which, by the way, people couldn't get out of, but you could get into?"

"You wouldn't believe me."

"Try me."

Carter leaned forward. They were in a private office, a hole-in-the-wall, really, and no one else was in sight. Still, he lowered his voice conspiratorially. "You remember that woman I interviewed a month or so ago? The one who watched her friend being abducted?"

Bryce groaned. "Not her again."

"What's that supposed to mean?"

"Come on, Carter, she's all I heard about for weeks. Don't tell me you two went off for a romantic weekend getaway."

"Not quite."

"You never learn, do you?"

"Don't go there," Carter warned.

"Backing up now," he said, holding both hands up. "So, how'd you end up at Ski Top?"

"Her son was stranded up there. I agreed to drive her, if she'd give me another interview."

"So you two went up there together to get her son."

"Yep."

"And you got another interview."

"Not quite."

Bryce groaned again. He hit the rewind button on the tape, tossed the remote onto the desk, and crossed the room to an aged coffee pot. He poured a cup so thick it could pass for oil. "Okay, Sir Lancelot, so you two get up to Ski Top and you rescue her son. Then,

just by a stroke of luck—" he looked sideways at Carter–
"they find the body of her missing coworker, not the
woman she saw abducted, mind you, but some guy who's
been missing even longer."

"That's about the long and the short of it."

"So you're sitting on the biggest story to hit DC
in—"

"Hours?"

"Weeks. And what do you do?"

"Let me guess. Report the story?"

"You leave." Bryce returned to the desk and glared
at Carter. Carter remained silent, and Bryce took a swig
of coffee. "Do you know how much trouble you're in?"

"No, I guess I don't," he answered smoothly.

Bryce pulled up a chair and leaned toward Carter.
"Every reporter in DC and half of 'em in Virginia, are
scrambling to get rides to a hole in the mountain that
nobody can get in or out of. But that doesn't deter them.
Nope, by God. There's a steady stream of traffic out
there, while every other news organization tries to climb
on the bandwagon that Carter Leigh is already on.

"There's a dead body at Ski Top Mountain, and
Carter's sittin' on it, the scoop of the year. Everybody
else is headed west, but for some unknown, whacked-
out reason, Carter starts heading east."

Carter fixed his eyes on a calendar that hung on the
opposite wall. It was last year's, but he kept it hanging
for the picture. He'd always liked looking at the model,
with her long hair and longer legs… Now he noticed
for the first time that her eyes were blue. They weren't
brown and sultry like—

"What I want to know, Carter, is *why*?"

"That's what I'd like to know, too," came a voice
from behind them.

Carter felt slammed forward into the present, but he forced himself to deliberately slide his feet off the desk and slowly roll the chair around as if he were fully in control.

"Don't let me interrupt you," Detective Munski said as he sauntered into the room. Carter watched as he crossed to the coffee pot, began to pour a cup, paused as he assessed the black goop, and then poured it back into the pot. He turned to Carter. "You were just about to tell Bryce why you left Ski Top."

Carter leaned back in his chair. "I was just about to tell Bryce that it's none of his business."

Munski strolled to the desk and placed both hands, palms down, on the aged metal frame. "Maybe it's *my* business."

The room was silent as the two men stared each other down.

Munski broke the silence. "Mind leaving us alone, Bryce?"

Without a word, Bryce made for the door. Carter caught a glimpse of him out of the corner of his eye as he paused in the doorway. Unspoken words seemed to hang heavy in the air before he disappeared down the hallway.

Munski crossed the small room and nudged the door with his foot. It closed with a thick thud, like the entrance to a tomb being sealed forever. The room was instantly stifling with the dry, faintly foul warmth that comes from aged heaters and perspiring bodies in the middle of winter.

Munski grabbed a chair and wheeled it around so the back was facing Carter. Eyeing him, he sat down, his legs straddling the chair, his arms resting over the back as he leaned toward the reporter.

"You're in a bit of trouble," Munski said.

"You're the second person to tell me that today," Carter said. "I must be on a roll."

"You're headed for more, too, pal."

"I haven't done anything wrong."

"Convince me."

Carter met Munski's even gaze. He'd first met him when Munski was in the Air Force, while he was dating his sister. He was ramrod straight even then, a man known for his honesty but also known for his impatience with folks living outside the norms of society. They were alike in some ways; they both came in contact with the dregs of society every day, both felt the same disdain for them. But while Carter reported on them, Munski locked them up.

"How can I convince you, when I don't know what I'm accused of?" Carter asked.

"I got a call yesterday. From an Officer Brinley."

"He's an idiot."

"Yeah? Maybe you'd better take a fresh look at him." Carter didn't reply, and Munski continued, "Anyway, seems you and Mrs. Olsen—name familiar, Carter?— were there at Ski Top Mountain, trying to convince him her son was missing. Gettin' plum nasty about it, in fact. Next thing he knows, you two are outta there like bats outta hell."

Despite himself, Carter dropped his gaze and inspected his hands as though they held a great deal of interest for him while he tried to ignore Munski's penetrating eyes.

"So, what's the story, guy? Did you two put in a false police report? Or did she decide she wasn't that committed to finding her son?"

"Back off, Ski."

"Thing is, Carter, I can't back off. Things are official now. They're not just between you and me."

"What are you talking about?"

"Brinley filed a police report on the missing boy. It was picked up by the press. If you cared to watch your own station, you'd have seen it on this morning's news." He reached in his pocket and pulled out a pack of cigarettes and thumped it against the back of the chair. "So you'd think the mother would stick around, help in the search, or at least go into hysterics where everybody could see her. You know, do the talk show circuit. But she doesn't."

Munski pulled a cigarette out.

"Don't light up that thing in here," Carter said. "My boss can smell a cigarette from a mile away."

The detective left the cigarette dangling from his lip. "I take it he doesn't smoke?" When Carter didn't answer, he continued, "Anyway, she leaves. In a big hurry, in fact. No explanations, and no kid with her. Looks pretty suspicious, especially when she runs off with another man."

Carter eyed him warily. "How long is this story? I've got work to do."

"Oh, things get even better. The cops start making a few phone calls, asking questions, tracking down Mrs. Olsen and her" —he paused— "reporter friend. So we start to nose around a little here and there. Talk to the kid who was with Mrs. Olsen's son—what's his name, Tim? Turns out, the kid thinks Tim left with his mother—and you."

Carter remained quiet. He was having increasing difficulty breathing in the closed room.

"So, what's the story, Carter? Was he hiding in the back seat of your car?"

"No."

"I'm all ears."

"Is this an official visit?"

"This is an official visit."

Carter took a deep breath and casually wiped his hand across his forehead. He hoped Munski didn't see the beads of sweat he wiped from his brow. He thought of opening the door, letting a little fresh air in, but thought better of it. "The kid left with somebody else. Called his mom on her cell phone, told her he'd left. She was so upset, we took out after him."

"And didn't tell Brinley?"

"I told you, he's an idiot."

"And I told you, you need to think again." Munski stood, stretched his legs, and pulled the cigarette out of his mouth. He twirled it between his fingers for a moment. To Carter, the silence was becoming as stifling as the forced-air heat.

"Then there's the little matter of Bernard Emerson," Munski continued after a long silence.

Carter raised one eyebrow and tried to appear nonchalant.

"The guy didn't die from exposure," he said. He stood in front of Carter and fixed him with a long, hard stare. Carter got the impression he was trying to gauge his reaction. "Looks like a professional hit, two bullets right between the eyes."

"What does that have to do with me?"

"Unfortunately, the more you hang around with that Olsen woman, the more involved you get."

"How so?"

"Do you know what that woman does for a living?"

"She writes programs."

"She *breaks* programs," he corrected. "Breaks, as in deciphers. She works for the CIA, Carter."

"She works for UCT—"

"A contractor. Rumor has it, the CIA is one of their clients."

"So? Doesn't that still make her one of the 'good guys'?"

Munski paced the small room. "Do you know how many feds have been in my office in the last twenty-four hours? I've got FBI, CIA, Homeland Security, you name it, on my doorstep. They're all asking questions."

"What kind of questions?"

Munski stopped mere inches from Carter, leaning so close to him that the reporter could detect the faint odor of stale cologne. "Joan Newcomb and Bernard Emerson were working on some highly confidential programs before their disappearances—"

"What kind of programs?"

"You think they'd tell me, a local cop? Anyway, large sums of money start flowing into their bank accounts. *Large sums of money.* We're talking five hundred grand in each account."

"I still don't know what that has to do with me."

"Joan Newcomb was Kit Olsen's best friend. She was the only one who witnessed her so-called 'disappearance.' The Olsen woman also worked right down the hall from Emerson."

"So did dozens of others."

"Then we have you and the missus showing up at the very same resort where Emerson's body is found, at precisely the time it's found. Then we have this matter of a false police report, claiming her son is missing."

Carter let out a hefty sigh and started to stand, but Munski waved him back down.

"Oh, it gets even better," he continues. "The crack reporter, the one who's right on the scene when the body is found, doesn't stay to cover the story. Instead, he flees the scene."

"I…"

"Looks mighty suspicious. Even more so when they return to the missus' house for a romp in the hay—"

"We didn't do anything—"

"Save it, Carter. There're witnesses."

"Witnesses to what?" he bellowed. Too late, he realized that anyone passing by the office door could hear him. He lowered his voice. "Don't tell me somebody's claiming they saw us—"

"Does 'the neighbor' ring a bell?"

"The neighbor?"

"The neighbor claims she walked in on you two goin' at it—"

"That's a crock."

"Why would she make it up?"

"Why don't you ask her?" Carter stood. "What's this all about, Ski? About being fortunate enough to find the kid after we reported him missing? Or about an affair between Kit and me? I'm just not following you here."

"The woman's a suspect. You hanging around her makes you a suspect, too."

"A suspect in *what?"*

"It doesn't look good, Carter."

"What doesn't look good?"

"She's a married woman."

"So what? If everybody who hung around with a married woman was prosecuted in this state, the courts wouldn't get anything else done."

"She's not just a married woman. She's *the* married woman."

"What's that supposed to mean?"

"Stay away from her, Carter. Off the record, from one brother to another."

"Now, that's real interesting, Ski. Seems I recall that we're no longer brothers. In fact, seems I recall that my sister accused you of a bit of philandering—"

"You know it wasn't true. Besides, this isn't about me."

"I've got work to do," Carter said, pushing past him.

The detective's cell phone rang. He pulled it off his belt and raised it to his ear as he said, "Be careful, Carter. It's out of my hands. I won't be able to help you."

Carter slung open the door and almost tripped over Bryce.

"We gotta go," Bryce said, his eyes clouded.

"Good," Carter said as he brushed past him and started down the hall. "I need some fresh air."

"I've already got the equipment loaded," Bryce said, struggling to keep up.

"What have you got?"

"Body found. Washed up from the Potomac, near Mount Vernon."

They reached the Expedition. "Give me the key," Carter said.

"Maybe I ought to drive, you seem a little upset—"

"Give me the key!"

Bryce tossed him the keys, and climbed into the front seat beside Carter. "Oh, and Stallworth called finally," he said. "We have that interview set up with him, a week from tomorrow."

CHAPTER 20

二十

The freight elevators were on the side of the building, down a short concrete driveway designed specifically for facilitating loading and unloading. There was already a moving van in place, but there was plenty of space alongside it for another. Kit pulled the minivan to the curb, rolled down her window, and motioned for the small van behind her to pull into the empty space.

It was just after three o'clock on Tuesday afternoon, but the cloud cover made it appear closer to five. It would soon be pitch black and the beginning of a long, cold winter night.

Kit turned off the ignition and joined the small team of movers on the ramp. As they slid open the door, she went in search of the person in charge of the other van.

She found him just outside the freight elevators, issuing instructions.

"Did you schedule these elevators in advance?" she asked without introducing herself.

"What's it to you?" the man answered, eyeing her curiously.

"There's been a mix-up. We were supposed to have them from three to five."

The man's eyebrows creased into one.

"How much do you have left to do here?" she asked.

"Five, maybe six trips."

She watched as the movers unloaded office furniture and boxes from the elevator and carried them to the waiting van.

"Tell you what," she said. "I have two trips to make, tops. We're moving some boxes in, nothing out. Let us ride up with these loads, and we'll be gone and out of your way."

The man hesitated. "I don't know—"

"Of course, I could call the management, and we could wait around while they get here. I believe Management is off-site? A few blocks away?"

The man glanced at the small van, where two workers were loading boxes on dollies. "How long will it take you?"

"Ten minutes, fifteen, tops."

Grudgingly, he issued instructions to his men. When the first elevator was empty, he motioned for her and stepped aside. In turn, she signaled for the movers.

The elevator was filled from floor to ceiling in less than five minutes.

She pushed the button for the top floor. As the elevator whisked them upward, she felt strangely calm. Not the way she would have expected to feel after almost twenty years of marriage.

The elevator doors opened to the insurance agency's lobby. Dorothy Bethel sat at the reception desk, her back to them as she fielded incoming calls. By the time she turned around, the first load was being wheeled off the elevator.

"Mrs. Olsen!" she blurted.

"Hello, Dorothy," Kit said as she beckoned for the movers to follow her. "Merry Christmas!"

Kit managed to hide a wry smile as she passed through the lobby on her way to Frank's office. As she turned at the end of the hall, she caught a glimpse of Dorothy picking up the phone. It didn't matter; she would be there quicker than anyone could respond to her call.

Miranda Wade was just hanging up the phone and rising from her desk as Kit rounded the next corner. Kit thought she detected a slight tic around the eyes, a nervous lip trembling.

"Hello, Miranda," she said as she approached. "Nice tan."

"Mrs. Olsen—"

"Right here," she instructed the movers, pointing to a corner of Miranda's reception area.

"I don't understand," Miranda said, coming out from behind her desk. "Is Mr. Olsen expecting this—?"

"If he isn't, he should be," Kit answered.

"But what—?"

"Frank's things, of course. He's moving in with you, hasn't he told you?"

Miranda's jaw dropped.

Kit was vaguely aware of the movers retreating down the hall in pursuit of the next load as she leaned over Miranda's desk. "You can have him," she said. "Just be sure to have his dinner on the table at the same time every night, or he can get pretty testy. Don't expect him to clean up after himself; he hasn't once in twenty years. He expects his shirts to be folded, not hung, and his socks rolled, not folded. Good thing you're in an apartment; Frank doesn't do yard work. I hope you can change a light bulb; he can't. Expect to spend a lot of nights alone. He travels a lot, and now that he has you full-time, he'll probably travel with someone else. It's the pursuit that's important to Frank, not the relationship."

The door beside Miranda's desk opened. Kit caught a glance of Frank's astonished expression before she realized that the hallway behind her was filled with his coworkers, all watching in stunned silence.

The door opened wider and Frank's boss stepped out. His eyes followed the activity behind her before returning to her.

"Hello, Barry," she said politely. Then, "Frank, here are all your clothes and personal things." She reached into her coat pocket and pulled out a business card. "I've changed the locks on the doors, filed for a restraining order, and also filed charges for your arrest on assault charges."

She stepped past Barry, who now stood like the rest of the staff, with his jaw dropped and his eyes wide, and offered the business card to Frank. She thought he looked stupefied, almost as if he were consciously willing himself to come out of paralysis in order to take the card from her. She continued, "That's my divorce attorney. From now on, you'll deal with her, not me."

She turned on her heels. "See you in court," she said as she marched down the hallway past the horde of spectators.

When Kit pulled away from Frank's office building, she thought she would feel some sense of satisfaction or relief. But she didn't. She felt heaviness, like a thick curtain descending on her. As she turned onto Greensboro Drive and headed for the Capitol Beltway, she couldn't resist the urge to glance in her rear-view mirror, to see his building growing smaller behind her.

She still loved Frank. She didn't know if it were possible to live with someone for close to two decades, to raise his son and share his life, and not love him. But loving someone and putting up with womanizing and abuse were two different things.

Maybe if he'd been contrite, apologetic, even communicative about his affair with Miranda, they could have worked things out. But not now. Not after last night.

She raised her hand to her chin, and winced as she touched the swollen skin. Instinctively, she moved her hand to the back of her head, where a scab was already forming.

She turned onto the slush and snow encrusted Beltway and started for home. Tim would be there, locked in his room, as he had been since last night. She'd heard his footsteps in the hallway during the night, listened as the door to the bathroom was gently closed, and got up when she heard it open. But by the time she'd reached the hallway, his door was closing, and the concerns she voiced through the door were met only with noncommittal, monosyllabic grunts.

She had to get her mind off of everything, if only for a moment, so she could return to her thoughts later with a fresh perspective.

She turned on the radio. She started to absent-mindedly hum a few bars and then realized she was listening to Whitney Houston singing *I Will Always Love You*. She switched stations several times, but as luck would have it, each one seemed to be fixated on a heartbreak theme. Finally, she tuned into WTOP, an all-news station.

"… six to twelve more inches of snow predicted in the next twenty-four hours," the broadcaster was saying, "as this storm stalls over the mid-Atlantic region…"

Wonderful, she thought. Only two of the four lanes on the Beltway were cleared of snow, but fortunately, traffic was almost non-existent. That was a miracle in itself, considering the congestion she usually encountered here. As if on cue, snowflakes began pelting the windshield, and she turned on the wipers, straining to see the road.

"… and we have this late-breaking news just in from our reporter who's on the scene in Fairfax County, where a body has been located that fits the description of Joan Newcomb, the Vice President of Universal Computer Technologies, who disappeared a few weeks ago…"

Kit gasped as she began to slide sideways across the road. She struggled to right it, throwing all of her concentration into turning southeast. She pumped the brake, trying not to panic, and battled her own instinct to overcorrect. When the minivan finally jolted to a stop, it was partially buried in snow a few feet from the concrete barricade separating the Inner Loop from the Outer Loop.

"… George Washington Memorial Parkway, just north of Mount Vernon at Little Hunting Creek…" the radio broadcaster was saying.

Kit backed into the cleared lanes, slammed the gear into drive, and sped off, passing the exit to Springfield and home.

CHAPTER 21

二十一

It took Carter over an hour to reach the turnoff to Little Hunting Creek. The official start of winter had only begun two weeks earlier, and he was already sick of the snow, now pushed three feet high along the road edge and completely blackened by soot and road debris. He'd spent the better part of his commute sitting in stalled traffic, impatiently contemplating a variety of alternate routes, but in the end, sticking with the main roads. Now the traffic came to a standstill again, just minutes before he'd reached his destination.

He saw the orange glow of the traffic wand before he spotted the officer. As he neared the intersection, he recognized Ned Strickland.

"What's going on, Ned?" he asked as he neared him.

"Diverting traffic onto Stratford Lane," he said. "We've got a homicide—"

"I know." He glanced around but couldn't see anything through the swirling snow. "Jerome here yet?"

It was a shot in the dark. Ned was a Fairfax County cop, but Little Hunting Creek was U.S. Park Police territory. That meant Jerome Randel from Park would most likely be handling the homicide investigation.

"Just got here," Ned answered. "He expecting you?"

"Yeah," Carter answered easily. "Where's he at?"

Ned pointed to the left. "Can't miss him," he said.

Carter turned onto a road narrowed by encroaching snow. He caught a glimpse of Ned in his rearview mirror, directing traffic onto Stratford Lane. It would be a nightmare commute tonight, and Ned would be soaked through before he got reinforcements.

The road curved to the right and dead-ended in a parking lot.

He turned off the windshield wipers and watched the icy precipitation strike the glass before turning off the ignition. They were expecting more, as if they hadn't had enough. Bracing for the cold, he turned his jacket collar up and jumped out.

Bryce was right behind him, as he knew he would be, gathering his equipment with the speed and efficiency of an old pro.

Carter subconsciously reached for his press pass, giving it a quick pat as a reminder that it was visible, clipped onto the outside of his jacket like a beacon that would lead him through doors that would otherwise be closed.

The fire truck and ambulance were at the edge of the lot, nearest the water. Probably from Fort Hunt, he deduced. Fire and Rescue would have been the first to respond, followed by Fairfax County and Park Police.

A fireman was climbing into the truck as they approached. "Leaving so soon?" Carter called out.

"No need to stay," came the response. "Body's DRT."

Carter turned toward the water and glimpsed a quizzical expression on Bryce's face. "Dead Right There," he explained as he brushed past him.

At most crime scenes, they'd be amongst dozens of reporters. The majority, he'd recognize. It was usually the same core group of reporters who covered these calls. The veterans would be even-handed, gathering the facts, as he would be. The others, mostly younger wannabes, would be looking for the dirt. They were in the same boat as paparazzi, as far as he was concerned; if they couldn't verify the facts, they'd blow things out of proportion, just to win the ratings war.

This scene was different. Ned would direct all but a choice two or three to the other side of the road, and they'd be left to guess what was happening while on air, appearing to be knowledgeable when they really didn't have a clue. Now that he was inside the outer police perimeter, he intended to make the most of it.

He could see a few officers on a towpath closer to the Potomac River, could hear the crime scene techs' cameras snapping and the hum of voices. This was a populated area, one that was frequented by joggers and bicyclists on better days.

The river was higher than normal, the waves lapping at the frozen ground like tired fingers trying to climb ashore. A half a dozen sparse trees lined this part of the Potomac before giving way to acres of natural woodlands. Their naked branches swung wildly in the increasing winds, spraying snow on the group below. The eastern sky was a light gray-blue, while directly overhead, black clouds were quickly claiming the remaining remnants of light. He shivered as a dark premonition that he couldn't quite put his finger on tugged at him.

The group's attention was on something at the base of a tree. Carter turned to Bryce. "Let me see that for a minute," he said.

Bryce reluctantly handed him the camera. It was already zoomed in, giving him a good view of the back of a snow-covered head leaning against the tree, the long blond hair streaming against the dark trunk like icicles. Then he saw the body, stretched out unnaturally, the arms at a ninety-degree angle, as if frozen in flight. The water lapped at the shoeless feet. Despite himself, he shivered.

He handed Bryce the camera and lost sight of the corpse as he descended an embankment and struggled to maintain his footing on the frozen ground.

When he was about 30 yards from the body, one figure broke away from the crowd and approached them.

"How's it goin', Jerome?" he called out.

"We're freezing out here," came the reply. "Don't happen to have any hot coffee with you?"

"Sorry, pal. What's going on?"

Jerome met him at a band of yellow crime scene tape stretched between the trees. He was a good cop, a straight shooter. He'd been with Park for only ten years, but he'd risen fast. They'd spent many an evening playing poker or watching Monday night football at the local Damon's. He didn't always give him everything he wanted to know about a case, but he always seemed to give him what he could.

Besides, his wife made a mean cheesecake, and it was worth staying in touch for that alone.

While he waited for an answer, Carter made a mental inventory of the people present: the police photographers, busily taking pictures from every angle; the uniformed cops searching inside the inner perimeter with metal detectors; the forensics crew…

He glimpsed a reporter from the *Post*, but he noted they had no other competition.

"Totally unofficial at this point," Jerome said in a low, conspiratorial tone, "but it might be that Newcomb woman."

"Joan Newcomb? The woman who disappeared—"

"Yeah."

"How do you know?"

"The body's in good shape; facial features match her description. Clothes are the same that Olsen woman described, too, who witnessed the abduction. She hasn't been dead long."

Carter pulled out his notebook and sheltered it from the falling snow. "What do you know?"

"Some guy walking his dog found her propped up against this tree," Jerome said, nodding toward a clean-cut young man talking to a uniformed officer some yards away.

He watched the golden retriever rooting through the snow, the flakes clinging to his muzzle, the owner struggling to maintain control with a flimsy leash.

"Walking a dog in this weather?" Carter asked.

"What, you're gonna tell a dog it can't go, because it's wet outside?"

He shrugged. "Was she murdered?"

Jerome raised one eyebrow and motioned toward the corpse. "From the neck down, there's not an inch we've seen so far that wasn't molested in some way. Cuts, bruises, burns… I'll give you ten-to-one odds, she wasn't killed here. She was tortured and dumped here, where someone'd be sure to find her."

Carter borrowed Bryce's camera again and stepped to the edge of the crime scene tape. From what he could see, the body was actually in pretty good shape, considering. It appeared swollen, but he'd seen worse. The clothes were beginning to strain at the seams. The collar was spread back; even from this distance, he could see the skin split open from knife wounds. Interesting, he thought. The wounds were more like slices than stabs.

"Fascinating, isn't it?" Jerome was saying. "Obvious signs of torture, but they didn't do anything above the neck."

"Why do you think that is?" Carter asked, unable to tear his eyes away from her face. Joan Newcomb must have been a real looker. Even after death, he could make out the high cheekbones and perfectly shaped eyebrows. Still, there were deep blue circles under her eyes, and the skin appeared pinched. Her mouth was open; two of her teeth were missing, which didn't fit the impression he'd formed of her.

Jerome shrugged. "They'll get a positive ID on her pretty quickly. She's wearing a bracelet, one of those medical ID things, you know what I mean? Has a name and a doctor's name—"

"Then you know she's Joan Newcomb."

"I know that's what the bracelet says. They'll run her prints, you know how it goes."

Carter's eyes wandered from her face to her arms, stretched out at her sides as if she had wings. The arms were swollen, but the fingers looked like his when he stayed in the pool too long. Not bad for a corpse. His eyes stopped at the wristwatch, then at the ring on her hand. Looked like an emerald, an expensive one at that. So robbery probably wasn't a motive.

"When will the autopsy be done?"

"I'll let you know later today. I don't think they've got a lot of stiffs in the morgue right now. Not too many suspicious ones, anyway. Besides, the Feds'll push this one through."

Carter glanced up in time to see Detective Munski making his way down the embankment to the water. He felt a twinge of satisfaction that he'd beat him to the scene. Their eyes met briefly before Carter turned his attention to the body. "Who's in charge of the investigation?"

Jerome chuckled. "Park Police, of course." He nodded toward Munski. "Closes his case. Fairfax County's just providing sector cops. Got a call that FBI's on their way…"

"Why are they involved?"

"If this is Newcomb, they've been paying a lot of attention to her and that guy she worked with, you know, the one found at the resort?"

"Yeah, I know which one you're talking about."

"Don't know much more than that, but they'll take a back seat to us, I guaran-damn-tee ya."

Carter turned his attention back to the body. The clothes were grimy, but looked like something out of Brooks Brothers. Black pinstriped dress slacks, pulled up around the knees, exposing calves that were covered in bruises, welts, and what appeared to be burns. A white blouse with contrasting black pin stripe. No jacket, no coat, although she surely would have been wearing one or both when she was abducted. Under her swollen breasts was a wide black leather strap. Carter pointed it out to Jerome. "What's that?"

"You just now noticing that? Wraps around to her back…"

Bryce let out an audible sigh, and Carter reluctantly handed him the camera. They'd have plenty of time to go back over the video, anyway. They'd zoom in on any part they wanted to further inspect.

His attention was distracted by a medium green minivan stopping just at the edge of the parking lot. The driver's side door was unceremoniously hurled open, and a figure leapt out. Right behind her was a Fairfax County police cruiser with lights flashing. The cop that jumped out and ran toward the woman was decidedly unhappy.

"Crap," Carter said under his breath as he took a step forward.

"Who's that?" Jerome asked.

Carter could see Munski out of the corner of his eye; he'd been talking to another cop a few feet away. Now he turned his full attention to the figure dashing toward them, screaming Joan's name as if she were still alive. In his mind's eye, he saw her running the police barricade past a horde of reporters stationed on the Parkway.

"It's Kit Olsen," he said. Then to Bryce, "We've got to get her out of here. They'll eat her alive."

Bryce hesitated, his camera still rolling. "You mean, *we'll* eat her alive, don't you? You *are* still covering this story, right?" He said incredulously.

Carter didn't answer. He'd already made his way past Munski and was nearing Kit. Still screaming, she tried to push past him towards the body of her friend, but his firm hands kept her back. He managed to turn her around and was forcefully guiding her back to her car. The uniformed cop, seeing Jerome and Munski, started to shout something, but Jerome cut him off.

"Hey, Carter!"

Carter pushed her into the front seat, curtly ordering her to slide over to the passenger side and at the same time, hoping she didn't continue right out the other door. As he started to climb in after her, he heard Jerome call him again.

"Hey, Carter, don't you want to know what's strapped to her?"

He hesitated, one foot already in the car.

"It's a laptop."

CHAPTER 22

二十二

They were heading north as Kit screamed, "What are you doing?"

"What are *you* doing?" Carter yelled back. "Are you crazy?"

"That's Joan out there; I have to go to her—"

"No, you don't," he barked.

Kit glanced in the side mirror as a slew of reporters reached the road. More than one had a video camera, and several had microphones. Carter turned left onto a side street, and the crowd disappeared behind them.

"You don't understand…" she began.

"No, *you* don't understand. You, of all people, cannot be seen anywhere near that body."

She groaned and slumped against the back of the passenger seat.

"She's dead, Kit. There's nothing you can do for her now."

Despite her objections, Carter headed for the Holiday Inn on Eisenhower Avenue. It was almost deserted. At this time of year, most of the travelers were businessmen, many of whom left town when the weather turned nasty. Across the street, the Hoffman Building, normally bustling with Department of Defense employees, appeared to be shut down.

Carter and Kit settled into the far corner of the lounge. While Carter ordered drinks, Kit used her cell phone to check on Tim.

"How is he?" Carter asked when she hung up.

She shrugged. "He won't open up to me."

"Has he told you anything? Given you a description of the guys he was with? Told you how he got to Alexandria?"

She shook her head. "No to everything. He doesn't want to talk about it."

"He's got to talk about it."

"I know. But I can't force him. He's obviously been through something very traumatic."

"What happened to you?"

She hadn't realized until now that she'd never told him what had occurred at the gristmill, or how she'd found Tim at Mount Vernon. He listened intently as she spoke, occasionally interjecting with questions.

She leaned back and finished, "I've been thinking a lot about that night. There's something more that's going on."

"What do you mean?"

"It was too easy. I gave him a disk; he let me have Tim. I could have given him a blank one, for all he knew. He never checked it. He didn't even have a means to check it."

"They know where you are. They can easily find you again."

"Maybe. But I don't think so. Otherwise, why go through all of that?"

"Scare tactic maybe?"

She didn't respond. The lounge was deserted, except for the bartender and the two of them.

Carter lowered his voice and leaned in close to her. "Listen to me, Kit." He waited until after the bartender set their drinks on the table and left. "If that's Joan—and they think it is—she was tortured before she died."

She gasped.

"These guys mean business. We're not dealing with some street punks here. Do you understand?"

"Yes." With all the strength she could muster, she grabbed her drink with a shaky hand and took a long, hard swig.

"Kit, what is it that you do for a living?"

She leaned back in her chair, shocked into silence. After a moment, she said, "You know what I do. I'm a programmer."

"What do you program?"

"I can't tell you."

"Why can't you?"

"Look, Carter, I appreciate everything you've done for me—"

"Don't placate me."

"I can't discuss specifics with you. I've never even been able to tell my husband."

"Well, you're gonna have to tell somebody."

"Why?"

"I don't know what the connection is between Emerson, Newcomb, and that disk you delivered, but there *is* a connection and they're closing in on you."

Kit felt her blood run cold. Despite herself, she glanced around the room, peering into the darkened corners. "Why do you say that?"

"We both know that program wasn't what they were after. At best—and it's a long shot—it was somewhat similar. But if I'm to believe you and Chen, neither one of you knew why they wanted it. It didn't have any secrets in it, right?"

"You mean—?"

"I mean like espionage."

Kit inched her chair around the table, closer to Carter. If there were anyone she could trust, it would have to be him.

He wrapped his arm across her shoulder. When she started to protest, he said, "Shhh. If anyone comes in, they'll think we're in love, or some crap like that," he added quickly. "Otherwise, we're gonna raise suspicions."

She nodded. Their backs were to the wall now, where they both had a clear view of the room. The bartender was facing away from them, polishing glasses as he put them away, his attention focused on a television set tuned to ESPN.

"UCT has several different divisions," she whispered. "Some of the programs we do are just run-of-the-mill, business-type programs."

"Like?"

"I don't know, like procurement programs or accounting systems."

"Is that what you do?"

"Sometimes. But most of the work I've done the past few years has been for the federal government."

"Who?"

She swallowed. "Mostly CIA."

"Are you involved in any covert activities?"

"Oh, no. Not me," she said quickly. "My life isn't that exciting. I just write programs that allow them to track certain kinds of information, that's all. I don't even see the data most of the time."

"Is that all?"

"Right before Joan disappeared, she reassigned me." She glanced around the room nervously. "They call it 'Customs', this division. They're code breakers."

She thought his hand squeezed her shoulder, but she wasn't certain. She knew she was treading on thin ice, and it was getter thinner by the second.

"So this is intercepted code, like secret transmissions?"

She nodded. "Sometimes, it's voice. But not this time. This time, they had a program that they'd gotten— I don't know how—and they were trying to figure out what it did."

"A Chinese program."

"Mandarin. A Chinese dialect," she added. "Chen could translate it, but they needed someone with more programming experience, I guess, to try and figure out what it was doing."

"So they assigned it to you."

She nodded.

He leaned in close to her, so close that she could smell the leather on his jacket. "This is the one that counted records, the one you described to me."

"That's the confusing part of this whole thing. It was a stupid program. I don't even know why they assigned it to me; Chen could have figured it out, a dozen others could have—"

"Were Emerson and Newcomb working on this same project?"

"I don't know." She wiped her forehead. As chilly as the room was, beads of sweat had broken out across her brow. "And now I'll never know." She took a deep breath. "But I do know this—it has to be that program."

"How can you be so sure?"

"I've gone over and over it. Chen had access to all of them—all of the programs—but they didn't come after him. They came after me, and I'd only worked on that one."

"Who else knew about it?"

"I asked."

"And?"

She shrugged. "Chen couldn't tell me."

They sat for a moment in silence before Carter said, "We're going to have to find out."

"Do you think they're going to come after me?"

He hesitated. "Yes. Yes, I do."

"Why?"

"Joan's laptop was strapped to her."

"What?!"

The bartender turned around, and Carter pressed his face against hers, burying her nose against his jacket collar. "Stay calm," he whispered in her ear.

She grabbed his arm with one hand and closed her eyes, trying to steady her nerves.

"Whatever it is they're looking for, they didn't find it with Joan. The laptop is a message, do you understand me? *The laptop is a message.*"

CHAPTER 23

二十三

Kit shivered as she tried to shield her face from the biting wind. The visibility had greatly diminished in the short time they'd been inside. Carter took her arm and led her through the parking lot. If she'd been with Frank, she would have pulled away, insisting she could easily navigate the rising snowdrifts on her own. Somehow, with Carter, it felt comforting to have him tending to her.

When they reached the vehicle, he brushed the snow away from the door, wrestled with the key in the near-frozen lock, and finally opened the passenger door. She was preparing to get in when he grabbed her arm. His sudden movement startled her, and she turned to him quickly, not quite knowing what to expect.

"What happened to your face?" he asked, his voice rising.

She sighed with relief. "Oh, it's nothing."

"The hell it's nothing. You've been cuffed. Did that guy at the gristmill—"

"No."

"Are you telling me the truth?"

"I have no reason to lie." She started to get in, but he still had a firm grip on her arm. "Do you mind?" she said, looking pointedly at his hand.

"Tell me who did this." His hold on her didn't lessen.

"I told you, it's nothing."

"I didn't ask if it was nothing; I asked who did this to you."

She sighed. "If you must know, it was Frank."

"Frank! That son of a—"

She wrestled away from him and climbed into the van. "It's over, Carter."

He slammed the door shut with such a vengeance that Kit jumped. His sudden rage caught her off guard. As he walked to the driver's side, his face was red with emotion, his lips pursed.

He got in and started the engine. "I have a real problem with that bastard hitting you," he said through gritted teeth.

"I told you, it's all over."

"Men who hit their wives don't just stop—they keep hitting them, until somebody *makes* them stop—"

"Listen to me, Carter." She grabbed his arm and waited for him to look at her before continuing. "When I said it was over, I meant the marriage. He's gone. Moved in with his girlfriend."

He sucked in his breath, his eyes fixed on hers. There appeared to be a myriad of emotions crossing his face, but she couldn't read them. She wanted him to say something, but she didn't quite know what. But before he could respond, his cell phone rang.

He let go with an expletive and yanked his phone from his jacket pocket. The volume was turned up, and Kit could hear the conversation almost as if she had her ear to the receiver.

"Where are you?"

"Sorry, man, I didn't mean to leave you at the scene like that," he answered. He mouthed "Bryce" to her, and she nodded her head.

"You're in deep trouble, Carter. You have no idea."

He leaned his head away from her, and she gazed out the window, pretending that she couldn't hear.

"I'll fix everything," he said in a low voice.

"It's too late to 'fix' anything. The boss wants you in the office, *pronto*. Every other station has already reported this story. You know what we got? Diddly. I'm freezing my buns off while you run off with half the story. What the hell is wrong with you?"

Carter didn't respond right away, but put the minivan in gear and headed out of the parking lot. "Where are you now?"

There was a hesitation before Bryce answered. "I came back to the office without you, Bud."

"Meet me at Springfield Mall, can you do that?"

"Carter—"

"*Can you do that?*"

Another hesitation. "Yeah. You there now?"

"I'll be there in ten minutes."

By the time they reached Springfield, visibility was reduced to a car length. Carter leaned forward, his face inches from the windshield. The wiper blades were at full speed, but they still weren't enough to keep the window clear.

Bryce was waiting for them at the corner of Target, the Expedition parked at an angle that appeared to give him a clear view of Franconia Road. Kit felt as if she were in the eye of the camera from the moment they pulled off of I-395 to the time that they parked alongside him.

Carter nodded to him in greeting. He barely moved his head in return. His brows were knit together, a constant tic and reddened cheeks revealing his anger.

"Will you be okay?" Carter asked Kit.

She nodded. "I'm not far from home."

"That's not what I meant."

She reached across the console and took his hand. She turned it palm up, and stared into it as if it held a great deal of interest to her. She ran her finger along the heart line, the top-most horizontal line that appeared across his palm. His hands were large and capable.

She didn't want him to leave, but she couldn't find the words to ask him to stay. She needed him, this confident man who seemed to show up just as her own life was falling apart. She glanced past him at Bryce, who appeared to be getting angrier by the second. "You'd better go," she said at last.

"Listen, Kit, I've been thinking…"

"You have?" she said, her voice sounding almost too eager. She swallowed. If she could take the words back, she would have. But it was too late; they were out there, hanging like a balloon in the air between them.

He blinked, and something akin to surprise passed across his face, but in the next instant, it was gone. "Kit, you can't stay around here. It's too dangerous."

She looked down at his hand again and tried to swallow her disappointment.

"Is there someplace else you can go?" he asked.

"My parents—"

"Do they live around here?"

"Chesterfield." His brows pulled together and she added, "About a hundred miles from here, near Richmond."

"Can you go there?"

She nodded. "We usually go on Christmas, anyway."

"Oh, yeah. Christmas."

"Tomorrow's Christmas Eve," she said, dropping her voice to barely over a whisper. For the first time, she realized how little she knew about him. She wondered where he would be, who he would spend the holiday with. "Do you have any plans?" she asked.

When he didn't answer, she raised her eyes to his. They were dark and veiled.

"Oh, yeah, sure." He shrugged. "Of course I do."

Just then, the air was filled with the rude sound of Bryce blowing the horn.

Carter glanced back at his coworker as if he wanted to give a stiff retort. But he seemed to think better of it, and he reluctantly opened the door. He was standing outside, ready to close it, when he leaned down and looked at her. "I'll call you, okay?"

She nodded. "Merry Christmas."

"Yeah. Merry Christmas."

He closed the door. A second later, he was in the Expedition. He'd barely gotten both feet in when the vehicle took off, spraying a cloud of soft white powder into the air. Through the near whiteout conditions, Kit thought she caught a glimpse of Carter's arm as he pulled the door shut, and then they were gone, disappearing into the snowstorm.

Blake Morley was an imposing figure on the best of days. On the worst of days, he seemed to loom like a demon over the newsroom, his shock of white hair pointing in every direction at once, his once-white shirt halfway pulled out of his trousers, his tie loosened and askew.

He was a no-nonsense man, not the kind of guy you'd chat pleasantly with upon arriving to work. His meetings were quick, brusque, and to the point. He hated time wasted. The news was happening all around them, and it was his job to pick out the stories that would grab the coveted top of the hour spots and everything in between.

For all the fear he instilled in his employees, he was also known as the best in the business. He'd come up the ranks from the bottom, switching to television after a twenty-year newspaper career. Now, after almost fifty years in the news business, he was a legend.

Carter caught sight of him as he stepped off the elevator. Bryce's anger had turned to an icy silence, and Carter was almost glad for the hustle and bustle of the news station until he spotted his boss. Morley was ranting at the top of his lungs at a poor young courier, who cowered in the larger man's shadow. He had just tossed a handful of papers in the air, shouting, *"Do it over!"* when his eyes met Carter's.

A thick finger jabbed at the air. *"You!"* he bellowed across the room.

Everyone knew what that meant, even as they lowered their heads and pretended to be busy. As Carter strode across the room, he pointedly looked at each person he passed, but not a single one raised their eyes to meet his.

At the end of the room, Morley stood beside his open door, watching Carter, his face fixed into a stony expression that was more alarming than his outbursts. Carter filed past him and tossed his coat on an empty chair, then pulled up another chair and sat down.

The door slammed behind him.

"You know what ABC and CBS are running as their top story tonight? Huh? Huh?"

Carter remained silent. He knew that Morley never asked a question he couldn't answer himself. Especially in this case. His boss would know exactly what the other networks would be reporting tonight, and they would, in turn, know what NBC was doing. It was too much of an incestuous, tiny community not to know each other's business.

"You, Mr. Hot Shot."

"I can explain."

"I bet you can. And if I had the time, I'd let you, just to see what you come up with."

Morley crossed to the door and ripped it open. *"You!"* he yelled before slamming it shut again.

There was a long moment of silence in which the air hung like a thick fog in the room. There was never silence in Morley's meetings; he considered it wasted time.

The door opened quietly and Bryce slipped inside.

Morley leaned against his desk, half-sitting and half-standing. "You two are reassigned."

"Excuse me?" Bryce said.

"You heard me."

Carter turned in his chair and looked at Bryce, but his coworker's eyes were fixed on their boss.

"Tomorrow morning, seven fifteen. Be prepared for your interview with Stallworth. We're gonna have to do it live. You've got seven minutes, with a commercial after three. You got that?"

Carter nodded.

"You got that?" he repeated.

"Yes, sir."

"Tomorrow afternoon, Stallworth leaves for Richmond. He's preparing for the inauguration; he'll be meeting with the outgoing administration, announcing his plans, you know the story. Be on the press bus. You're going with him."

"Both of us?" Bryce asked.

"Both of you."

Bryce shot Carter a look that could kill. "I understand *him*, Mr. Morley, but why me?"

"Because he needs a babysitter."

Carter groaned.

"But tomorrow's Christmas Eve—" Bryce protested.

"News doesn't take a holiday," Morley barked. "Now get out of my office."

Bryce stood for a moment with his mouth agape. Then, shaking his head, he yanked the door open.

Carter listened to his heavy footsteps as they crossed a completely silent newsroom.

"That goes for you, too," Morley said.

"Please don't punish Bryce," Carter said. "It was all my fault; he had nothing to do with it—"

"I don't care." He leaned slightly toward Carter. "This is not a face that cares."

"I'm working on a big story—"

"Sell it to *Playboy*." Then, almost as an afterthought, he added, "But do it on your own time. Not mine."

Carter fought to remain calm. Despite his efforts, he could feel his right hand thrusting itself into a fist, releasing, and then balling up again, almost as if it had a mind of its own.

"I can't tell you to stay away from that woman," Morley said, "but while you're in Richmond, you'd better decide what you'd rather have—her or your job."

Before Carter could respond, Morley abruptly crossed the room to the door. Without even a glance behind him, he continued into the newsroom. "What are you gawking at?" Carter heard him bellow. "Get busy! We've got news to get out!"

CHAPTER 24

二十四

Kit intended to leave for Chesterfield and her parents' house first thing in the morning. But last night when she arrived home, the media was already camped around the house. She felt like an insect trying to navigate a spider web as she dodged past them. The flash of cameras going off all around her was disconcerting, to say the least.

The questions came from every direction—*what were her thoughts when she found out Joan had been found? What did she think of her friend being tortured?* It took all her willpower to keep from shouting back, *How would you feel? What would you think?*

She'd closed all the blinds and drapes and spent the remainder of the evening a prisoner in her own home.

Tim stayed in his room, and her efforts to bring him out and talk to him were to no avail. He did manage to make an appearance at dinnertime, just long enough to fill up a plate with food and return to his cave.

Now he was upstairs, presumably packing, while she sat alone at the dining room table, Joan's laptop open in front of her and her untouched breakfast beside it.

It was only a matter of time before law enforcement found out that the laptop strapped to Joan belonged to Kit. Her brain was buzzing with concern that went in all directions at once. In fact, she'd been up half the night, tossing and turning, trying to get her worries out of her head so she could get some sleep. Finally, around four am, she'd given up and come downstairs. Since then, she'd been going through Joan's laptop in minute detail, looking for anything that would provide a clue.

Her job was over; she knew that now. Once they found the programs on her laptop and realized what sensitive information she'd carelessly carried home with her, she'd be dismissed on the spot. Removing top-secret information was unforgivable, especially after high profile cases like Robert Hanssen, John Walker, and Aldrich Ames. They'd take her in for questioning, at the very least; at the most, she'd be accused of spying.

She'd never be able to explain why she didn't come forward when she realized the computers had been switched. Why she hadn't confessed to taking home sensitive information, and why she never told another soul that she had Joan's laptop.

And Joan's captors had known. The man's reference to her laptop at the gristmill left her convinced that Tim had been kidnapped by the very same people who'd tortured and killed Joan.

Carter was right; the laptop was a message. She'd turned on the news early this morning, but every channel was interviewing so-called experts who were speculating in grisly detail how Joan may have been tortured.

Now she glanced at the television in the living room. A picture crossed the screen, but the sound was muted, as it had been for the past hour.

So they tortured her and they killed her, and they strapped Kit's laptop to her when they dumped the body.

Were they trying to get the password into the computer when they tortured her? And Joan couldn't give it to them, because it wasn't her laptop. Or had they been able to hack their way into it, only to find that Kit's computer didn't have any of the programs they were after? Is that why they kidnapped Tim, because by that time, they knew that she had the information they needed? But then, why didn't they ask for the whole laptop, instead of a single program?

She grasped her head in her hands as if by doing so, she could rid her brain of all the questions. She was trying to apply logic to something she didn't know enough about, to people who might defy logic. But the questions wouldn't stop. They continued until she thought she was going to go crazy.

Was the man who met her at the gristmill "Toy," the man Joan mentioned in her email? Had Joan been doing some sort of business with him? What was it he said about Joan and Bernard's greed?

She sighed. It was approaching seven o'clock. Her boss wouldn't be in yet, so this would be a good time for her to call and leave a message.

She dialed the number to the office, got the after-hours recording, and punched in his extension. After listening to his outgoing tape, she left a message reminding him that she'd planned to vacation this week, and left a number where she could be reached. She hoped her voice sounded light, as if she were simply an employee excited about going on vacation.

Then after she hung up, she worried that she sounded *too* nonchalant. After all, Joan's body had just been found. And he had to know that she knew, after seeing the news footage of Carter pushing her back into her vehicle, and later, of her picking her way through the press to get into her own home.

Now what should she do?

She reached for the phone, preparing to call again, when it rang. She jumped. She hadn't realized how quiet the house was.

Maybe it was her boss calling back.

"Kit, it's Carter."

Her heart skipped a beat. She could at least find solace in his voice—his confident, sometimes arrogant voice.

"I'm glad you called," she said.

There was a slight pause. "I'm leaving for Richmond later today."

"Why?"

"I'm on assignment. I'm covering Governor-Elect Stallworth. Anyway, he's going to Richmond, and I'm to stay there to cover the events through the Inauguration."

"You won't be far from my folks' house."

"Can you—will you—give me their number?"

She complied without hesitation. "Carter, I need to tell you something, something important."

"Hold on."

She waited. She realized after a moment that she was holding her breath. Should she tell him over the phone that she had Joan's laptop? Or should she arrange to meet him somewhere? What if someone were listening in on her conversation?

"I've got to go," Carter said.

"Can you—?"

"I'm sorry. I'm doing an interview of Stallworth. Turn on your TV; it'll be broadcast live. If you care," he said as an afterthought.

"Of course I'll watch."

"Talk to ya soon."

"Yeah."

She heard the dial tone before she jerked herself out of the cloud she was in—a cloud that seemed to get darker and more forbidding as each minute passed.

She couldn't keep this a secret any longer. She'd have to tell someone what she had, what she'd done.

She picked up the remote and turned on the volume. The co-hosts bantered light-heartedly before announcing that an interview with the Governor-Elect would take place after a commercial break. She nibbled on a slice of bacon and waited.

Carter hung up the telephone, deep in thought. He didn't dare request leave time, not after his run-in with Morley. But every inch of him wished he were there with Kit, even if there was nothing he could do to help her.

It seemed like a lifetime ago when he had this brainstorm of interviewing Stallworth. God, was his life really that boring? Talk about a slow news day. How did this cockamamie idea get approved anyway? Whoever heard of a serious interview about sister cities?

Somebody beckoned him to the set where the interview would take place; his mind was so far away, he didn't even remember who it was. He strode to the set as if on autopilot. He'd have to shake this feeling and do one hell of an interview, or he was toast.

He shook hands with Stallworth. They seated themselves across a coffee table, making idle chitchat as they clipped on their microphones.

God, he wished he were anywhere else.

The fingers were up—four, three, two, one…

Then he was introducing Stallworth, as if anyone watching wouldn't know who he was, welcoming him to the show—and then the reporter in him kicked in.

"Sir, you've expressed a great deal of interest in forming a relationship with another nation, perhaps a country that's comprised of a number of starving children—"

Stallworth's expression didn't change; his smile remained fixed as he smoothly answered, "I'm advocating a step up from a wonderful program called Sister Cities, in which two cities from vastly different cultures can join together to promote international goodwill and understanding."

"This Sister City project, do you see this happening in Virginia, under your governorship?"

"Oh, it's happening already, with many cities in Virginia."

"How would you propose to step up this program? Perhaps there're starving kids that need our help—"

"What are you doing?"

The words came from Carter's earpiece; it was Morley's unmistakable voice. Carter knew it wasn't a question he was supposed to answer, but rather a directive to stop him from going in an odd direction. But if Stallworth's trigger was starving children, he had to mention it enough to get him riled, no matter what the voice in the booth said.

"Actually, I'd love to see something like a Sister State, between Virginia and another state or province."

"Do you have one in mind?"

"Yes, I do, Carter. I'd like to form a relationship with a region of China."

"China?" Carter was acutely aware of the camera that remained focused on his face. He knew in the control booth, they were watching several cameras at once: at least one was trained on his face, one or more on Stallworth, and another showing both of them from a slight distance. They would instantly cut from one to another, providing the viewer with the best shots of the interview. No matter what, he couldn't allow his expression to give anything away. "What region, in particular?"

"Tibet."

"Tibet." I'm repeating everything he's saying, Carter thought. Morley's gonna hack me to pieces on this one.

It occurred to him that he hadn't prepared for this interview. Rule number one in live interviews: know the answers to the questions. He'd been so busy with Kit, he hadn't given the interview a second thought. And now it was showing.

"But Tibet isn't in China," he said. "It's a separate country."

"Oh, but it *is* part of China," Stallworth laughed. "It's been a part of China for centuries, long before the birth of Christ."

"That's a farce; Tibet was never a part of China."

Stallworth continued without missing a beat. "For a time, China allowed them to rule themselves, but unfortunately, an upper class materialized that gained control of the country and enslaved the majority. In 1951, China liberated the Tibetans, and now they enjoy all of the freedoms that Chinese citizens enjoy—"

"*Freedoms?* You understand we're talking about a communist country with a horrific human rights record?"

"You know, Carter, it's well documented that the United States made a mistake at the end of World War II, when Mao Tse-tung was gaining in popularity—"

"Chairman Mao," Carter interjected for the benefit of the viewing audience. "The Communist leader."

"We backed the then-current regime," Stallworth continued, "under Chiang Kai-shek, who we now know was a crook—"

"How was he a crook?"

"He stole millions of dollars. It's well documented. The United States sent more than four billion dollars in aid to China, and almost a quarter of that was put in Chiang's own pocket. Even President Truman said we were backing the wrong party. But by then, McCarthy was plunging the U.S. into mass hysteria, and we couldn't see the forest for the trees, to use an old expression. The Chinese people were starving, and we backed the oppressor."

The Chinese people were starving. The words reverberated in Carter's head.

"They had no alternative," Stallworth continued, "but to get assistance from the only other superpower that existed."

"Soviet Russia."

"Yes, the Russians. Who backed the winner, by the way. And as a consequence, the Chinese people were freed from oppression."

"Do you honestly believe the Chinese people are not oppressed today?" Visions of Tiananmen Square flashed before him, and he felt his cheeks grow hot in anger.

"And then they freed Tibet." Stallworth sat back smugly, as if he'd announced that he personally had accomplished something great.

"They seized control of Tibet," Carter corrected, "burned—by some accounts—up to ninety-five percent of their temples, maimed, raped, and killed monks and nuns in the streets—"

"Oh, please." Stallworth waved his hand as if to dismiss his allegations. "You've been watching too many movies. Why, all you have to do is look at Tibet today, to see how far they've come. Before the peaceful liberation of Tibet—and I want to stress the word *peaceful* here, because it certainly was—more than ninety percent of the country was owned by less than five percent of the population."

"The country was governed by a diplomatic partnership between religious leaders and noblemen."

"You've got to be kidding me, Carter! The vast majority of Tibetans were serfs—slaves—in circumstances so horrible, it overshadows the darkest days of serfdom in Europe's Middle Ages!"

The voice in Carter's ear had been counting down the seconds to the commercial break. He didn't want to lose momentum, but he had no choice. The advertisers paid the bills here, something he was reminded of daily, so he reluctantly cut to the commercial.

Stallworth's aids rushed forth to wipe non-existent perspiration from his brows and whisper in his ear. Try though he did, Carter wasn't able to hear their conversation.

Morley was no longer in the control booth. He was standing near the corner of the set, eyeing Carter. Carter met his eyes evenly, perhaps a little rebelliously, but Morley's expression didn't betray any emotions.

The fingers were up. Four, three, two, one...

"And we're back with Governor-Elect Stallworth, who's been informing us of his desire to unite Virginia with Tibet as a step-up to the 'Sister Cities' program. You were telling us, Sir, how much better off Tibet is under Communist China's rule?"

"Oh, come now, Carter. Let's not get melodramatic. But the fact is, Tibet has flourished under China's leadership."

"How can you say they're better off under a repressive communist regime?"

"Let's look at the facts and not get emotional. Take their roads, as one example. Great Britain presented the

Fourteenth Dalai Lama with an automobile, sometime around 1950. Do you know where he drove it? Nowhere. Do you know why? They had no roads. Tibet did not have a single, solitary road in the entire country. Today, they have an infrastructure."

"An infrastructure at what cost to the Tibetan people?"

"It was done entirely without bloodshed."

"Without bloodshed?" Carter shouted. He struggled to remain seated. "In one battle alone, the Chinese slaughtered almost 6,000 Tibetans! There are documented accounts of torture, of nuns being raped in the streets, of electric batons inserted into every opening in the human body—"

Out of the corner of his eye, he could see Morley, leaning against the wall, watching him. This was the interview they should have had during the campaign. Stallworth wouldn't have had a chance.

"I can't let you sit here, Governor-Elect Stallworth," he spat, "and tell the American public that China 'peacefully liberated' Tibet. I won't back down on this one." Despite his training, Carter turned and glared pointedly at Morley, whose expression remained unreadable. "The only reason the average American doesn't know more about the cruel and inhumane treatment of Tibetans is because China has an iron grip on that country. And I, for one, don't understand why our government won't do something about it."

"There is absolutely no evidence of torture or of mistreatment of a single Tibetan citizen. It doesn't exist! The nobles and monks in Tibet fabricated it in a failed attempt to bring the United States into a war against China. And we didn't take the bait!"

"In recently declassified information, there's evidence the United States tried to provide Tibet with covert support—both before and after the communist takeover."

"Are you telling me the U.S. tried—and failed—to fight a covert war against China? That's ludicrous! Rather, it was a half-hearted attempt to keep the communists out of Tibet, to keep them from reuniting their country. It was done purely out of the panic that Senator McCarthy plunged this country into—which we now know was *wrong*."

The adrenaline was flowing. This was the interview of the year—if not the decade. Who could have imagined a newly elected governor defending a communist regime?

Stallworth continued, "In the 1970's, Richard Nixon, who by most accounts, was the most knowledgeable man in America on foreign policies— especially concerning Asia—forged a friendship with China."

"Yes, but we now know why," Carter interjected. "We now know that China and the U.S. entered an agreement to spy on the former Soviet Union's nuclear and atomic capabilities and testing during a critical time in our own nation's history. China agreed to share that information with us."

"You are quite correct," Stallworth said. "It was information we could not have obtained otherwise. And," he added, "I don't have to remind you, it was information that ultimately led to the fall of the Berlin Wall, and the collapse of the Soviet Empire."

"But now we know that China has replaced the former Soviet Union as the world's next great superpower and as the single greatest threat to America. China remains, *I don't have to remind you, Governor-Elect Stallworth,* a communist nation."

"Now, now, Carter," Stallworth laughed, "The 'commi-hunter' was an invention of McCarthyism. We know now that communism doesn't have to be such a bad thing, after all. Isn't communism the antithesis of a dictatorship? Where every person owns his own business, his land, his home, instead of slaving away to provide riches to the wealthy?"

"What planet are you living on?" Carter bellowed. "The Chinese people—and the Tibetan people—don't own anything! That's capitalism—something communists are adamantly opposed to!"

Stallworth laughed. "Apparently, not the planet you're living on. The fact is, there are more than forty-three thousand businesses in Tibet today—owned by Tibetans. Private businesses, not government owned businesses. Owned by people who were, themselves, slaves fifty years ago, whose parents were born into slavery and serfdom and who had no hope whatsoever of getting out of it."

"I don't believe it, and I can't believe our viewers will buy this hogwash either." Carter had wanted to use a different word, something he knew the control room could remove in the short delay before his words went out over the airwaves, but he refrained. He didn't want a single word cut out of this interview.

"Believe it, Carter, because it's true. The land that was once owned by a minute percentage of the population, consisting entirely of nobles and monks, was given back to the people. Their economy is booming; they've learned modern agricultural skills; they own stores and businesses that less than a century ago, they dared not even dream about."

"Computer businesses?"

Stallworth's eyes widened, the first hint of any kind of surprise that Carter detected. "Yes, they probably do own some computer businesses."

The time was counting down in Carter's earpiece.

As if Stallworth was aware the interview was winding down, he leaned toward Carter and said, "I'm not the only one who believes in China's goodwill toward the United States. You want to talk Sister Cities? Right here, Washington, D.C., the capital of the free world—do you know who the Sister City is for D.C.?"

Carter barely shook his head.

"Beijing. That's right, Mr. Reporter, it's the capital of *China*. It could have been the Sister City to almost any city in the world, but they chose *China*. And the capital of Tibet—Lhasa, once the home of the Dalai Lama and the monks and nobles who would enslave their entire population—yes, Carter Leigh, they are also a Sister City—to Boulder, Colorado."

"Thirty seconds," the control room reported.

"You're out of step, Carter. Out of step with the rest of the country, out of step with the *future* of our great country. And when I become Governor of this great state of Virginia, I will do anything within my power to help China, to forge good—no, excellent—relations with the government and their people, to encourage imports and exports, to establish a Sister State, and to bind our two countries together as the allies we should have been all along."

CHAPTER 25
二十五

Kit leaned back in her chair, so stunned it took a moment to realize her jaw had dropped open. When the interview was over, she remained transfixed to the television set but her mind was thousands of miles away.

Then she bolted up and climbed the stairs two at a time, calling for Tim.

She was in her bedroom with the drawer to the nightstand open when he appeared in her doorway.

"What's up?" he said.

She withdrew the gun from the drawer and checked the bullets. "Are you packed?"

"For Grandma's house?"

"Of course."

"Yeah."

She glanced up then realized he was watching her curiously. "Get your suitcases downstairs. We're going out the back door."

"What's that for?" he asked, pointing at the gun.

"Never mind what it's for. Just get your stuff downstairs, do you hear me?"

He remained in the doorway.

"Do you hear me?" she shouted.

He left without replying. She grabbed a box of bullets, checked the supply—a full box—and was in the hallway as Tim was headed downstairs with his bag.

She was poised to descend, when she withdrew back into the upstairs hallway. She glanced toward Tim's room. Quietly, she made her way down the hall.

His door was closed. She carefully turned the doorknob and gently opened it. It snagged on something, and she tried pushing to open it further. Something was preventing it from moving. Finally, she squeezed inside, flipped on the light, and turned around. The dresser had been dragged behind the door.

Quietly, she closed the door and surveyed the room. It was in total disarray. His chest of drawers had been moved in front of the window, completely blocking it. He'd made himself a virtual prisoner in his own bedroom—or perhaps he'd made himself a safe room.

She felt a heaviness in her chest, as though her heart were being crushed. After a moment, she opened the door, squeezed back through to the hallway, and started downstairs.

Once there, she slipped the gun and the bullets into the laptop case. Besides the laptop, she had two bags and Tim had one. Enough to carry in one trip. They couldn't evade the press; they were everywhere. But at least they'd only have to run the gauntlet once. Thank God Carter had replaced the car battery for her; otherwise, she'd be sitting in the driveway, surrounded by the media, trying to rouse a dead horse.

It was snowing again, the fourth time in as many days. Interstate 95 between Washington and Richmond was usually packed with vehicles. When they weren't stopped in one of the Washington area's infamous backups, traffic was generally whizzing past at seventy-five miles an hour, well over the posted speed limit. But today, the road was so vacant it looked surreal. The windshield was plastered with a mixture of snow and ice; as soon as the wipers cleared it, it was covered again.

They hadn't spoken in almost an hour. Tim was sprawled across the back seat, his face hidden behind a book ironically titled *China Run*. Kit wondered just how much of it he was actually retaining; he was wearing a headset, his portable CD player turned up so loudly she could hear a muffled version of it in the front seat.

Her neck and upper back ached from hunching forward, tensely watching the road, carefully scanning what little bit of the pavement she could actually see. Her mind was reeling.

The CD paused between songs, and she reached to the seat behind her and nudged Tim's leg. She glimpsed him in the rear view mirror as he lowered his book.

"Turn off your music," she said.

"Why?"

"I want to talk to you, that's why."

He let out an audible sigh, switched off the CD, and closed his book with a thud.

She watched him in the mirror as he sat up and leaned forward in the center of the back seat. She adjusted the mirror so she could see his face clearly.

"What happened at the ski resort, when you disappeared?"

He shrugged. It may have been Kit's imagination, but she thought his lower lip was trembling. "I don't know."

"We're in this together, Tim. You have to trust me."

He peered sideways at her.

"How did they get you to go with them? Did they grab you?"

"No."

"Then what happened?"

"One of the security guys told me you were waiting for me, that you were ready to leave."

"Where was Jason?"

He shrugged and stared at the ceiling. "I don't know."

"Weren't you two together?" Kit wished she didn't have to concentrate so hard on driving, so she could pay more attention to getting information out of her son. On the plus side, though, he was a captive audience.

"We were, and then we got separated."

"How?"

"I don't know. We were helping the security guys search for—whatever."

Kit was quiet for a moment. "The word went around that they needed some help finding somebody's medicine, wasn't that what happened? And I told you to stay with me, and you two went anyway."

"You were asleep."

"So what? You think when I tell you to do something, I mean to do it only when I'm awake?"

He didn't answer, and Kit concentrated on the road. There was a road plow in the left lane. She moved to the right and breezed past him.

"So you two go to help, and you get separated. And somebody tells you that I'm waiting for you. How did you know that he was security?"

"He was wearing one of those jackets, I think it had an orange stripe."

Kit thought of the time she spent standing in the security office, wondering and worrying where he was. Now she wondered if anyone in that room had known what had happened to him, if they were in on it.

"When you told us to stay with you, I never thought—well, I never thought what happened would happen."

It wasn't her imagination. His lower lip was trembling, even more now than it was before. Her voice softened. "So when did you find out that I wasn't waiting for you?"

He half shrugged and turned his head. After a moment, his hand wiped at the corner of his eye. Catching her reflection in the mirror, he coughed and lowered his head.

"Tim, I have to know. We might still be in danger, and I need your help. Where did they take you?"

He took a deep breath. "They took me on a ski lift, to a building at the top of the hill."

"You got on a ski lift with them?"

"They said you'd driven up there, and you were waiting to pick me up."

"Didn't you think that was odd? Do you not have a sixth sense or something, that tells you when things aren't right?"

He stared at the floor, and she wished she could take back her biting remark.

"So you get to this building. Then what?"

"They locked me in a room."

"Did they tie you up?"

"No."

"You couldn't get out?"

"No."

"What kind of room?"

"What do you mean, what kind of room?"

Kit knew she was pushing it. He'd already said more than he usually said in conversation—at least with her. "Okay, so there was no window you could crawl out of?"

"Remember when you first started programming? That room you worked in, that was so cold, and it didn't have any windows?"

Of course she remembered it. She'd spent years in that windowless room, working on mainframe computers... It was as cold as a refrigerator in that room. "That's what it was like?"

"Yeah. It even had a raised floor. I pulled up a couple of tiles, looked underneath, but there was a firewall all the way around. Anyway, they took my shoes."

"They took your shoes?"

"That's crazy, isn't it?"

Kit fell silent. She met a CIA agent once, who had been captured during the Viet Nam War. He told her that Americans were immediately stripped of their shoes when they were captured. It turned out that most Americans had soft soles, too soft to go very far in bare feet, particularly in the jungle. What would have happened if Tim had wandered out barefoot? Was it cold enough for him to get frostbite? Would his feet have frozen to the point where he wouldn't have been able to continue walking? Would they have been cut and bleeding?

She shivered, remembering how long it had taken for her own feet to warm up the night she'd left her shoes at the gristmill, and how painful it was until they did. "Were any of the men oriental?"

"Oriental?"

"Asian. Like Chinese."

"No."

"They were all Americans?"

"I guess. They looked American." When she didn't respond, he asked, "Mom, what's going on?"

"I don't know," she answered. She glanced at him in the mirror. His forehead was furrowed and his eyes were clouded. The sight of his room and his furniture blocking the entrances loomed before her. "Don't worry, Tim. We'll be safe at Grandma's house."

"How could you let them take me like that?"

"How could I…" She swallowed hard. "I won't let them take you again. I promise."

They were approaching the Richmond city limits. Kit's parents lived in Chesterfield County, bordering the southern part of the city. It would be another half an hour before she'd be there. She flexed her fingers. She'd been gripping the steering wheel for so long, her hands were stiff.

So Tim had been at the ski resort, further up the hill, when she'd left with Carter. That's why there'd been no tire tracks along the road. Had they needed her out of the area, so they could get him out without detection?

"Were you there the whole time?"

"Where?"

"In the room with no windows."

"No." He stared out the window.

"Where did they take you?"

"They blindfolded me. I don't know where we went."

"How long did it take for you to get there?"

"Not as long as it's taking us to get to Grandma's house."

She settled into her seat and tried to relax her shoulders, but she immediately hunched forward again as if by doing so, visibility would improve. They could have stopped any number of places south or west of the city.

"Can I read my book now?"

Kit could no longer see his face in the mirror, but his voice said enough. "Go ahead."

He sighed and then fell silent.

She longed to ask him more questions, but that would come soon enough. She would have to contact somebody—someone in law enforcement, who could arrange for composite sketches of the men he'd been with. And she would just have to figure out a way to tell somebody what had happened to Tim, and what was happening to her.

What *had* happened to her. After all, it was over with now.

Less than an hour later, she turned onto the two-lane road leading to her parent's house. The road hadn't been plowed at all, and driving was treacherous. As she rounded a corner, she pulled to a stop.

"What's up?" Tim asked, leaning forward to look out the front window.

"The road's flooded," Kit answered in awe. "It's never been flooded before."

They sat at the top of a small hill, looking at a steep dip in the road. Exactly where the road reached its lowest point, a one-lane bridge passed over a small creek. Kit couldn't remember how many times she'd gone fishing in that creek. It had never overflowed its banks, even during the wettest seasons. It had come close to drying up a few times, but...

"What are we gonna do?" Tim asked.

Kit put the minivan in reverse. "We're going a different way," she said as she backed into the nearest driveway and turned around.

CHAPTER 26
二十六

Kit trudged up the stairs behind Tim, her shoulders weighed down with the laptop and her suitcase. At the top of the stairs, they parted; Tim automatically went to the left, to the room he always used when visiting his grandparents, and Kit continued down the hall to a room on the right.

This had been a farmhouse at one time, when this part of Chesterfield County had been mostly agricultural. It was white clapboard, set back from the road, with a small lawn bordered with giant oak trees and holly and surrounded by tobacco fields. Now the fields were dwindling, as the farmers sold off bits and pieces to a new generation of Virginians, outsiders attracted to the beauty that was central Virginia.

Her father had never been a farmer; he'd been a banker and a friend to the old-time locals. He'd looked the other way when farmers came across bad times, not calling in loans when he probably should have.

It had been a sweltering August day when two young men had wandered away from the Interstate and found the tiny bank nestled into a sleepy row of businesses.

Her father had given them all he had, but they'd still shot him and left him for dead. The doctor said it was a testament to his will to live that he survived, although he would never walk again.

He worked for a time, a familiar sight in his wheelchair. Then a series of droughts and stiff competition forced Old Man Cabot to give up his family farm. He had only one request: that the O'Reillys move into the home instead of selling it to a stranger, and somehow or other, he would buy it back. Any other banker would have scoffed at the idea, but not Kit's father. He sold their own modest home and moved the family into the old Cabot place.

It was supposed to be a temporary arrangement. The children—Kit and her two brothers—were warned not to write on the white walls or pick at the peeling wallpaper, because they were living in the house only until the Cabots could afford to move back in.

That was more than thirty years ago. Old Man Cabot had passed on a long time ago, followed shortly after by his wife of sixty years. Their children had scattered to the far ends of the country.

Eventually, her father's bank was sold to a larger one in North Carolina, and Mr. O'Reilly retired on disability.

But the walls still had the same peeling wallpaper on them; those rooms that had once been painted white were now yellowed and dingy with age. The house had a musty smell to it, an odor more associated with antique stores and flea markets.

Kit plopped the luggage onto the floor. "It's hot as a fire poker in here," she said.

Mrs. O'Reilly leaned against the doorframe. "Don't adjust the radiators," she cautioned. "Every time the wind blows, the power goes off. You'll be glad the rooms are so warm, when the power goes out and the house holds in that heat."

Kit fought the desire to run to the window and throw it open. "How long has it been snowing here?"

Her mother shrugged. "Off and on for two weeks now. It alternates between rain, snow, and ice. Been a real mess, if you ask me."

"I had to come around the back way," Kit said. "The main road was flooded."

"I heard tell the water's higher than it's been in fifty years. Good thing the house was built on a rise."

Kit laid a suitcase across the bed, opened it, and began to unpack.

"How long you figure on staying?"

"I don't know. A few days, a week."

"Frank gonna join you?"

Kit shook her head.

"He called last night, you know."

"No, I didn't know."

"Said you threw him out. Now Kit, why'd you want to go and do a fool thing like that?"

Kit opened the dresser drawer and neatly placed her clothes in before answering. "Did he tell you the situation?"

"Of course he did, Dear." Mrs. O'Reilly sat on the edge of the bed. "Don't act so rash. Men sometimes wander; you should know that."

"He can wander all he wants now," Kit said curtly.

"You're a fool for letting him go."

Kit held her tongue, although she would have loved to have told her mother just what she thought of Frank and his 'wandering.' She snapped the suitcase shut, and started to pull it off the bed. "What's that?" she asked, pointing to a brown envelope propped against the pillows.

"Oh, a courier brought that for you this morning."

Kit leaned across the bed and pulled it toward her. It was a standard brown nine-by-twelve envelope, but it was bulky as if it had something other than papers in it. Her name and her parent's address were typed on the front label. There was no return address.

"When did you say this came?"

"This morning. Around eight o'clock. I'd barely gotten out of the shower."

She didn't know why the room felt so cold, when only a moment ago she'd been as hot as if she'd had a fever. It was as if a chill had started at the nape of her neck and was working its way throughout her body. Her fingers were clammy and stiff as she opened the package.

She barely heard her mother's voice; it sounded distant and muffled. When Kit sat on the bed, her hands trembling, she was startled to find herself alone. Tearing her attention away from the package, she vaguely heard her mother and Tim talking as they descended the stairs.

The envelope contained a videotape and a single sheet of paper. She unfolded the note and read: *"Watch the tape alone. You will be contacted within twenty-four hours."*

She turned the paper over, but there was no name, no signature. Just the two neatly typed sentences.

She crossed the room, pushing the door closed as she went, and turned on the television and VCR in the corner. She popped the tape in, and sat down at the end of the bed to watch.

The film was dark, the objects hard to make out. There was no talking, no noise. Something large loomed in the background; as the moon shifted, she was able to make out the roofline of a building and a few naked branches of aged, craggy trees.

Then a sliver of light that widened; an arm outstretched, propping open a wooden shutter.

The camera zoomed inward, locking on two figures silhouetted against the window.

"What do you have for me?" one figure asked, his face obscured by the brim of his hat.

The other figure held out an object that shone in the moonlight: a CD case. Kit gasped as the camera moved in closer, revealing the face. The blood seemed to drain out of her as she recognized that face as her own.

"What is it?" the man asked.

The camera remained focused on her face. "It's the program, the one you wanted," she answered clearly.

"How do you know it's the right one?"

"It's the Chinese code."

"How did you get it?"

"Never mind that. I got it. That's all that matters…"

She heard the man chuckling in the background, although the camera remained riveted on her. "Hold it up," he said, "so I can see it."

Kit watched the video as her image held it in front of the window, where the gold cover appeared like a beacon in the moonlight.

It was a moment before the man reached out, seeming to pause just short of touching it. The pause seemed as if it lasted forever, and all the while, the camera was riveted on the jewel case. Finally, with a slight chuckle, he took it from her.

"Has anyone missed your laptop?" he asked.

She hesitated. "No."

"No one has questioned you about it?"

"When do I get it back?"

"It has some very valuable information on it. Information we can use. Information the CIA would be hard-pressed to explain, if they find out we have it."

"Keep it," she said.

The images were abruptly replaced with gray static. They knew they had her laptop, and they had to know that she had Joan's. The gravity of their brief conversation had been eclipsed in the surrealism of the moment and the rush to get her son back.

She stared at the static for a long time, until she came to her senses and popped the tape out of the VCR.

She crossed the room to the wastebasket, where she yanked the videotape out of the reel with an angry vengeance. When she was finished, the tape lay in a brown heap in the wastebasket, the plastic reel broken.

It wouldn't be the only tape; of that she was certain. They had the original. As cunning as they were, they would have it in a secure place, a place she couldn't begin to imagine.

They'd never wanted Tim. And they'd never wanted the program, or the CD. They wanted *her*, and she'd played right into their hands.

CHAPTER 27

二十七

It was almost 3:30 when Carter Leigh slid a suitcase into the hallway of his building and turned to lock his apartment door.

He tried phoning Kit's house soon after the interview with Stallworth ended, but her answering machine picked up. He didn't leave a message. He reasoned that she was probably on her way to her parents' house; he would be there soon enough and could talk to her in person.

Stallworth had been whisked away by his staff so quickly and cleanly, that the news staff were left scratching their heads and wondering what had happened. He could still see the look on Morley's face; their eyes had locked across the room, their expressions mutually incredulous. Carter didn't know if the look of suspicion in his boss' eyes was directed at him or at Stallworth, but Morley didn't speak and didn't hang around for Carter to find out.

Carter spent the morning replaying the tape of the interview, time and time again. It was too coincidental with everything going on with Kit, for Stallworth to bring up the subject of China. Carter wasn't an expert on Chinese matters or on Tibet, but he'd read enough to have formed an opinion of the regime and it was decidedly different from Stallworth's. He also had a strange sensation, one he'd experienced before—a feeling that defied logic, that made him feel as if an apparition's chilling breath was blowing down his shirt collar. It was a premonition, something that told him he was on a collision course with Stallworth and somehow, Kit was, too.

He grabbed the suitcase and strode briskly down the hallway to the elevator. Bryce would be there any minute. With any luck, they'd be in Richmond before dinnertime.

The elevator doors opened and Carter immediately stepped forward, running headlong into Munski.

"Going someplace?" the detective asked, eyeing his suitcase.

"An assignment," Carter answered, trying to sidestep him.

Munski held his arm across the elevator.

Carter stepped back. "What do you think you're doing?"

"I just want to have a word with you."

"You already did that."

The elevator doors closed. Carter pushed the button again, then jammed it two or three times just for good measure.

"Look, Carter, we've known each other a long time."

"Yeah. So?" Carter stared at the lights over the elevator. Two were at the ground floor, and another appeared permanently parked on the eighth.

Munski gently grabbed his arm. "Carter, we've been through a lot together. Don't let something come between us now."

Carter sighed and glanced at Munski. His sandy eyes, usually so piercing and rigid, appeared softer now—or at least as soft as a detective's eyes could get.

"What do you want?" Carter asked.

"Things aren't looking so good," Munski said.

"Oh?"

"We've got a frickin' can 'o worms with this case."

"The Joan Newcomb case?"

"Yeah."

Carter shrugged, trying to look disinterested, but his antennae were fully erect. "Now that the body's been found, it should make things easier. You get forensics, an autopsy—"

"You'd think it'd be easier. But that's precisely the problem."

Carter pulled out a pack of cigarettes and offered one to Munski. The elevator came while they were lighting up, but they both ignored it, just as they ignored the "No Smoking" sign posted clearly above the elevator buttons.

"You've dealt with bodies a lot more mutilated than hers," Carter said.

"It's not the condition of the body that's a problem. It's jurisdictions and agency maneuvering."

"Yeah? How so?"

"Newcomb was abducted in Arlington County," Munski said. "My jurisdiction; my case. Only she worked at a company that I swear to God, I think is a front for the CIA."

"A front?"

"I don't think UCT is a private company at all. Fact is, I can't even find information on the owners; it just leads from one corporation to another, and I think some of them consist solely of a mailbox."

"What do you mean?"

"Most of them have addresses on K Street, right downtown, prime location. But when I check it out, it's one of those mail houses, you know, that has rows of mail boxes and no businesses."

"It's a popular thing to do. A one-man shop opens up in a garage, and they get a K Street address to make it look like a conglomerate."

"Yeah, but they don't own Universal Computer Technologies."

Carter nodded. "You got me there."

"That's not all. I've had the CIA breathing down my neck ever since this Olsen woman reported the abduction. It's like they don't want me to really investigate the case."

"Are they hindering the investigation?"

Munski took a long drag on his cigarette before answering. "Off the record."

"You know I won't report anything until you give me the green light."

"*Unless* I give you the green light," Munski corrected. "I've got three more years till retirement, and I don't want anything screwing it up."

Carter nodded.

"These CIA guys, they've been looking for something, but I don't know what. I wanted to talk to people Newcomb worked with, but they blocked me. Later, I read in the *Post* that the police interviewed the UCT employees. Only we haven't interviewed anybody except the Olsen woman."

"Yeah?"

"Now Jerome's telling me they're going ape over the laptop. That's a weird thing to find with a body, isn't it? A frickin' laptop. Not even beside her, but strapped to her."

"So, are they trying to get the laptop away from Park Police?"

"They told Jerome they're going straight to the Director. Now they've got a political football on their hands, you know what I mean?"

The impact of Munski's words hit him like sighting a meteor right before it crashes through the window.

"What's so important about this woman?" Carter mused.

"Not the woman. The computer. CIA's claiming it's a matter of national security. They think there's classified information on it, and they don't want Park Police—or anybody else—to get to it before they do."

"But the Park Police has to get forensics first," Carter said.

"Yeah, and Park has jurisdiction. But get this: FBI's poking around, too."

"What do the Frisbees want?"

"Weird, isn't it? They won't tell me anything, but," Munski leaned forward and lowered his voice, although there wasn't another soul in the hallway, "I recognize one of the agents; name's Davidson."

"Yeah, I remember him. Didn't he work some case on the trucking industry last summer—kickbacks or something?"

"That's right; only now he's working in the espionage division."

"Espionage!" Carter exclaimed before catching himself.

"So what does that tell you, pal?" Munski continued. "They want the laptop as much as CIA and Park."

"And Davidson's not talking to you?"

Munski shrugged. "All I know is, I'm off the Newcomb case. I'm too far down the totem pole."

"Oh?"

Munski put out his cigarette. "My case is over. It was an abduction, anyway. Now that a body's been found, it's changed to homicide."

"Yeah, but—"

"And now that the Feds are involved, there's no way I'd be handling the murder case. Wasn't found in my back yard, anyway."

The elevator doors opened. Munski held out his arm to prop the door open. "Going down?" he asked.

They rode the elevator in silence. When they reached the lobby, Carter peered outside, but Bryce hadn't yet arrived. "So, what do you do now?" Carter asks.

"I still have another matter I'm working on," Munski said.

"What's that?"

"While it's not my jurisdiction, it holds a bit of interest for me. That's the alleged abduction of the Olsen boy."

Carter glanced up. "I figured you would get around to Mrs. Olsen sooner or later."

"Look, Carter, I was there for you when Teri died. I know how hard it was for you—"

"Don't mention her."

Munski hesitated. The Expedition pulled up in front of the building, and Carter reached for the suitcase. Munski's hand blocked him. "Carter, don't do it again. Don't get involved with this woman. I'm telling you not as a cop, but as a brother."

Carter shook off his hand. "You stopped being my brother when my sister divorced you."

"Listen to me, Carter. They're watching her; we're watching her. Something's not kosher about this woman."

Carter picked up his suitcase and headed for the door.

"I checked out her bank accounts."

He stopped with the door partway open and looked back at Munski.

"Turns out," Munski continued, "the bank tells me her accounts have attracted a whole lot of interest. *A whole lot of interest.*"

"What are you saying, Ski? Are you accusing her of murdering her boss? Or murdering Emerson?"

Munski shrugged. "I'm not accusing her of anything—yet."

Carter let out an expletive aimed in Munski's direction as he exited the building, the door slamming shut with a bang behind him.

CHAPTER 28
二十八

Kit steadied the ladder while Tim balanced the angel light on the top of the tree. Christmas music played softly in the background. In prior years, she'd always been moist-eyed on Christmas Eve, remembering the days of her childhood when she'd listened to the same songs, now updated from 33 RPM LP's to the O'Reilly's new CD player.

But tonight, her thoughts were miles away. Her father's voice, directing Tim from his wheelchair in the corner, was no more than a low hum in the distance. And when her mother entered the room with a plateful of warm cookies, she barely smelled the fresh gingerbread and spices. She shook her head when she was offered one of the delectable morsels.

"Are you sick?" her mother asked.

"No. Just not hungry," she said as Tim climbed down the ladder and grabbed a handful of cookies.

"But you love these," her mother said.

Kit glanced at her mother's eyes, filled now with worry. Like a dutiful daughter, she took one of the gingerbread men, carefully decked out in green, white, and red icing. She nibbled on it until her mother's expression turned to relief, but she barely tasted it.

She'd called every courier service in central Virginia. No one had delivered a package to the O'Reilly house— not today, not ever.

She'd waited all day for a phone call. She jumped every time the phone rang, but they were mostly calls from neighbors or relatives, wishing them a happy holiday. Her cell phone remained conspicuously silent.

The holiday banter faded as the voices inside her gained momentum. She'd gone over everything, knowing she had to accept the logical explanation even if her heart didn't want to.

He'd been waiting for her at the police department the night Joan was abducted. When Tim needed her at the ski resort and her car wouldn't start, he'd shown up almost instantly. For all she knew, he'd rigged it so she'd have to accept his ride. He was there with her—and Tim—when she fell asleep and Tim was kidnapped. And he'd accompanied her back to her house that night, making sure she got there in time for her next set of instructions. He'd stayed there while the program was reconstructed. And he'd driven her to the bank, to pick up the instructions—the very ones that explicitly directed her to go to the gristmill alone.

That left him free to film the meeting. He was a television reporter; of course, he'd have easy access and the knowledge to film them in the dark.

And he'd phoned right before the interview with Stallworth. It was planned, right down to the last detail. The interview was a message to her, a message that told her in no uncertain terms that there were people in high places behind all of this.

Nothing else would have convinced her to venture out in a snowstorm, to piece together a program that even she didn't fully understand, to meet someone in the dead of night, to hand over a disk as ransom—except her son. And they knew that. Tim would be the only way they could set her up. And now they would blackmail her.

Unless she turned the tables on them first.

There were only a handful of people who knew she was here: Frank, who was too busy with his love interest to give her a second thought; Jack, her boss, who she'd known as long as she'd been with UCT... and him.

The blackmailer had to be Carter.

By the time her cell phone did ring, she was almost in a trance. It must have rung several times before she emerged from her thoughts; her mother was saying something to her, tugging at her arm.

Mechanically, she pulled the phone from the belt clip. It was him. He hadn't blocked his number; the caller ID clearly provided it, along with his name.

She couldn't talk to him now. Not now.

She held the phone in her hand, listening to it ring, watching the name on the faceplate as though it was hypnotizing her.

Then she snapped out of it.

She had to talk to him. If he was part of all this, he was calling to give her more instructions. She'd have to play along with him until she figured out what she would do, and how she could turn the tables.

She pushed the on button, and raised the phone to her ear. It was too late. Either he'd hung up or her voice mail had already picked up.

She was getting ready for bed when it rang again. She answered it on the first ring.

"Kathryn Olsen," the voice stated.

"Yes." She was surprised her voice sounded so calm.

"Be at Iron Bridge Park, precisely at midnight. Come alone. We'll be watching."

"Where do I meet you?"

"Take the trail behind the tennis courts. Bear left beyond the picnic area."

"I'll be there," she said.

Then the line went dead.

Kit lay in bed, the covers drawn up to her neck, watching the curtains sway in the draft created by the air vents. The room was stifling. She could feel the sweat popping out at the roots of her hair; she found it more difficult to breathe as the minutes crept past.

The grandfather clock at the end of the upstairs hallway chimed the eleventh hour. Only a few minutes passed before the television set downstairs went silent, but each minute felt like an eternity.

She heard her mother's footsteps on the stairs, and then padding softly down the hallway. They stopped first at her door, as she knew they would. The door was opened quietly. "Kit?"

"Yes, Mom?"

The door was opened wider, allowing a swath of yellow light into the room, stretching like tentacles across the bed. "Good night," her mother said softly.

"Good night."

Then the door was closed as quietly as it was opened. Her mother's footsteps headed back to the stairwell, stopping once more before descending. Kit wondered if Tim were awake, or if her mother would awaken him to tell him good-night, as she'd done with her so many, many times, like the hospital nurse who wakes up the patient only to give him a sleeping pill.

The light seeping in under her doorway eventually disappeared, and Kit quickly slung the covers off of her. She was dressed all in black—black turtleneck, black sweater, black jeans, even socks. She slipped on her boots, then stuffed pillows under the covers to make it appear as if she were in bed. She pulled the parka off the hook behind the door. Instinctively, she reached into the deep pocket and touched the gun. It was there, as she knew it would be, locked and loaded.

She eased the door open, slipped into the hallway and gently closed the door behind her.

Her breathing was heavy and labored; it sounded like a freight train as it echoed in the hallway.

She crept to the top of the stairs, hesitated briefly, held her breath and waited. No sound from Tim's room, no telltale light under his door.

She peered downstairs, catching sight of a swath of dim light and a hum of voices. Then that light gradually narrowed until it faded, and she heard the soft click of her parents' bedroom door closing. It had been the den while she was growing up, before her father was sentenced to life as an invalid. Now it saved him from the steep stairway to the second floor.

She slinked down the stairs, barely resting her foot on each step. She crossed the front hallway silently, grasping hold of her mother's key ring on the corner table, unchained the front door, and slipped outside. The door closed quietly. She'd made it.

Tim had shoveled a narrow path earlier out of the deep snow, leading from the house to the detached garage a hundred feet away. The thin layer of snow left behind had turned to ice, and she found herself sliding more than walking toward the darkened building. A gust of wind buffeted her as she hurried between the two structures.

She raised the garage door, wincing as it creaked on rusty hinges. Her mother's Silverado pickup truck awaited, salt and snow covering the dark brown exterior.

She jumped inside and slid the truck into neutral, holding her breath as it rolled backwards downhill. When it was a car length from the garage, she slid it into park, jumped out, ran back and closed the garage door. Back inside the truck, she eased it forward until she reached the bend in the driveway. Once there, she couldn't avoid the inevitable; she started the engine, quickly shifted it into gear, and backed across the crunching ice and gravel, where she turned around and headed off down the quiet road without turning on her lights.

This part of southern Chesterfield County was rural and isolated, the roads narrow and winding. She could barely make out the yellow lines at the center; she knew there were no shoulders on these roads, only deep ditches obscured by the piles of blackened snow left by the plows. There were no streetlights and in the moonless night, it was difficult to see the houses she knew were nestled beyond the tree line.

Nervously, she clutched the four-wheel-drive stick. Many a vehicle slid off these roads, even in the best of conditions. Not a season would go by without another cross popping up in memory of an ill-fated drive on an ill-fated night.

Finally, she reached Iron Bridge Road. The light was red, as she knew it would be. As she gently slid the truck to a stop, she glanced in both directions. The road was well lit and deserted. She wiped the sweat from her forehead. The light turned green; she cautiously eased through the intersection and turned left.

She saw the sign at the corner of Iron Bridge Road and Whitepine Road long before she reached it, a brick and metal sign that looked as if it could withstand a hurricane. She turned right on Whitepine, turned off her headlights, and entered Iron Bridge Park.

She'd spent many an evening at this park. When Tim was younger, they frequented its softball diamonds, soccer fields, tennis and basketball courts.

Now it was desolate, the street plowed only because a subdivision beckoned at the end of the road. She drove past the tennis courts on her right, peering through the darkness at the parking lot beyond. She continued down the gently winding road, past a half dozen more parking lots. She slowed at each one, carefully examining it, looking for a vehicle. There were none.

At the golf course, the road abruptly turned. She continued until she reached a residential neighborhood, looking closely at the darkened houses and the occasional blue flicker of a television set.

She reached a side road and turned the truck around. The drive back to the tennis courts was just as slow, just as labored. This time, she pulled into the parking lot nearest the tennis courts. The virgin snow layered with ice crunched under the tires as she pulled behind a crop of evergreens. With any luck, she and the truck wouldn't be spotted.

Her boots provided a firm footing in the snow, although she was painfully aware she was leaving a trail that wouldn't be obscured until the snow melted or more fell. Curious, she scanned the surrounding parking lot and the trail behind the tennis courts. It was all virgin snow, unmarred by a single set of footprints.

A solitary light behind the tennis courts shone, feebly illuminating the entrance to a trail. Directly to the left was a picnic table, forlorn and cold under a darkened wood roof lined with icicles. She swallowed hard as she passed it.

Just beyond, the trees parted. In sunnier days and warmer days, the path would be clear, although she couldn't remember now whether it was gravel or dirt.

This part of the county was normally filled with evergreens that made spring always seem as if it were just around the corner. But tonight, as she turned left onto an adjoining path, there were no evergreens; just craggy, naked limbs from aged oaks drooping dangerously low under the weight of ice and snow.

She passed a fitness stop on the right; she recognized the benches placed almost in an L-shape, now buried by glistening snow. Just beyond, the trail took a sharp turn to the right.

She reached deeper into her pockets, her right hand fingering the Glock, the metal cold even through her lined leather glove. With each breath, she sent out a frosty cloud.

She heard a noise like a twig snapping, and she jerked her head to the right. At that same instant, she was grabbed from behind. Her right arm was wrenched out of her parka and almost out of its socket, dropping the gun into the depths of her pocket. Another arm wrapped itself across her face, yanking her head backward and blocking her mouth, stifling her instinctive scream.

She could smell leather and the thick odor of horses as she was dragged, kicking and fighting, into the woods.

CHAPTER 29
二十九

When Kit was six or seven years old, she'd gone to the James River with her family. They'd taken southern fried chicken, home-fried potatoes and cole slaw made from homegrown cabbage. Afterward, Kit and her brothers had ventured onto the rocks that wound their way across the James toward Hollywood Cemetery in Richmond, their shoes off and voices squealing as the cold rapids licked at their heels.

She really didn't know what happened first—if the current had caused her to lose her footing, or if she'd slipped on the slimy rock and tumbled into the waves crashing over the rocks.

She didn't have time to be afraid. As she slid under water, her head hit the jagged rock full force, knocking her unconscious. When she awakened, she was propped against a tree, her legs splayed out in front of her, blood oozing down the side of her head as her mother worked feverishly to stop the flow. She vaguely remembered her father in the background, confined to his wheelchair, offering advice, but it was her mother's strong voice and stronger hands that she remembered most.

Only now her mother's calming touch was nowhere near. She could feel the tree against her back, the rough bark penetrating the heavy parka, her legs stretched out before her in a decidedly un-ladylike pose.

Her eyes flew open, the movement causing her to gasp in pain.

Not four feet away was the man from the gristmill, the same dark gray hat slightly cocked on his head, the brim barely above his brows. In the darkness, she couldn't make out his eyes but she knew from his chuckle he was watching her.

She strained to sit up as pain shot through her head.

"I could have killed you," he said calmly.

"Yeah, then you could prove to the world that you're stronger than a girl," she said with more conviction than she felt. She sat up straighter and rubbed her head.

"I heard you were spunky," he said.

He was bent down, his coat brushing the snow beneath him; he was dark and large, and loomed menacingly over her.

"What do you want with me?" she asked.

"Isn't it more like, what do you want with us?" he answered evenly.

"I don't understand."

"Don't play games with me. You've stolen a laptop and a very valuable program, and I want to know why."

Kit was silent. She suddenly realized her hands were not bound. The bottom of her parka reached midway to her knees, but she couldn't feel the pistol against her leg. Although his face was obscured, she knew he was watching her. Slowly, she moved her hands to her lap.

"I haven't stolen anything," she said.

"I know you switched computers with the *late* Joan Newcomb," he hissed, "what I don't know is, why you did it."

"I didn't switch them on purpose. It was a mistake; they were both together, and we grabbed the wrong ones."

"That's pretty weak. You expect me to believe that?"

"I don't care what you believe."

"You should. Your life depends on it."

In that instant, she shoved her hand into her pocket and grasped the Glock. Through the material, she aimed it directly at his head. It would blow her parka to bits and the sound would reverberate through the woods, but with any luck, she'd hit him point-blank. And then she'd have fourteen more bullets in the clip to unload in him.

"I wouldn't do that if I were you."

The voice came from behind her. Startled, she jerked her head to the left as a figure walked into the small clearing.

"Jack!" she gasped.

"Pull your hand out of your coat," her boss ordered.

It was then that she noticed both his hands remained in his pockets. The other man was still a few feet from her, staring directly into her face. She caught a glimpse of cold, steely gray eyes, eyes that didn't blink but remained fixed on hers. She'd seen those eyes somewhere before—

Slowly, she pulled her hand from her pocket.

"Keep your hands where we can see them," Jack directed.

"How can you be a part of this?" she spat.

"Things are not always as they appear," he answered. "For example, I thought you were a hard-working, honest employee. I never thought you'd turn out to be a thief."

"So is this your idea of an employee conference? Call me to a deserted area in the middle of the night to beat me up?" she retorted. "Somehow, I think if you were everything I thought *you* were, none of us would be here."

She pulled herself to her feet, trying not to wince from the pain in her head.

Jack waited for her to steady herself before continuing. "I want the laptop, and some reassurance that you'll never discuss the program you gave Toy at the gristmill."

She gasped as he nodded toward the man with the steely eyes.

"And if we get the laptop and you keep your mouth shut, there's a promotion waiting for you," he said. "Just continue like nothing happened."

"But…" Kit struggled to find the words. Carter had been right. The laptop was a message—a message to her and her alone. Maybe the message was if she didn't remain quiet, she would be found just like Joan. But it was only a matter of time before the authorities would realize her laptop had been switched with Joan's, only a matter of time before the feds would be investigating her, bringing her up on charges…

"No one else will ever know you switched computers," Jack added, "as long as you do what you're told."

"You murdered Joan," Kit said.

"Joan committed suicide," Jack said. "So did Bernard."

"Two bullets—"

"They may not have pulled the trigger, but it was suicide just the same," Toy said. "You can learn a lot from them, Kit. They got greedy, and they tried to double-cross us. It isn't possible. You take what we give you, and you don't make up your own rules. Understand?"

The reality of the situation began to take hold, like a tsunami forming far from shore, rolling toward her, gaining in momentum as it approached. There would be plenty of time for her to sort through all of this, to figure everything out, but she couldn't do it now. Now she needed to get out of this alive, to make them believe she was on their team—no matter the cost.

"I understand," she said.

Toy nodded. "We've made the first installment."

"What do you mean?"

"A hundred thousand dollars has been deposited in your account."

"Why?"

"Isn't it obvious? We're buying your silence."

"Why not just kill me?" she asked. "You're smart enough to find Joan's laptop yourself. Then you don't have to pay me, and you don't have to worry about me."

Toy chuckled. "Maybe you're worth more to us alive."

"Besides," Jack added, "we have the power to charge you with two murders, and if that weren't enough, we can charge you with spying. But of course, we won't do that."

"Of course you won't," she said, "because I'll remain silent."

A long moment passed before she added, "If that's all, I'm leaving now." When they didn't respond, she took a deep breath and turned away. Deliberately, she began walking, each step excruciatingly painful as she envisioned a gun pointed at her back, imagining the sound of it filling her ears any second...

"Just one more thing," Jack said.

She stopped and turned back. To her surprise, neither one had a gun leveled at her. In fact, they appeared not to have moved.

"This is bigger than any of us," Jack said. "You can't imagine how far-reaching this is. For every one of us you meet, there are a thousand more you'll never see. There are people in high places, in all walks of life...*in all walks of life.*"

Kit nodded, swallowing hard despite her best efforts to remain calm. After a moment that felt like forever, she turned away and started back down the path toward the tennis courts. At the corner, she turned back, but they were gone. There was nothing in the clearing except naked trees with jagged branches swaying in the wind.

Her parents' house loomed before her in the dark, the ancient oaks hovering over the two-story structure, their stripped branches reaching out in the night like tentacles. The truck's headlights cast ghostly shadows as Kit wound her way to the side of the house. As she got out to open the garage door, the cry of a bobcat pierced the air.

Hurriedly, she opened the door and drove the truck in. She couldn't shake off the eerie feeling she had as she closed the garage door. Although she was certain she hadn't been followed, she couldn't resist glancing behind her as she rushed along the slippery path between the garage and the house.

She fumbled with the key, her fingers stiff and cold. Finally, she opened the door. She stepped inside and adjusted her eyes to the darkness.

At first, the house seemed still and silent, but once she closed the door, it felt as if it had come alive. It creaked and moaned with the change in temperature; the icemaker dropped a load of ice into the bucket with a sound like rattling chains; and the heater came on with a sputter and groan that filled the rooms.

Cautiously, she stepped toward her parents' bedroom. There was no light under the door, no indication that they'd been awakened.

She climbed the stairs, holding her breath as if by so doing, she could avoid a creaking board. Upstairs all of the doors were closed tight, sealing out any light. She felt her way along the wall until she reached her room.

Quietly, carefully, she opened the door, stepped inside, and closed it.

Finally, she heaved a sigh of relief. She leaned against the door, resting her eyes. Every bone in her body ached.

"What's going on?"

She jumped. A shadow moved in the corner.

She flipped the light switch.

"Mom!" she cried, her hand instinctively moving to her chest. "You scared me to death!"

Her mother remained in the rocking chair at the far end of the room. Her lips were pursed, her eyes almost glowing. She pulled a quilt tighter around her, as if she felt a chill.

"What are you doing here?" Kit asked.

"The question is, young lady, where have *you* been?"

Kit bit her tongue and peeled off her parka, returning it to the hook behind the door. "How long have you been here?" she asked.

"Long enough."

"Long enough for what?"

"You've been up to something, and I want to know what it is."

Kit sat on the edge of the bed and pulled her boots off. "Mom, I'm not sixteen anymore."

"I don't care how old you are, you're under my roof now, Missy, and I know something's up. I know cow dung when I smell it."

"Jesus."

"Yes, now you call the name of our Lord!"

"I'm going to bed. You can sit here and watch me snore if you want. But I don't feel like talking, and nothing's gonna keep me from this bed."

"You're seeing someone," her mother announced.

"What?"

"You can't fool me. I know you're sneaking around, seeing somebody. *He's* been calling here."

"Who's been calling here?"

"It ain't Frank."

"When did he call?"

"Don't matter. I told him he had the wrong number, ain't nobody here by that name."

Kit's head was throbbing. "Yes, Mother, I am seeing someone. I wasn't ready to tell you yet, but you caught me, fair and square."

"I knew it! You'd better beg the Lord's forgiveness!"

Kit stopped undressing to peer at her mother. "Didn't you just tell me yesterday, that people sometimes wander? You didn't seem to think there was anything wrong with it then!"

"I said *men* sometimes wander; there's a big difference."

"Oh, so it's okay for Frank to fool around, but it isn't okay for me?"

"I raised you better than that! You sneaking around, like a slut in the dark…"

"Oh, Mom, give it a rest." Kit pulled off her slacks and climbed into bed. She reached for the light switch, abruptly turning the room into a black abyss. "I'm going to sleep."

It was the rain pelting against the windowpane that awakened her. Her first thought was to check the rocking chair. It was empty, the quilt neatly folded in the seat. Her second thought was to check her watch. It was almost ten o'clock.

Half an hour later, she bounded into the kitchen, where her father was busy fixing a broken radio. She kissed Tim on the cheek and then her father. For a brief moment, the room was filled with holiday wishes, and then Tim dragged her into the living room to open her gifts.

The tree was ablaze. A garland twinkled as it wound around the room, and the sound of Christmas music wafted everywhere. Freshly baked cinnamon buns, a family tradition, sat under a glass dome on the coffee table.

But somehow, it didn't feel like Christmas. It felt hollow, like opening a box expecting to find a surprise and finding instead it was simply an empty box.

When her mother walked into the room a few minutes later, her lips pursed and stiff, Kit wished she were somewhere else.

It was no wonder Kit's two brothers never came to visit. Mrs. O'Reilly had ruled her husband and her family with an iron hand ever since Kit could remember, and her personality hadn't mellowed one bit through the years. The tensest Christmas she'd ever experienced was in this house the year both her brothers brought their new brides for the holiday. Kit hadn't seen either of her sisters-in-law within an hour's drive of her mother since.

Tim was excited about his gifts for her, and hovered over her while she opened them: a mousepad with a picture emblazoned on it, taken of her at Cozamel the previous summer, a Mayan pyramid forming the backdrop behind her; an angel figurine; a box of Godiva chocolates, her favorite candy; and a bottle of cologne,

Ralph Lauren's *Romance*. Her mother clucked when she saw the last gift, but Kit ignored her, and reached across to hug Tim.

He had already opened the gifts from her, probably at the crack of dawn: the new *Dungeons and Dragons* software; the *X-Files* and *Austin Powers* DVDs; too many sweaters and socks and jeans for Kit to remember them all now; and his favorite present, as she knew it would be, a gift certificate from a local sporting goods store.

The phone rang just as she was getting ready to bite into a cinnamon bun. Her mother remained fixed in her chair. She could hear the wheels on her father's wheelchair as he made his way from the kitchen into the living room.

"Want me to answer that?" Kit asked her mother.

She shrugged, and Kit walked to the table beside Mrs. O'Reilly's chair and answered the phone. It was Frank, calling to wish his son a merry Christmas. Kit was icily cordial. She set the phone on the end table. "It's for you, Tim. It's your dad."

"I don't want to talk to him," Tim said. "I hate him."

"Tim, don't say that," Kit said. "He's your father. He's calling because he loves you."

"I don't care." Tim got up. "You can't make me talk to him, Mom. You can't." It was more of a plea than an announcement.

Her mother exhaled sharply. Kit whirled her head in her mom's direction. She wasn't looking at either of them, but upward as if having a silent conversation with God, her face almost bloating with rage right in front of Kit's eyes.

"Just for a minute, Tim. Just wish him a merry Christmas, or let him wish you one, and then you can get off the phone," Kit said.

"You see what you've done to your family!" Mrs. O'Reilly exploded.

"What are you talking about?" Kit said.

"You—you find some man to have an affair with, and you tear your whole family to pieces. I can't stand it! I just can't stand it!" Wailing, she stomped through the room to her bedroom.

Tim stared at Kit with wide eyes.

"Tim, I didn't..."

"I know *you* wouldn't do that. Dad would!" Tim said firmly, his eyes misty. Before Kit could respond, he walked to the phone and picked it up. "Merry Christmas," he said, "have a nice life." And with that, he hung up.

CHAPTER 30

三十

Kit bent over the computer printouts. She'd finally become accustomed to the guard stationed in the corner. He never made a sound, simply stood there like the guards at Buckingham Palace: a somber, silent figure who never moved but who, she assumed, observed everything.

She bent over the desk as though her mind was totally focused on the code before her, but she was neither reading the code nor thinking about the programs.

It was January 13, a blustery, bone-chilling day that was setting record low temperatures across the region.

Not that she could observe the snow falling yet again, or the whiteout conditions she knew were just beyond the room. She stole a glance at Chen, seated at the next desk. She was locked into this high security office like a forty-hour-a-week prisoner, as she had been for weeks: a captive in a room where the world's most secret programs were held under lock and key, where nothing came in and nothing left, except what she held in her own memory.

She'd purchased a new laptop in Richmond and backed up Joan's entire hard drive to the new one. On her first day back in the office, she deposited Joan's computer in Jack's office, setting it in the center of his desk while he silently watched her, his face expressionless. Her promotion had been waiting for her, along with a hefty pay increase.

She'd visited the bank's ATM and checked her bank balance the day after Christmas; Jack hadn't been lying. The balance reflected precisely one hundred thousand dollars more than she knew she should have. She'd destroyed the receipt from the ATM; lit it afire in the front seat of her van and watched it burn into blackened dust in the ashtray.

She hadn't done anything with the money. She'd just left it there, until she could get her thoughts in order.

Which was more easily said than done. The truth was, she'd spent endless sleepless hours reliving that night at Iron Bridge Park, analyzing every sentence uttered.

Since returning to work, she'd seen Jack countless times, in impromptu hall meetings, standing at the water cooler, or on his way to or from the elevator, and he acted like he always had. He was so calm and so cool that she was tempted to question whether that fateful night had happened at all. Then she stopped herself, realizing that beyond a doubt, it had happened.

The piles of work she had accumulated on her desk were reassigned, and she was sent to work in Customs full-time. Chen never mentioned the program he helped her develop, never questioned whether it was accepted by the kidnappers, and never asked her what transpired after he left.

Carter had called numerous times, but she hadn't picked up and hadn't returned his messages. Thank God for caller ID. She was totally conflicted about his intentions. A part of her wanted to run to him, to feel as if they were partners in this whole mess, to have at least one ally. Another part was still suspicious, still thought he could be a part of this conspiracy. And Jack's words still rang in her ears: "For every one of us you meet, there are a thousand more you'll never see. There are people in high places, in all walks of life…"

She stole another glance at Chen. He was busily typing away, his fingers flying over the keyboard, his shoulders rounded as he leaned forward.

He couldn't be involved.

She'd been through this chain of thoughts so many times she knew exactly where it would lead. It was just too convenient to think he was linked to the kidnappers because of his ethnicity.

This room contained the most classified information on China that existed in the CIA. She learned no one gained access to this room and the banks of information lined up in the adjoining vault unless Chen personally approved. For all his youth, he had important ties to important people that kept him in charge. And whatever he was in charge of, the kidnappers needed.

Even Jack could not cross the threshold into this room. Joan had never been here either. But Bernard had. Bernard had worked side by side with Chen for years, like a modern day Mutt and Jeff; Chen, with his proper and formal ways, and Bernard… well, Bernard like an overflowing dumpster.

He'd sat in this very seat, worked at this very same desk, possibly on the same program she was working on. And whatever it was he found out, he tried to extort money from Jack and Toy in return for his silence. And that extortion got him killed.

She absent-mindedly thumped her pencil against the computer printout. What had he uncovered? Had he discovered that Jack was a spy? And now they thought she held the same information.

As the minutes ticked past, she analyzed the computer code in front of her in a completely different way. For her entire career, she'd focused only on what the programs did and how they did it. Now, her life would depend on finding the programs of interest to China, and finding the ones so important that people who had knowledge of them would die.

There was increased chatter in the Far East. American operatives and their allies always assumed something foul was in the air when voice and data transmissions quickened their pace.

And now, the Israelis were intercepting transmissions believed to be from Mongolia. At the same time, agents in the field were intercepting lines of computer code. As Customs kicked into action, Kit was seeing a side of espionage she'd only imagined. It was now her job to figure out what purpose the code served.

And she found herself wondering, day after day, if each line of code that crossed her desk was something Jack and Toy needed.

She had to think like the enemy.

Kit drew the curtains as if her life depended on it. One by one, the heavy drapes in the living room and dining room were pulled tight, obscuring the pale winter moon and the yellow streetlamps, enveloping the rooms in darkness. She hurriedly pulled the blinds in the kitchen, involuntarily shivering as she remembered Lisa's face at the back door.

She had retrieved her new laptop from the bank deposit box, where it had remained out of sight since she'd returned from Chesterfield County. Now it was booting on the dining room table.

She muted the sound, even though she knew it didn't matter; Tim was upstairs, locked in his room, where he'd been since finishing dinner. It had been days since she'd heard from Frank. Presumably, he was busy with his new love. Whenever Kit thought of the two of them in each other's arms, she felt sick. It was much easier to ignore it and concentrate on the code. Later, when she'd connected all the dots and extricated herself, she would piece the rest of her life back together.

In contrast, Carter didn't appear ready to give up on her. At times, she felt guilty for ignoring him, and at other times she wanted to call him so badly that it actually hurt. But her logical alter ego had kicked in, and she was now convinced she would be better off determining how he fit into this puzzle, before allowing any contact with him.

Her first stop was the *Windows Explorer*, where she painstakingly sifted through every folder, like a gold miner searching for gold. And just like the gold miner, she found herself with mountains of useless stuff—a technical version of dirt and stones and rubble that led nowhere.

She narrowed down the possibilities into three categories: emails, word processing documents, and programs.

Since she'd previously found emails between Joan and Bernard that referred to Toy, she started with them. She worked her way backward from the day Joan disappeared, reading each email, deciphering each sentence, trying to find the hidden meaning in each piece of correspondence.

There had been other after-hours meetings between Joan and Bernard, always occurring off-site, out of the

office. Midnight encounters, weekend rendezvous…
And for the first time, she thought of Bernard's widow.

She felt a pang of guilt; she hadn't considered his
widow before now. She didn't even know her name. She
knew they had children, who were now without a father.
But how many, and what their ages were, she hadn't a
clue. Kit thought she might have met her at a company
party, maybe a Christmas party a year or so ago. She
couldn't picture what she looked like; she's been
nondescript, the type of woman who fades into the
background. She couldn't remember ever having talked
with her.

She switched to the Internet and ran an address
check. Bernard had lived in Arlington, not far from the
office. Prime real estate, right outside of the District.
Kit jotted down the address and the phone number,
and glanced at her watch. It was too late to go there
tonight, and besides, she wanted to continue searching
the computer files. With any luck, she could make it
there tomorrow evening, after work. She and Mrs.
Emerson would have a nice little chat; perhaps she could
shed some light on what her husband may have been
involved in.

The minutes ticked by as she read each email, one
by one. She got up once to stretch her legs and pour a
cup of orange pekoe tea, but hours later, the tea sat
untouched, the cream turned into cold specks that
floated along the surface.

She opened every word processing document she
could find. Many of them were personnel related. Before
her meeting with Jack and Toy, she would have bypassed
those. Now she read each one, looking at salaries and
benefits, searching for any aberrancy, anything that
appeared out of the ordinary.

In a spreadsheet, she listed the employees whose salaries far surpassed their counterparts—eleven in all, out of more than sixty. Interesting, considering the government made public the grades and associated salary ranges. Could they also be part of the conspiracy, bribed into silence and compliance? Some of them, Kit knew on a professional level; none of them she knew socially. Another trip to the Internet's white pages revealed several of the addresses and phone numbers, information that could be useful as she pieced together the puzzle.

There were other documents tracking the progress of programs Joan had been supervising before her disappearance. Some of them involved the same people on Kit's newly compiled list.

She drew a diagram, linking the programs with the individuals. Many of them overlapped. But only three of them involved Bernard. And only one of those had been worked on right up to the time of Bernard's disappearance: the elections program.

"I'm going to bed, Mom," Tim announced. His voice startled her, and she realized for the first time how engrossed she'd become in her research.

"Okay, Tim," she said, trying to calm her rapidly beating heart. "Sleep good tonight."

He hesitated at the doorway, as if he wanted to say something else.

"What is it?" she asked.

"Nothing." He looked toward the staircase, and then glanced back at her. "Are you coming to bed soon?"

"I'm finishing up some work," she said. "What time is it?"

"Almost midnight."

"I'll be up shortly."

He didn't reply, and a couple of minutes passed before Kit realized he was still standing in the doorway.

"Are you okay?" she asked.

"I'm okay." He glanced at the stairs again. "I'm going to bed now."

Kit pushed her chair away from the dining room table. "What are you afraid of?"

"Nothing… We're safe here, right?"

"Of course we are. Come on, we'll check the alarm system together," she said, jumping up and grabbing his arm. She walked with him to the back door, where they set the alarm. As the familiar computerized voice announced the alarm status, she began to question whether she was doing this for his benefit or for her own.

"What if somebody was inside the house?" he asked timidly.

"What do you mean?"

"Like, they'd gotten in before the alarm was turned on."

"Did you hear anything?"

"No."

"You're just worried?"

He nodded, avoided looking at her.

"Don't be afraid," she said, wrapping her arm around his shoulders. "Take my cell phone. Go upstairs, search your room, and then lock yourself in. If you hear anything, or if the alarm goes off, call the police. Okay?"

"What about you?"

"I'll be okay. I promise."

He took her cell phone and started toward the stairs. "Mom?"

"Yes?"

"Is it okay if I spend the night at Jason's tomorrow?"

She didn't hesitate. "Sure. I think it'd be good for you."

"Thanks."

She watched as he started to ascend the stairs. "Tim," she called. When he turned to look at her, she said, "I love you."

"Yeah," he said. He took a couple more steps before adding, "Same here."

A moment later, his door was closed and locked, and she heard the sound of heavy furniture being dragged across the floor. She thought of the dresser Tim used to barricade himself in, and the chest of drawers that blocked his window. What a time for Frank to be gone.

She unplugged the laptop. Carrying it under her arm, she made her way through the house, checking the doors. Funny, the door leading into the garage was unlocked. They never even used the garage. It was so filled with Frank's workbenches and power tools that a vehicle wouldn't fit inside. In fact, she couldn't even remember the last time she'd used that door.

Tim's words hung in the air. As she looked back, a dim light had settled over the room, causing shadows in the corners that took on a life of their own. She couldn't resist glancing over her shoulder as she made her way upstairs.

The silence in the hallway was oppressive. She felt as though the walls had eyes. She made her way to Tim's door, held her breath and listened. The only sound was her heartbeat. "Tim?" she called softly.

"Yeah?"

"Are you okay?"

"Yeah, Mom."

She hesitated momentarily, and then padded down the hall to her bedroom.

She usually slept with the door open, especially since Frank had moved out. She guessed it gave her the feeling that she was closer to another human being. For the first time since he'd been gone, she wished he were there.

Somehow, she was never afraid when he was home, even when he was snoring away, oblivious of anything going on around him. Maybe it was just his physical stature; she knew it would take two men to bring down his six-foot-plus frame. And now, it was just Tim and her; both of them together weren't close to Frank's size.

She had a feeling she couldn't quite put her finger on, a heightened awareness that convinced her she wasn't alone, that made her want to constantly turn around and look behind her.

She gently pushed the door to and locked it. Then she thought of Tim down the hall and unlocked it. She stood for a long moment, engaged in an internal debate on whether the door should remain unlocked or locked.

Then she remembered a wind chime that hung in her bathroom. It was designed to hang outside, perhaps on a porch or a deck, but it had beautiful, intricate shells along the top that made her hang it in the bathroom where she could glimpse a reminder of the beach and lazy days long past. She ran her fingers through it, listening to the brass melody.

A moment later, it was hanging on the doorknob. She was a light sleeper; if anyone even so much as turned the doorknob, the chimes would awaken her. And Tim could still get to her if he needed her.

She checked the clip in her Glock and set it on the nightstand.

Really, she thought, I'm getting as bad as Tim. Next thing you know, I'll be pushing furniture against the door.

She tossed her clothes in the hamper that stood just inside her walk-in closet. As an afterthought, she turned on the light and peered inside. Against the far wall was a built-in chest comprised of a half-dozen drawers. One wall was empty except for a solitary rod, now that Frank's clothes were gone. The other wall was completely filled with her clothes, arranged neatly so the dresses were grouped together, followed by her slacks and blouses. The floor was covered with pairs of shoes.

She gingerly stepped inside and pushed the dresses to the side, checking the shoes. One square foot at a time, she checked the entire closet.

Finally, she turned off the light and closed the door. A few minutes later, she was in bed, the pillows propping her into a seated position, the computer in her lap.

The elections program was just as she remembered it when it was unveiled at the office. They'd made a big production out of it. After the 2000 fiasco when half the population thought Gore had won and the other half thought Bush had, it was obvious something needed to be done. The age of chads, in all their configurations—pregnant, dimpled, hanging, or otherwise—were obsolete.

The technology age was here.

The program was simple, the premise even simpler.

Kit could picture the polling booth in her mind's eye, with its drapes drawn across the entrance. The voter would turn to a simple push screen. A diagram they called the "start screen" would be displayed, prompting the voter to press the screen to begin voting.

Candidates were listed, and the voters simply touched the name of the one they wanted. If they changed their mind, they merely touched another name. It was impossible to select two candidates, and you couldn't move forward to the next screen without voting or choosing to decline a vote on the prior screen.

And one by one, the voter would be provided with other issues or sets of candidates: governors, senators, congressmen, and referendums. All personally developed and customized for each jurisdiction by Universal

Computer Technologies. Was it possible the CIA was controlling the votes?

A major part of the CIA's role, although it was something she'd never been involved in personally, was covert operations in foreign countries. They'd been behind the overthrow of the Iranian government when they placed the Shah of Iran in power, as well as countless other countries, making it appear as if a democracy of the people had chosen a new leader, when the leader had been skillfully selected by the American government. Could they have taken it a step further, and developed a program to rig the votes? And could they now be using that program *inside* the United States as well? Otherwise, why would the CIA ever have been involved in writing it in the first place?

She felt a chill creep up her back, and she found herself holding her breath, listening. She hated the way the house creaked and moaned in the night. It was too easy to let her imagination run wild, to imagine footsteps on the stairs, making their way to her room.

She watched the wind chime for a time, her mind alternating between floods of emotion and stunned blackness.

Then she logged out of the elections program and searched for a back door, a way into the guts of the program. By the time she found it, the room was getting lighter, dawn peaking around the edges of the blinds. But her heart sank when she tried to open it. It was password protected. She had known deep down, it would be, but had hoped this version, at least, wouldn't.

It could take hours, days, or weeks to crack the password. Unless…

She deliberated. She could use the same technology she applied in her office to crack code. It was just a matter of writing the program, a simple one that would loop through literally millions of character combinations until it hit on just the right one. When it did, it would open the back door and deposit her right inside. Just like cracking a safe.

Ninety minutes later, the program was done. She tested it with a couple of baby-step tasks, and then set it to unlock the back door to the elections program. She slid the laptop under the bed, made sure the overhanging bedspread concealed it, and then started the shower.

She was due at work in an hour.

CHAPTER 31

三十一

Winter skies are always blacker than summer skies. Kit didn't think it was a matter of the sun setting earlier, although it was dark by five o'clock. It seemed the stars didn't twinkle as brightly; the moon, even when full, didn't cast as much light. And tonight, for the first time in weeks, there wasn't a cloud in the sky. It was as if someone had painted the air with a single black brushstroke.

She glanced nervously at the notepad she held in her hand, even though it was unreadable and the address was etched into her brain. In her rearview mirror, she could still see her office building rising in the dark, each window lit like a burst of white light. And then she turned off of Wilson Boulevard and the building vanished behind some trees.

Bernard's house was in a cul-de-sac. Kit stared at his home. It was afire with multi-colored holiday lights and a plastic Santa in the front yard; a Christmas tree sparkled gaily in the window. It just didn't seem right, with Bernard dead; he wasn't even buried yet, his body still in the hands of the coroner.

Finally, she took a deep breath and trudged to the front porch. A moment after ringing the bell, two young girls opened the door. Kit gasped; they were identical twins, four or five years old, with blond hair that caught the light like halos, and wide-set blue eyes. For a moment, she thought she had the wrong address; and then, from the back of the house, she saw an older heavy-set boy, shuffling his way to the door. He looked as she would have envisioned Bernard some thirty or forty years ago.

"Ma gave at the office," he said, starting to close the door.

Kit pushed the door open. "I'm not a salesperson," she said briskly. "I'm here to see Mrs. Emerson."

He glared at her for a moment, and she defiantly returned his glare. "Wait here." With that, he disappeared.

Kit waited only a few seconds before stepping inside and closing the door. She wandered down the hall, the twins on her heels. Amazingly, every room in the house was decorated in a blaze of color.

She turned the corner at the end of the hallway and almost ran smack into Bernard's wife. "Mrs. Emerson," she said, holding out her hand, "I'm—"

"I know who you are." Her brown eyes were brooding and dark. "Please leave."

"I worked with Bernard," Kit continued. "I'm so sorry about your loss."

"Sure you are," she answered, pushing past Kit. "Go upstairs," she said to the twins.

"It's terrible, what happened to him," Kit said. "I wonder if you could just talk with me, for just a moment. I have a few questions."

She let out a dry, humorless snicker. "You, and everybody else."

"Who else has been here?" Kit blurted out.

"Who *hasn't* been here?" Mrs. Emerson shrugged. "The police, the FBI… reporters at every window…"

Mrs. Emerson was several steps ahead of her, opening the door. Kit lunged forward and pushed it shut.

"Please," Kit said. "Give me one minute."

"What do you want to know that hasn't been plastered across the front page of *The Washington Post*? What could possibly be left to tell you?" The words were angry, biting.

"What are they asking?"

"Who?"

"The police, the FBI—"

"Why should I tell you?"

"Please," Kit said. "I'm not here to upset you. It's just that—well, the same people who murdered your husband are after me."

Mrs. Emerson laughed. "Now I've heard everything." She reached for the doorknob and then turned back to face Kit. "I'm glad to be rid of him, to be perfectly honest. He never told me anything. For twenty years, he went off to work every day before dawn. For the first ten, he called every night to tell me he was working late. For the next ten, he didn't even bother. I knew he wasn't always working, and I knew he was having an affair, although I could never figure out how he could ever be attractive to anybody."

"Then why did you stay married to him?"

"Because I didn't care." She opened the door. "He paid the bills, and that's all I wanted. I didn't need him out of my life; he was already out of it. If you ask me, some jealous husband shot him dead, and he deserved it."

Speechless, Kit stepped past Mrs. Emerson into the cold night air.

"The only thing that gets my gall," she continued, "are the accounts I never knew he had. All these years of barely scraping by, thinking he was underpaid, when he was bringing in big bucks."

Kit wondered how she considered herself scraping by with a Cadillac in the driveway and a home in a trendy section of Arlington, but thought better of it. Not that she could have gotten a word in edgewise, as Mrs. Emerson continued.

"And if his lover got her due, then more power to the man who did it," she was saying. "Anything else you get from me, you'll get from *The Post*." With that, she slammed the door in Kit's face.

It was only a few minutes past eight when Kit pulled into her driveway, but it may as well have been midnight. One glance at her house, the windows darkened like sunken eyes, and she was sorry she'd given Tim permission to stay at Jason's. Then she berated herself for being a wimp.

She almost wished Lisa's face would appear at her window; it would at least indicate that someone was listening to the comings and goings, like a modern Mrs. Kravitz. But no one appeared. In fact, the houses on both sides of her were darkened and seemed empty.

She let herself in, and then turned on the lights as she moved through the downstairs to the kitchen. Once there, she poured herself a glass of water and grabbed a box of crackers and a half-eaten beef stick left over from the holidays. Leaving the lights on, she went upstairs.

Inside her room, she locked the door and set the food on the table in the corner. Then she carefully pulled the laptop out from under the bed, as if she were removing a priceless artifact from a pharaoh's tomb.

Her program had stopped. She could barely contain her excitement when she viewed the sequence of characters that comprised the password. With shaking fingers, she entered the back door.

Carter stared into his glass as if the golden liquid held the answer to a riddle. Bryce sullenly sat across the table from him. Between them were the remains of an extra-large pizza, the crust now hardened and cold.

"We're closing," the waitress said as she cleared the table. "Can I get you anything else?"

Carter shook his head without looking up as Bryce replied, "Just the check."

When they got up to leave, Carter was surprised to find the restaurant empty. It seemed only a few minutes ago that Ledo's had been bustling—kids crying, parents scolding, couples here and there engrossed in conversations. As they headed out, one of the employees hurried behind them to lock the door and turn the sign to Closed.

Carter and Bryce stood on the sidewalk for a moment, both appearing to survey the near-empty parking lot.

It was raining again. Carter thought this was the wettest place on earth. If it wasn't raining, it was snowing, making for wicked driving and depressingly gray, filthy accumulations.

"Can we…?"

"No." Bryce answered emphatically.

Carter sighed. Bryce was right. It was hopeless. He thought it had been a good plan, when they first arrived in Richmond; instead of checking into the downtown hotels with the other press, they opted to stay at the Homewood Suites in Chester. It gave him an excuse to be in Chesterfield County, where maybe, just maybe, he would run into Kit at a restaurant or a bank or the post office. But the county proved to be bigger than he realized, and he was no closer to finding Kit than he'd been to finding Tim.

And Bryce was tired of the long drives after dinner, drives that often took them on corkscrew roads that twisted in so many directions they easily became lost. They marveled at how desolate the area was, how few vehicles they encountered, and how dark things became on those country roads. The houses, for the most part, were set back behind acres of trees and brown vines that crept along the ground and wrapped themselves around everything, an omen of the thick underbrush that must occupy the land in warmer months. But nowhere had they even come close to spotting Kit and her dark green minivan.

If only her mother didn't hang up on him every time he called.

Carter pulled his collar up to shield him from the rain, and they made a dash for the Expedition. Once inside, he cranked up the heater.

"She's not here," Carter said.

"What?"

"She's not here."

"Christ. Not that again."

It was a straight shot from the restaurant back to the hotel, nine miles of a mostly deserted four-lane road. They drove in silence, Bryce staring out his window with his arms crossed over his chest.

Carter pulled into the circular driveway at the front of the hotel.

"What are you doing?" Bryce asked.

"Letting you out."

"Since when do you drive me to the door?" Then without waiting for an answer, he mumbled, "I'll walk from the lot."

"Get out, Bryce."

When Bryce peered at Carter, his brows were knit together, his face dark.

"What stupid thing are you going to do now?" Bryce asked.

"Get out."

"No. Not till you tell me what you're gonna do."

Carter sighed. "The less you know, the better things'll be."

"You're going after her, aren't you?"

Carter stared straight ahead.

"You're gonna get yourself killed." When Carter didn't respond, Bryce continued, "Have you not learned *anything*?"

"Get out of the car, Bryce."

"What is today?" he asked suddenly.

Carter jerked his head in his coworkers' direction but didn't answer.

"That's what this is all about, isn't it?"

"What are you talking about?" Carter asked in a tone that clearly indicated he didn't care to hear the answer.

"It's been five years, hasn't it? Five years ago this month."

"I don't know…"

"Five years ago, you were hot and heavy over that socialite, what was her name? Carey? Mary?"

"You know damn well what her name was."

"Say it, Carter. I want you to say it."

"Get out of the car!"

"It was Teri, wasn't it? You've got a thing for married women, don't you, pal?"

"I swear to God, if you don't get out of this car, I'm gonna kick your—"

"Teri wasn't so happy in her marriage either, was she? Only her husband wasn't so willing to let go—"

"I'm warning you—"

"You remember that night, don't you? The night you went to her house, snuck in the back door—how'd you get her to come downstairs, to talk to you in the middle of the night, while her husband slept upstairs?"

Carter's jaw was popping now, the grinding of his teeth adding to his anger.

"Only her husband wasn't sleeping. And when he came downstairs and saw you two together, he was ready, wasn't he, Carter? Ready with a bullet meant for you— only what happened? Did you duck? Or did she throw herself in front of you?"

Carter's fist caught Bryce squarely on the jaw with such force that Bryce's head bounced off the side window. Carter stared at him with a fury he hadn't felt since that night so long ago. His chest felt as if a quarter ton pickup was parked on it, and he realized in a flash that the weight had never really gone away; he only thought it had for brief, all too brief, moments.

Bryce rubbed his jaw and opened the door. Once outside, he turned around and looked at Carter with an expressionless face. "She's not Teri, Carter. She'll never be Teri. You have to accept the fact that she's gone…"

The car took off so suddenly Bryce jumped back, the tires missing his feet by inches. Carter sped through the parking lot toward the interstate, the passenger door swinging open in the wind and rain.

The minute hand on the wall clock ticked toward three o'clock in a monotonous rhythm that only served to make her eyelids heavier. The elections program comprised thousands of lines of code that were only slightly more exciting than balancing her checkbook.

The sleepless nights of the past weeks were catching up with her, and for the first time she realized how bone-tired she was, how her neck ached with tension, how the weight in the pit of her stomach seemed to grow like a cluster of boulders.

But still, she plodded on, her weary eyes scanning each line of code without reading it and without comprehending it, just continually skimming it like the rocks she used to flick over the surface of the James River.

Her eyes had begun to close, her lids like a trap door on heavy hinges, when she saw it.

She sat up straight, the adrenaline pumping through her like a bolt of lightning.

It couldn't have been clearer. Lines upon lines of a foreign language, a language she'd seen all too many times by now—

In the midst of the election software that was to become more American than apple pie and red, white, and blue, rested a distinct Chinese program.

A program she herself had attempted to recreate.

She flipped to the Windows Explorer and pulled up the document she'd written that fateful night when she was terrified she'd never see her son again. And then she opened the document that Chen had translated from English to Mandarin. Copying the program, she dragged it over the top of the election software and watched as the words lined up almost exactly.

"Oh, my God," she whispered.

CHAPTER 32

三十二

Kit yanked her jeans on, the telephone nestled between her neck and her shoulder. "What do you mean, you haven't seen him all night?" she demanded. "He *lives* there, for Christ's sake!"

She cut the guard off before he could offer an explanation. "Tell him I've got to talk to him. Tell him it's urgent."

A sudden *beep, beep* sounded in the phone line, and her next words froze on her lips. She clicked the phone off and tossed it onto the bed, staring at it as though it were a tarantula crawling out from under a rock.

It's not this phone that's bugged, she thought wildly, trying to calm her racing heart. It's the one at the office; it has to be. That would make more sense.

She crammed her feet into her shoes and grabbed her parka and the laptop. She hurriedly opened the bedroom door and slipped into the hallway, her leg brushing the heavy weight in her right pocket. She instinctively moved her hand toward it. Her fingers had just brushed the handgrip when she heard it—the sound of footsteps on the hardwood floor below.

She held her breath and strained to see through the darkness. Then she gingerly backtracked into the bedroom and softly closed and locked the door.

If they wanted her, simply locking the door wouldn't keep them out. It wouldn't take Hulk Hogan to splinter it or rip it off its hinges, and she'd be standing on the other side caught like an insect in a web.

She lunged for the phone on the bed and quickly dialed the police. She was straining to hear the intruder, trying to gauge his location, before she noticed that the phone wasn't ringing. She tried clicking the phone off and then back on, but there was no dial tone. Her mind raced to the phone downstairs. They'd taken it off the hook.

And her cell phone was on the dining room table beside her purse.

Her eyes came to rest on the laptop. She set it on the table, and with the swift fingers of a computer professional, she deftly popped open the casing. She heard the stairs creak; in her mind's eye, she envisioned someone purposefully moving up the staircase. Her fingers shook as she pulled the hard drive out and unhooked the wires. Then she slid the drive into the inside pocket on her parka, zipped up the pocket, and as silently as humanly possible, snapped shut the laptop case.

She hurried to the window and parted the curtains. She skimmed the street below, mentally registering each vehicle. Most of her neighbors' cars were tucked into garages and hidden from view. A few more were pulled deep into the driveways, where there was no question as to their owners. Only a few were parallel parked by the curb. The front grill of a white vehicle caught her eye; could it be Carter? She shook her head. Wishful thinking.

She squinted into the darkness. There appeared to be thin layers of ice on all the windshields. Just as she thought they'd all been there too long to raise suspicion, she noticed a movement. She stifled a gasp as she instinctively pinched the curtains closer together.

In front of her neighbor's house was a dark vehicle, its nose pointed away from her. Had it not been for the movement in the front seat, she wouldn't have detected him. Now she frantically tried to see what he was doing, but the streetlights were too dim.

She could hear the footsteps now, moving down the hall in the opposite direction. Thank God Tim wasn't home.

On an impulse, she slid the laptop between the mattress and box springs.

At the rear of the bedroom was a master bath with double sinks, a dressing area, and a separate shower and whirlpool bath. Within seconds, she'd climbed into the bathtub, her fingers shaking and her breath heavy as she opened the large window above it.

She'd hated that window when they moved in; she'd thought it was impractical in the midst of this urban jungle. Now it might save her life. She climbed onto the roof of the garage, and then slid the window closed.

She hesitated, her eyes scanning the upstairs windows. She stifled a gasp as she caught a glimpse of a shadowy figure methodically moving down the hall, pushing each door open and pausing as if peering within. She crouched low and held her breath.

The roof was slick with ice and dew, and she found herself hanging on to the gutter pipe. She knew if she started to slide, the whole gutter could tear away. She closed her eyes and inhaled. There was no getting past it; she'd have to jump. She could only hope that the deep snow would break her fall.

She hit hard, the ground knocking the wind out of her. The snow did nothing to cushion the impact, but she didn't have time to contemplate the bruises forming on her backside. Swallowing the pain, she rose and darted to the side of her house.

She could plainly see the car now and a man in the front passenger seat. As she watched, he turned toward her. She jumped back and flattened against the wall.

She'd have to move in the opposite direction, toward Lisa's house. She could hide in their garage or shed, just long enough for the men to leave...

She inched away from the corner of the house. She turned to run and collided headlong with Jack.

"Oh, thank God!" she cried and flung herself into his astonished arms. "Thank God you're here! There's a burglar in my house!"

She could only interpret his silence as shock.

Her face was pressed against his jacket, and she knew he could hear her heart beating wildly against him. He can't get suspicious now, she thought frantically. Not when I'm so close...

"Someone's in my house," she repeated. "Help me!"

She sat in the corner of the living room while Jack remained motionless in the opposite corner, like two boxers eyeing each other before a bout. Thank God the light was dim; she knew her cheeks must be flushed even as her blood seemed to have drained out of her knuckles. She kept her face in the shadows, her eyes hidden, even as she felt his eyes hot upon her.

The floorboards creaked upstairs as Toy moved from room to room, presumably searching for the intruder.

She wondered just how long this ruse would last, while she tried not to think about what they would do to her if they found the laptop and turned it on.

She kept her arms crossed in front of her, the parka making her so hot she was soaked with sweat. But she dared not remove it. She could feel the metal pressing against her chest through the fabric—and she could also feel the gun against her side.

"There's no one else in the house," Toy announced as he entered.

"You're sure?" she asked in her best imitation of a pitiful woman.

"Where's Frank?" Jack asked abruptly.

His question caught her off-guard. In a split second, she went from wondering how he knew her husband's name to realizing that of course Jack would have every piece of information about her at his fingertips. Besides, there'd been any number of times Frank and Jack had shared stories over an office party drink.

"He's gone," she said. "He left me for another woman."

She said it matter-of-factly, without a tinge of emotion, which surprised her. She thought she detected a slightly raised eyebrow. It didn't matter. She was probably the hot topic of conversation in Frank's company; why not be one in her own office as well?

Toy unbuttoned his leather coat and sat on the couch, as if he'd been invited to a leisurely get-together. After a brief moment of silence, he asked, "Who did he run away with?"

"His secretary," she answered, beginning to bristle. "I'd be surprised if you knew her."

"Oh, would you now?" he answered smoothly.

Jack leaned forward in his chair. "Don't go to Bernard's house again."

"I wasn't planning to."

"Good."

In the awkward silence that ensued, she marveled how she could have missed them following her, and she wondered just how much they'd seen or heard.

Toy leaned forward. "You're becoming a bit of a problem for us, Ms. Olsen. You don't want to end up like your friends, now do you?"

Carter's hand was on the car keys before he abruptly let go of them, allowing them to dangle from the ignition with the gentle sound of a wind chime. He'd arrived at Kit's house several hours earlier, had driven like the devil himself was hot on his heels. But once he arrived, he found himself unsure what to do.

So he turned off the ignition and just sat there. He noticed the downstairs going dark, as if Kit were moving through the house, switching off lights. Then a single light upstairs came on. The temperature dropped as the minutes turned into hours, but he made no move toward the house and made no effort to call her.

If only Bryce hadn't mentioned Teri. If only he hadn't said her name. Strange, that both Munski and Bryce would mention what happened, that they would bring her up after all this time, all this time of trying to forget.

It had been a cold night like tonight, but the roads had been dry and there hadn't been an inch of snow all winter. They'd been together earlier in the evening. Not like Kit and he had been together, but *together*, wrapped in each other's arms. He could still smell the fresh fragrance of her hair, could still taste her lips. And it drove him crazy when she'd left to go home.

She'd been having problems with her husband, and had been for quite some time, long before he ever laid eyes on her. It wasn't as if he was breaking up their marriage; it was already broken and beyond repair. Carter reasoned he'd just given her the extra courage she needed to tell her husband she was leaving.

She wasn't expecting him. The plan was for her to tell her husband she was leaving, pack her bags, and drive to Carter's apartment. He was supposed to be there waiting for her.

But as the minutes ticked by, he knew something was wrong. He could feel it in every bone.

So he drove to her house, parked outside and watched, just as he was doing now with Kit. He could see Teri and *him* through the downstairs window. Although he couldn't hear them, they were obviously in the throes of an argument. Even in the darkness and across the lawn, their faces were red, while their hands carried on whole spastic conversations.

He saw her go upstairs. He watched her through the filmy bedroom curtains, pulling out suitcases and unceremoniously tossing her clothes in, saw her husband begin to climb the stairs, one foot after another, in a calculated, deliberate manner that caused Carter to sit straighter, his eyes riveted on the hulking figure.

She was near the window when he punched her. Her head hit the wall behind her, and he pinned her there with one hand while he slapped her with the other, over and over again. The shock hadn't worn off of Carter before his feet were flying across the lawn and taking the front steps two at a time. The door was locked, but in seconds, it was lying in splinters and chunks.

When he made it through the doorway, she was rushing downstairs, screaming for him, screaming his name. He pushed her behind him, gruffly ordering her to go to his car.

He didn't see her husband coming down with that gun in his hand. He saw her shocked face, saw the blood drain out of it, leaving it lily white, saw her violet eyes widen. In a fraction of a second, she'd screamed and lunged for Carter, pushing him onto the floor. Then the shot had rung out.

She fell on top of him, but in an instant, he'd rolled out from under her. And in the next instant, he had the smaller man's wrist locked in his grasp. He threw his arm against the wall until he lost count, until the gun had slipped from his fingers and slid across the floor, and then he'd pummeled him until his head was bloody, shouting all the time for him to fight a man for a change.

It had taken three police officers to pull him off of Teri's husband.

And when they were finally separated, he unclenched his bleeding fists and turned back to Teri, but she was lying on the floor, her body curled as if in sleep. The officer shook his head, said something that Carter didn't understand, his mouth moving and his voice deep and slow as if the world were stopping around him. And then Carter was cradling her in his arms, telling her to hang on, that she was going to make it…

He saw the car drive slowly past, appearing to linger in front of Kit's house before it continued down the street, only to return a few minutes later. It parked a house or two down. It sat there idling for a long time, two heads in the front seat occasionally moving as if they were in conversation. He watched until their windows fogged up.

A few minutes later, a man exited the car and walked to the side entrance of Kit's house, to the kitchen door where Lisa had been watching them that day that now felt like a lifetime ago. He let himself in with a key. Carter could see him through the window, disarming the alarm system. Then the door was closed and the man disappeared into the bowels of the house.

Carter's eyes traveled from one window to the next and then moved slowly to the car, where one man remained seated. Then a movement caught his eye, and his eyes returned to the house just as Kit's face appeared at the bedroom curtain.

He reached across the front seat to the glove compartment and popped it open. Inside was a shiny black Sig Sauer, fully loaded with an extra clip. He slid the gun and the clip into his pocket.

His hand was on the door handle when he saw Kit creep around the corner of the house and peer at the car down the street. Then a shadow appeared behind her. Carter grasped the gun, in one deft movement pulling it out of his pocket.

He was a split second away from yanking the door open and firing a warning shot across the lawn when Kit threw herself into the man's arms. In stunned silence, he let the gun slide out of his hand onto the car seat.

He could see the three of them through the living room window, could see them talking like three familiar friends.

Bryce was right. She wasn't Teri. She would never be Teri.

And he was a fool for even coming here.

He cranked up the vehicle and pulled away.

CHAPTER 33

三十三

She went to the only place where she knew they couldn't reach her. She went to Customs.

It was nearing nine o'clock, unusually late for her to arrive at work. But then, this was shaping up to be an unusual day. Somewhere in the back of her mind, she knew the office was teeming with the normal hustle and bustle of another workday, the clicking of computer keypads, and the office conversations.

She turned at the end of the hall just in time to catch Jack standing at the other end, watching her with narrowed eyes. He nodded to her in a brief, almost imperceptible movement. She hoped her own face remained emotionless.

An employee stepped between them, garnering Jack's attention while they skimmed a stack of computer printouts. Then with a final backward, Jack led him into his office.

In another moment, she would be protected inside the cocoon of Customs, but she would also be rendered incommunicado. With a watchful eye on Jack's office door, she whipped out her cell phone. Every second counted now, and she knew just who she needed to call.

Carter folded his newspaper and took a final sip of his tepid coffee. The hotel restaurant was almost deserted now, employees busily clearing the breakfast buffet. An hour earlier, it had been swarming with military uniforms, government employees, and contractors ready to tackle another day at the Hoffman Building on Eisenhower Avenue.

He dropped a tip on the table and headed for the cash register. At least now, with a bit of sleep and a full stomach, he felt a tad more refreshed. When he'd left Kit's house, he opted to get a room at the Holiday Inn instead of tackling the long drive back to Richmond. He must have been exhausted; he fell asleep sprawled across the top of the bed, fully clothed, having intended to watch a few minutes of ESPN before hitting the sack. He was awakened four hours later with a curt but curious call from Bryce, inquiring on his whereabouts.

Now, as he headed into the frigid air, he planned his day. By mid-morning, he'd be at The Homewood Suites in Chester. After a shower and a shave and a change of clothes, he'd leave with Bryce for downtown Richmond to cover a luncheon for the incoming Governor and other newly elected officials. Back to the room for a quick snooze, and tonight he'd be covering a pre-Inaugural Ball in honor of Governor-Elect Stallworth.

He was letting the car warm up and the windows defrost when the cell phone rang. Bryce is so impatient, he thought as he grabbed it. Then he stopped, the phone still ringing in his hand, his eyes riveted on the caller ID.

It was Kit.

He thought of not answering it, of letting his voice mail pick up, of listening to her message later when he was miles away, stronger, and more detached. Then he clicked the *On* button.

"Carter, it's me, Kit," she said. Her words spilled out rapidly, her voice low, as she continued, "I need your help. How soon can you be here?"

"What do you need?" he said.

"Pick up Tim for me. He's at Lee High School, off Franconia Road—"

"I know where it is."

"Get him out of here, check him into a hotel, and tell him to stay there. I'll be in touch later. Don't leave any messages on my cell phone, okay? If I don't answer, call me again later."

"What's going on?"

"I can't talk right now. Just trust me."

He thought of asking why he *should* trust her, why the guy she was hugging didn't pick up her son. He thought of telling her that he was still in Richmond, and he couldn't get to Lee High School today. He thought of a dozen excuses why he couldn't help her.

"Can you do that for me?" she was asking.

"Yeah," he said. "I'll take care of him."

Then he clicked off his cell phone, tossed it into the console, and headed out of the parking lot.

Chen was sitting at his desk, as she knew he would be.

"We need to talk," she said as she entered the room.

Without a word, he rose from his desk and crossed to hers. She pulled out the program she'd been working on and laid it in the center of her desk.

"Where did you get this?" she asked.

"I'm not at liberty—"

"Cut the crap, Chen, and level with me."

"You cracked the code."

"Yes, I cracked it. But before I tell you what it does and why it does it, you're going to have to answer a lot of questions."

He opened his mouth, but before he could respond, she added, "And for starters, I want to know how you came to wield so much power in this room."

There are times when it's obvious that someone is lying. Their eyes wander, or they develop a nervous tic, or their skin turns a shade lighter or darker. But as Kit peered across the desk at Chen, she couldn't be certain whether his words were the truth or fiction.

If he were a plant, he'd know his assumed identity like the back of his hand. Telling his story to her in this setting would be a cakewalk. He would have rehearsed so thoroughly that his story would stand up to untold acts of torture by enemy forces; he would be prepared to go to his death reciting a life that wasn't his.

And now as she stared at him, she realized that every choice she'd have to make would depend on whether she could trust him, and trust his story.

He began his story in 1949, twenty-six years before his birth, with the communist takeover of China. His grandfather had been an aid to Chiang Kai-Shek. Although the United States officially backed Kai-Shek and provided billions of dollars in aid to his regime, they secretly planted spies in key positions. His grandfather, a Chinese nationalist, was one of these spies, reporting first to the OSS and later to the Central

Intelligence Group, or CIG, the forerunner of the CIA. His specialty inside Kai-Shek's regime was atomic energy.

The world was stunned when the atomic bombs were dropped on Hiroshima and Nagasaki during the Second World War, not only because of the devastation they inflicted but because they elevated the United States to superpower status. Chinese officials had joined with the Allies out of necessity; they were losing the war against Japan, and would have partnered with the devil himself to defeat their ancient foe. Even as the Chinese celebrated when Japan's cities were destroyed, Chinese officials knew they could not afford to be without the atomic bomb themselves. One day, they could find themselves on the opposite side of American interests, and their savior might very well come in a uranium package.

While Kai-Shek's regime openly cooperated with the United States, secretly they plotted to steal the plans for the atomic bomb, and to locate the necessary materials needed to build it. Chen's grandfather would find himself drawn to China's western borders, to a closed society suspicious of all foreigners and protected by the tallest mountain range in the world—Tibet.

For it was in Tibet that they discovered the world's richest uranium resources, the key ingredient to building the atomic bomb.

In 1949, the United States was beginning covert plans to arm the Tibetan government against a Chinese invasion, but they walked a thin tightrope. The Tibetans were no more inclined to accept American aid than Chinese overtures, and in the beginning, they rejected arms or protection of any kind. And while Chen's grandfather assisted the Chinese in moving closer to Tibet, he also assisted the Americans in attempting to arm the Tibetans.

All of that was to change in 1949, when Mao Tse-tung overthrew Kai-Shek and gained control of China. Chen's grandfather was arrested one black, cloudless night. In the confusion, his grandmother escaped with her infant son—Chen's father.

They would escape to Tzahu, near Inner Mongolia. They would never really know the fate of his grandfather. Although they would hear that he had been tortured to death in a makeshift prison, one of hundreds that sprang up overnight and became death camps for Kai-Shek's followers, the rumors would never be substantiated. Chen's grandfather, like millions of other Chinese, would simply vanish.

Ironically, it would be CIA operatives who located Chen's grandmother eighteen years later. And it would be the same agents who had worked with his grandfather who now recruited his father.

The Cultural Revolution was beginning when Chen's father made his way to Peking, by now called Beijing. And with the help of other CIA operatives on the inside, he'd worked his way up from a lowly government employee to a direct servant for Chairman Mao. Mao believed that Chen's father was illiterate and uneducated, fit only to attend to Mao's basic needs. Because of his feigned ignorance, he overheard much that he would pass on to the Americans. And it would be the Americans who would train him to look for items of importance and listen to conversations that would be useful.

The summer of 1975 found Chen's father in the unusual position of overhearing Mao complaining of a spy in their midst and reciting subject matter that he'd learned had been passed to the Americans. Now Chen's father knew that a double agent existed within the palace, and it would only be a matter of time before he was exposed. He had two choices: he could remain and, if found, would most certainly be tortured and executed—or he could flee.

So he enlisted the aid of trusted confidantes and soon found himself living in America and working directly for the CIA. His specialty became Tibetan matters, specifically with regard to uranium mining.

While working at CIA Headquarters, he met and married Chen's mother, an American of Irish descent; Chen was born one year later.

In 1998, Chen's father traveled to Hong Kong for a clandestine meeting with another CIA operative. He never returned.

"It was debated whether he ever made it to Hong Kong," Chen was saying now. "The operative he was to meet claims he never arrived. Yet he was seen boarding a direct flight to Hong Kong." He shook his head. "We'll probably never know what happened to him."

"And you? Were you recruited by the CIA?"

"I never imagined working anywhere else. I started here part-time while I was in college. The agency recruited me full-time, helped me get my degree… my specialty is obviously China—her history, government, and dialects."

Kit pondered this. "I remember when we moved to this facility, when I saw Customs for the first time—from the other side of the guard desk, that is."

"Shortly after I was recruited full-time," Chen offered.

"They built this room for you?"

"They built this room for the knowledge that would be housed here."

"Why not at Langley? With the history of political murders in your family, why would they have you working here?"

"Precisely because of those murders."

"I don't follow."

"China took a back seat during the Cold War, while America was focused on the Soviet Union. The Chinese were thought to be heathens, uneducated barbarians who posed no threat. Gradually, the CIA learned that China was more educated and more resourceful than they'd given them credit. And with the fall of the Soviet Union, China's been emerging as a major threat to world peace and democracy." Chen hunched forward. "Think about it. Who do you think is backing North Korea? The only war America ever lost was against China."

"Viet Nam."

"Precisely. And it was done without nuclear power. Now we know that China and North Korea both have the bomb, that they are fully capable of supplying nuclear warheads to anyplace they believe that anti-American sentiment will result in destroying their most formidable enemy—"

"Us."

"Precisely."

"And the reason you're not at Langley—"

"Is because it's easier to recruit spies outside of Headquarters."

"Spies that would still know enough to help bring down America."

Chen nodded.

"And is that the goal?" Kit asked. "To destroy America? Or is it to control America?"

Chen appeared surprised. "There would be nothing to gain if they destroyed it. But everything to gain if they could control it."

"Interesting," Kit said.

"So tell me… how can a program that simply counts, control America?"

He smiled as he leaned toward Kit, but she fought the instinct to return his attempt at camaraderie. Assuming everything he told her was true, her emotions were caught between her personal feelings and professional assessment. On the personal level, she empathized with the pain his family must have endured as both his father and grandfather were murdered for their western alliances. She also felt more respect for Chen, and for the courage it must have taken for him to follow in his father's footsteps.

But she knew that her personal feelings must take a back seat to her professional assessment, and professionally, she remained skeptical. Even if he'd told her the truth, his story was ancient history. So much had happened since the fall of Kai-Shek, Mao's rise to power and subsequent death, and the Cultural Revolution, that even if everything he said could be substantiated, it made little difference. Even as they spoke, a younger generation of Chinese politicians was assuming power, America was importing a record number of Chinese-made products, and any chasm that once separated the west from the east was narrowing.

But if she were to believe that China and the United States were true allies, there would be no need for the work they currently performed...

"You hand picked me for this job," she said.

He nodded. "Yes. I did."

"Why?"

He leaned back in his chair and rubbed his chin. "That requires a long answer," he said.

"I have all the time in the world," she bluffed.

Chen glanced at the guard in the corner. "We've known for some time that there are individuals within the agency who" —he seemed to struggle with the words— "have leanings toward China."

"Spies," Kit said without flinching, her eyes locked on Chen's.

He nodded slowly. "Possibly. Although it extends beyond passing information to the enemy."

She motioned for him to continue.

"Your background was thoroughly checked. It's flawless."

Kit nodded. "So you knew I wasn't a spy."

He shrugged. "As far as we could determine."

"You're a programmer," Kit said, leaning toward him, "and the program you assigned to me wasn't all that complicated. If you could translate the code from Mandarin to English, you could easily figure out what it did. So why did you need me here?"

He hesitated. His eyes wandered slowly around the room.

"You set me up," she said.

He glanced at her, and then focused on an imaginary speck on his shirtsleeve.

"You planted me in this room, because you knew I would be contacted," she continued. "There's something here that somebody on the outside wants, and they want it bad enough to threaten me and my family."

He didn't respond, but continued staring at his shirt.

"And you knew I wouldn't give it to them."

His words were barely audible. "Don't you think you need to tell me what the program does?"

"You know what it does. You knew before I ever stepped foot in this room."

"I know it counts, and I know it counts incorrectly. I also know that it's harder to write a program that counts badly than it is to create one that counts correctly."

"What you don't know," Kit said, fighting back anger, "is where this program originated. And for that, you were willing to sacrifice an innocent boy—"

"What 'innocent boy'?"

"My son."

"Your son isn't in any danger."

"No? Then where were you when he was kidnapped? Where were you when I handed over the disk, and found him half frozen, waiting for help? Where the hell were you when men entered my house last night—"

Chen held up his hand. "If you tell me what you know, I can help you."

"How do I know that?" she spat. "How do I know I can trust you, when I couldn't, up to this point?"

"Yes, I set you up—*we* set you up. We know there's an inner circle within the agency who's working for China. But we can't take them in—yet. If we did prematurely, we'd never know the extent of their plot. We had to let it go a certain distance—and yes, we did bring you in here because we knew they would contact you. They would never contact me; we all know that. We needed someone in here they thought they could get to—"

"Someone with ties," Kit said hotly. "Someone with something to lose."

He shrugged. "Possibly."

"Where did you get the program?"

Without hesitation, he responded, "After Bernard Emerson disappeared, a disk was mailed to my home."

"But who—?"

"And since less than a dozen people know where I live, it was easy to figure out where it came from."

The question froze on Kit's lips.

"It was Joan Newcomb," Chen answered. He appeared to be watching her closely, and Kit glanced away, her mind reeling. "I don't know why she sent the program to me," he continued, "and now I'll never know. But for whatever reason, she sent only a piece of the program, enough for us to determine what it accomplished, but not enough for us to establish where it could be used."

"But you knew that Bernard used it."

"Yes."

Kit looked at her watch. The time was ticking by. Carter would soon have Tim. She'd have to get her parents to a safe place. But then what? What would she do, knowing that an inner circle at the CIA was searching for her, searching for them all? Knowing that whether it took hours or years, they would eventually find her? It didn't matter how much or how little she knew; what mattered is what they *thought* she knew. And the only way she could protect the ones she loved would be to turn the tables and destroy them.

She looked back at Chen, who appeared to be eyeing her curiously. When she spoke, her words came rapidly. "You waited too long. The program has already been used. It was used to elect our own government; it took votes away from those who aren't in China's pocket and applied them toward those who are. They've staged a technological coup; they've gained control of our country without firing a single shot."

CHAPTER 34

三十四

Carter took the steps two at a time. Funny how, after all this time, a school still had the power to turn his insides to putty.

It looked like the one he'd attended so many years ago, but then, he supposed they all looked the same: tiled floors, wide hallways, bulletin boards in every direction, lockers lining every wall.

It wasn't difficult to locate the principal's office; maybe he'd been so accustomed to being sent to one that even after all these years, his feet found their way automatically.

The secretary greeted him. "May I help you?"

She had large, friendly blue eyes. He returned her smile. "Yes, I'm Frank Olsen. I need to pull my son out of class; we've had a family emergency."

"Oh? Who's his teacher?"

Carter leaned across the desk and whispered conspiratorially, "You know, I'm a really bad father. My wife usually takes care of all the school stuff, and I'm kind of out of my element here. Can you help me? I don't know whose class he's in."

"Sure." She pressed a few keys on her computer keyboard. "Tim Olsen?"

"That's right."

He tried to catch a glimpse of her computer screen but she clicked out of it.

"You look familiar," she said, glancing at him before her thick dark lashes obscured her eyes.

He thought he detected a slight blush on her cheeks. "I've been here before," he said. "It's just been awhile."

"You'll need to complete this form," she said, pushing a piece of paper toward him. "Need a pencil?"

"No," he said, before noticing she was twirling her hair with one. He pulled his pen out of his pocket. "Thanks anyway."

He completed the form quickly. Most of it was standard information—name, date, reason for leaving. He wrote "death in the family" and immediately felt a cold chill climbing his back.

"Anything wrong?" she asked.

"No. Yes." He returned the paper to her. "We've had a death in the family. I'm in a hurry to get Tim."

"I'll let him know you're here," she said. She left the form on the desk and walked down the hall.

He waited until she was out of sight and then started to reach across the desk to retrieve the paper, when a stout woman entered the room.

"Anyone helping you?" she asked briskly.

"Yes, thank you."

He inched his way to the doorway and wandered into the hall, cooling his heels while he tried to appear calm. He saw the secretary exit a room, followed closely by Tim. Even from this distance, he could see a dark scowl on his face, as though he'd tasted something disagreeable. For the first time, he realized that Tim could give him more trouble than he'd bargained for.

Tim slung a book bag—or maybe it was a laptop case—over his shoulder as he plodded toward Carter. It was as if he knew his father was standing at the end of the hallway, and he was purposefully avoiding his gaze. Tim was almost upon Carter when he looked up. His astonishment was obvious; his eyes widened and his face paled. He cut his eyes toward the secretary and then stared at his shoes. Carter could tell that the boy's mind was turning over at a hundred miles an hour.

"Your mom's waiting for you," Carter said hesitantly.

Tim nodded but didn't look up. "Where you parked?"

Carter kicked into high gear. With two long strides, he was at the front door, Tim close on his heels. He waved to the secretary as he opened the door. "Thanks."

"I'm going to remember where I've seen you before," she said coquettishly. "I know it wasn't here."

He smiled and held the door open for Tim. Once outside, he broke into a brisk walk. "Let's get the hell out of here."

Carter turned on the heat and was immediately met with a blast of warm air. He reached to the curtain above the heater, started to draw it closed, and then hesitated. The hotel room faced west toward Interstate 295 and the James River. In the distance, he could see the water. The weather was warming at a record rate, with a high expected tomorrow in the mid 60's. Freakish, considering all the snowfall and rain in the last few days. With the snow expected to melt and more rain on the way, there were flood warnings throughout the Richmond area, the problem even threatening to eclipse the coming inauguration of Virginia's first Independent Governor.

He scanned the parking lot and surrounding buildings. Not really sure what he was searching for, but not finding anything that appeared out of the ordinary, he closed the drapes and turned back to Tim, who was sprawled across the bed, already channel surfing.

"Listen, Tim," Carter said, sitting on the edge of the bed. "I don't want you to feel like a prisoner here or anything, but I'm gonna have to ask you not to leave the room or use the phone."

Tim glanced at him out of the corner of his eye. "Is my mom here?"

"Not yet," Carter answered. He handed Tim his cell phone. "You can use my phone to call her."

"I can use this phone," Tim said, "but I can't use that one?" He nodded toward the hotel phone.

"We can't have the calls traced. If anyone else sees the caller id, we can't risk them knowing where you are. Even if they see the call's from me," he tapped the cell phone, "they won't know where I am—or you."

"First," Tim said, sitting up, "you *can* trace a cell phone to the nearest cell tower, so that theory's got a hole in it. And second, what kind of trouble is my mom in?"

"Code red!" Chen shouted to the guard, coming to his feet so quickly he almost tipped the computer off Kit's desk. "Lockdown!"

He raced to the door, Kit on his heels. Code red was the highest alert, usually reserved for terrorist attacks or wartime invasions. But in the few times she'd heard it used, she'd never heard it followed by a lockdown.

She heard the horn sounding in the hallways as she exited Customs, the sound bombarding her from all directions. Employees were racing at fast-forward—all computers were shut down, all projects immediately locked up, and everyone on standby for shredding orders.

Only Jack was absent.

"Where is he?" Chen shouted as he rushed from office to office. "Anybody see where Jack went?"

The employee who had been conversing with Jack earlier was busily powering down the equipment in his office. Kit grabbed his arm. "Where's Jack?" she asked frantically.

"He's not here," the employee answered, pointedly staring at Kit's fingers gripping his shirt. "Said he had something to take care of."

The uniformed CIA officers were piling out of the elevators like a SWAT team. As each group exited, the elevator was shut down, the lights turned off, the doors permanently opened. As Kit watched, uniformed officers rushed into the stairwells, searching for individuals attempting to leave, the doors locked tight behind them. Her heart sank as she thought of Tim. She had to get out of here.

Chen and Kit met back at Customs, both empty-handed.

"Get Kyle Ralston on the phone," Chen ordered the guard.

Kit sucked in her breath. Chen was going all the way to the Director. "I've got to call Tim," she said abruptly. She started away from Customs, toward her old office, but Chen stopped her.

"I can't let you do that," he said. "No phone calls. In or out."

"Tim could be in danger," she said, throwing his hand off her. "And so could my parents. You got them into this mess. You owe it to me—and them—to get them out of it."

"It's out of my hands now," Chen said.

"I swear to God, if anything happens to them…" her voice faded, her hands clenched and eyes narrowed. Chen had turned back to the desk and was now speaking on the phone. Kit looked around in desperation. *There is no way in hell they're going to keep me here.*

"I thought you were gonna shave or something," Bryce said.

Carter finished closing the door and checked to make sure it was secure. "Yeah, well, you thought wrong."

Bryce shook his head as they started toward the elevators. As they passed Tim's room, Carter could hear a television set and what sounded like the Normandy invasion. He hoped he could trust the boy to stay put.

"I'm gonna need some cash," Carter said when they reached the car. "I saw an ATM up the street; it'll only take me a minute to pop in, before we head downtown."

The ATM wasn't working, and after it spit his card out for the second time, Carter decided to go inside. Bryce was antsy, but he'd just have to suffer through it. Credit cards left a trail, so he'd have to make all of Tim's purchases, including the room, in cash.

The tellers at the BB&T were friendly and fast, a far cry from the service he was used to in Northern Virginia. He got a thousand dollars in fifties, and was stuffing it in his wallet on his way out the door when he heard someone call his name. He turned and almost dropped his wallet and his jaw when he saw Munski standing in the doorway across the lobby.

"What are you doing here?" Carter asked when he regained his voice.

Munski strode to the door. "I should be asking you that."

"I'm working," Carter said. "Covering Stallworth's inauguration."

"From Chester?"

"We're on our way downtown, to a luncheon—"

"We?" Munski peered outside.

"Bryce is in the car."

Munski turned back to face the lobby. Carter noticed an attractive woman standing in the doorway the detective had just vacated. Now Munski addressed her. "Can we use your office?"

"Bryce is gonna wonder what happened to me," Carter was saying as he sat in the leather chair in the bank manager's office.

"I won't keep you but a minute," Munski said. "I just need for you to see something." He pulled a set of papers from the inside pocket of his overcoat and handed them to Carter.

"What the…?" Carter mumbled as he opened the papers. It was a computer printout of bank activity; he found the names on the account almost immediately. Frank and Kathryn Olsen. *Christ.* Of all the banks he could have gone into, he had to choose theirs.

"So what is this supposed to tell me?" he asked nonchalantly.

"Look at the balance," Munski replied calmly.

Carter did a double take. "There's—there's over a million dollars in this account."

The detective didn't respond. Carter looked up, their eyes meeting over the papers. Munski had an "I told you so" look, and Carter knew his own expression was incredulous.

"Her husband rich?" he asked.

"Guess again."

"Family money?"

"Strike two. One more and you're out."

"This is Kit's?"

"Well, now you've hit a home run," Munski said. He jabbed his finger at the paper. "Money started rolling in shortly before Bernard Emerson disappeared. Steady money, a hundred grand at a time. Over half a million has already been withdrawn, transferred to an overseas account." He pulled the paper from Carter's fingers. "She won't be taking any more money out. We've frozen the account. This one, and two others here, including one that had a hundred grand deposited on Christmas Eve. Some Christmas gift, huh?"

"What gives you the right to freeze those accounts?" Carter said, coming to his feet. "Is there a law against having too much money?"

Munski folded the papers and tucked them into his pocket. "We're back on the case, pal. Got a call from Park Police. Kyle Ralston refused to go to Chief MacKearney—"

"That's the Park Police Chief?"

"You got it. CIA tried to get the laptop before Park could do anything with it, but the CIA Director decided—for whatever reason—that Park could keep it. So guess what?"

"Oh, come on, Ski. Give me a break."

"No, take a guess, Carter. Take a wild guess."

Carter glanced out the window. "Bryce is gonna kill me. I don't have time to play games."

"The hard drive's missing from the laptop."

"So there's no data."

"No data, but there is a serial number. Want to know who it traced back to?"

Carter felt a hardened, sick sensation forming in his gut, the same kind of feeling he had in college when he was tackled on the football field by none other than "Hudson" Humphrey, the guy with a chest the size of a '46 Commodore. He was out of the bank manager's office in two seconds flat, crossed the lobby and was halfway through the main door when he heard Munski's voice echoing through the quiet lobby.

"It belongs to Kit Olsen."

CHAPTER 35

三十五

Bureaucratic wheels turn very slowly. In an age of technology where knowledge is only a keyboard click away, communication flies at lightning speeds, and the world grows smaller with every new invention, the federal government has the ability to slow progress to a pace even the Pony Express could surpass.

And so it was in one building in Arlington, where Kit watched the clock's hand tick by every excruciating second. Although the clock was several feet away from her, the sound reverberated around the room, matched only by the thump of her heart and her ragged breathing.

Never before had the phrase "hurry up and wait" meant so much. After the initial flurry of activity, everything came to a complete standstill. With their computers shut down, all paperwork under lock and key, and the telephones disabled, there was nothing left for the staff to do except sit and stare. Kit supposed in some offices, meaningless chatter had started while employees tried to pass the time. But in her office, she was alone with the silence.

In her mind's eye, she pictured each office that housed those employees whose salaries were inordinately high. She wondered what they were thinking, and whether anything in those offices could indict them. She glanced at the camera mounted on the wall. No doubt security was particularly interested in what each person was doing while they awaited further instructions. No one would dare attempt to destroy anything now.

There were guards posted at every exit. There was no escape. Somewhere, most likely at Langley, a group of men in dark suits were discussing their fate. The meeting might last minutes or hours. And in the meantime, they were captives...or sitting ducks.

Kit straightened. Then with a start, she took off down the hall in search of Chen.

She found him exiting Customs.

"We need to talk," she said hurriedly, pulling him into a nearby office. Once she'd pushed the door closed, she continued, "Who's coming here now?"

"What do you mean?"

"They're not just going to open the office back up. Somebody has to come here, to investigate—who will it be?"

Chen shrugged. "I don't know."

"Listen to me. Just hear me out. Joan had the highest rank in this office, right? Besides you, of course."

"Right."

"And Jack the second highest?"

"Yes."

"Then how do you know how high this conspiracy goes? How do you know that the men who are discussing—right this minute—how to proceed, aren't part of it?"

Chen shook his head. "That's not possible," he said, avoiding Kit's eyes.

"You've thought of it, too," she challenged. "We're helpless here. If the guys on our side show up, we're fine; we'll be cleared in no time, and we can go on our merry way. But if the *wrong* guys show up, we're through. We could disappear without a trace."

His eyes were clouded when he looked at her. "That won't happen. The Director knows."

"The Director knows what you told him. Don't you think somebody else has his ear? Somebody that could facilitate our disappearance and explain it away at the same time?"

"What are you suggesting we do?"

"We need to get to the Director. We need to talk to him face to face, with nobody in between."

"That's not possible."

"Everything is possible; you know that. You have to get us out of here."

"I can't do that."

"If anybody can do it, you can. You owe it to yourself."

Chen stood straighter. "My commitment is to the agency, not to myself."

"That's where you're wrong, Chen Ling. Your commitment is to your family. Don't make your mother go through *another* disappearance. Don't do that to her."

His eyes widened before he looked away. "I'll make a phone call."

They stood at the guard desk in front of Customs, while the guard opened a locked drawer and pulled out the red phone that connected directly to Headquarters.

Chen lifted the receiver and asked for Ralston's office. While he waited, he breathed a heavy sigh.

"Mr. Ralston?" he said, furrowing his brow. "I need to speak—"

He hesitated. Kit thought his lower lip trembled slightly. "Who is this?" he said.

Slowly, he lowered the phone to the cradle.

"What is it?" Kit said, grabbing his arm.

"Ralston left a few minutes ago."

"He's coming here?"

Chen looked her straight in the eyes. "He left for the Middle East."

Kit had never been in a physical altercation, had never boxed or wrestled, nor been in a street fight… But now, as she stared at Chen's unblinking eyes, she felt as if she'd just gone eight rounds with a heavyweight champ, and he'd just landed a punch directly to her abdomen.

But with Chen's next statement, she felt as if she were hanging from the ropes, unable to fight back, while her opponent went for the knockout.

"That was Jack on the phone."

The Jefferson Hotel was a shining jewel in Richmond's crown, and never more so than today. Carter and Bryce arrived late, barely making it inside the Franklin Street entrance before the downpour began. The thick structure muffled the sound of the rain pelting against it, and as Carter made his way into the lobby, he forgot about it entirely.

The lobby was decorated in a bygone era, the rich tapestries and dark wood catapulting him instantly to a time when Richmond was the capital of the Confederacy and its streets filled with Southern society. Before him lay an expansive staircase with a genteel red patterned carpet, flanked by elaborately carved, massive columns.

His eyes drifted upward to a breezeway on the second floor that framed all four sides. He searched door after door until his eyes fell on a set in the far corner, where the media was gathering.

"Up there," he said to Bryce, pointing.

Bryce took one glance and hurried to the staircase. Carter passed him halfway up, and was at the door before Bryce had made it around the corner.

"Speeches are just finishing," one of the reporters said in response to Carter's question.

"Anything earth-shattering?"

The reporter snorted and didn't reply.

"I take that as a 'no'," Carter said, moving into the room.

The crowd was politely clapping as a middle-aged man whom Carter didn't recognize, was returning to his seat from the podium. Another man approached the microphone. Carter glanced behind him. Bryce was removing the lens cap and preparing to film.

"Thank you, Mr. Glenhaven, and thanks to all our speakers here today," the speaker said.

"Who is that?" Carter whispered to a reporter.

"Retired Judge Gayle," he answered. "You'd know that if you'd been on time."

"And of course, special thanks to this man" —Gayle extended his arm in Stallworth's direction—"who we will all be calling Governor Stallworth this time tomorrow!"

The crowd broke into thunderous applause. Stallworth remained seated, but beamed and nodded his head. As the applause died down, the speaker continued, "And on behalf of all the businesses in Virginia, may I say we're excited about your plans to open more avenues of trade with China…"

Carter didn't hear the rest. At that moment, he was striding purposefully toward the front center of the room. He could feel the audience's eyes upon him, and his adrenaline was flowing with the knowledge that Bryce was taping.

"*Governor* Stallworth," Carter said, his voice booming through the room even without the benefit of the microphone. "Isn't it true that by opening more 'avenues of trade' with China, it will actually mean the end to many businesses right here in Virginia?"

Stallworth's expression didn't change, but Carter thought he detected a raised eyebrow.

"Sir, if you'd been here *on time*, you would have heard Stallworth's eloquent speech," Gayle said disapprovingly. "Unfortunately, we don't have time to stage a press conference—"

"That's quite all right," Stallworth said, rising to his feet. His eyes didn't waver from Carter's as he took the podium. "Mr. Leigh, the United States is already exporting over sixteen *billion* dollars of goods annually to China, including many items that are made right here in Virginia—machinery, appliances, data processing machines, aircraft…"

"That's a deficit of over eighty-three percent, isn't it, *Governor?*" Carter interrupted. Before Stallworth could answer, he stepped closer to the microphone and continued, "Didn't the United States *import* over one hundred billion dollars of goods from China just in the past year alone? And didn't we *import* machinery, appliances, and data processing equipment? And wasn't trade with China cited as the number one reason why five major shoe manufacturers in the state of Virginia closed their doors last year?"

Gayle stepped in. "Young man, we're not going to turn this luncheon into a—"

"Isn't it true that the United States government has repeatedly classified China as a Special 301 priority foreign country, because they fail to recognize United States patents and copyrights, and isn't it true, *Governor* Stallworth, that they're one of the major producers of pirated software in the world? What do you intend to do to protect the hundreds of technology-based companies in Virginia, who stand to lose billions of dollars to China's pirated products?"

"This meeting is over!" Gayle called wildly. Carter had the impression he would have pounded his gavel if he'd had it. The judge turned to an assistant. "Turn off these microphones!"

"What do you intend to do, *Governor* Stallworth," Carter boomed, "to protect the employees of Virginia against losing their jobs and livelihoods, while we import billions of dollars in substandard clothing and electronics, from a country that uses slave labor?"

"Get him out of here!" Judge Gayle waved angrily.

Carter could feel the rush of bodies toward him, but his eyes remained locked on Stallworth's, who stood silently beside the podium, his face expressionless.

"Is it true, *Governor* Stallworth, that you've accepted bribes from Chinese officials, for the right to import mass quantities of goods into this State—?" He shouted. Someone grabbed his arm, but as he fought against their hold on him, he was grabbed from the other side. It felt as if a half a dozen men were escorting him from the room, pulling him backward as the flashbulbs popped around him. Video cameras were in his face and all around him. Somehow, through the maze of bodies, he glimpsed Bryce with his camera, steadily trained on Stallworth.

"*She* is Dr. Kathryn Olsen, and *Dr. Olsen* is also expected in the Director's office. Unless, of course, you'd like to skip the chain of command," Chen spat, "and call Ralston directly for instructions?!"

"Good God, we're wasting the Director's time! He's waiting for us!" Chen bellowed.

Jansson nodded at one of his guards. "Bonelli, you'll drive. Mr. Ling sits up front with you. I'll sit in the back with Dr. Olsen."

It took less than five minutes for them to reach the vehicle. She knew they weren't en route to the Director's office. But now what? They were sandwiched between two armed guards, and Headquarters was only minutes away.

Jansson firmly escorted Chen to the front seat, while Bonelli walked Kit around the vehicle to the other side. Once she was situated in the back seat, the guards climbed in, closing their doors simultaneously. Kit wondered if the back doors opened from inside or if, like police cars, she was a captive.

As they pulled away from the curb, she focused on the back of the driver's neck. Even if she had the nerve, she didn't know if she could grab him from behind; Jansson would be on top of her in seconds. And he was armed.

She felt her heart quicken. *She* was armed. She felt the Glock's hard metal against her thigh. She'd walked right into the building that morning, wearing her parka and carrying the hard drive and her pistol, depositing it all in her locker before going through the usual uncompromising inspection.

The driver took the radio microphone and called the dispatcher. "En route to Headquarters from UCT," he announced. The dispatcher acknowledged receipt of the transmission.

CHAPTER 36

三十六

All eyes were on Kit and Chen as they marched down the hall to the elevators. With all the guards, it looked as if martial law had been declared.

Chen marched up to the officer in charge. "Bring a car around front," he directed.

"Nobody leaves. We're in lockdown."

"Who do you think declared the lockdown?" Chen answered impatiently. "I've been ordered to appear before the Director ASAP. You can drive me yourself, if you want."

Kit glanced at the guards, who were all watching them. The officer in charge was locked in a glare with Chen, who wasn't backing down.

"My orders are—"

"Your orders are to obey your superiors. And I'm ordering you to take us to the Director's office—*now*."

The officer glared at Chen and then Kit. Kit peered pointedly at his nametag—Officer Martin Jansson. She hoped her own expression was as confident as Chen's.

"All right," Jansson answered slowly. "Just you and me. *She* stays here."

Out of the corner of her eye, Kit examined Jansson. He was watching the road, his eyes focused somewhere between Chen and Bonelli. They slowed as they rounded a curve on the entrance ramp to I-395; then the car sped up as it merged with traffic.

Her heart quickened as they took the Washington Boulevard exit without slowing. As they moved into the curve, Chen grabbed the steering wheel with lightning speed, sending them careening onto the shoulder of the road as traffic around them swerved to avoid hitting them. Just as quickly, Jansson lunged forward, his hand on his weapon.

Her hand was in her pocket and back out again, the pistol firmly in her grasp. She braced her legs against the back of the front seat, fighting to stay in control even as they pitched about.

"Freeze!" Kit shouted through the commotion. "Get your hands in the air!" she screamed, leveling her pistol at Jansson's chest.

Jansson was slung backward in his seat as the car lurched back onto the highway, his pistol catapulting to the floor. Kit kept her gun trained on him, knowing if she glanced away for so much as a second, he could have control of his own weapon and it would all be over. Twice, he slowly lowered his arms, and twice, Kit shouted at him to raise them higher.

Bonelli's head was hitting the window on the driver's door now, as Chen struggled to overpower him. A shot rang out from the front seat, and instinctively, Kit fired. Jansson's right arm flung against the glass, smearing it with blood.

She glanced toward the front seat, frantic to find out who had been shot, as the car careened toward a concrete barricade. She screamed as they hit it with the left front fender, spinning off it, out of control into the center of the road. When they came to a stop, Bonelli was hunched over the steering wheel, his arms limp at his sides. Kit heard a groan as Chen sat up, his forehead bloodied.

"You've been shot," she said.

"No," he answered shakily. "Just banged up." He glanced at the back seat. "Get his gun."

Kit hurriedly grabbed Jansson's gun as the officer held his arm and groaned. He appeared to be losing consciousness. She tore his jacket away from the wound and peered at it. "Oh, God," she said. "Right through the armpit. Jesus."

Chen was busy in the front seat.

"Is he dead?" she asked.

"Unconscious." He took Bonelli's gun, sticking it in the back of his belt.

"Where'd you shoot him?"

"I didn't. It went through the seat."

It was then that Kit noticed the back of the seat was ripped. She jerked her head to look at her own seatback. Barely an inch from her head was another hole. She jammed her fingers into it, extracting the spent bullet. *"Jesus."*

Jansson was getting his wits about him now, and was sitting straighter, his eyes wide and searching. Kit could see through the window behind him; there were stopped cars now, and at least one person on his cell phone.

"We've got problems," she called to Chen.

"Get out of the car," Chen ordered.

Kit climbed out, her gun still trained on Jansson. Chen pulled the key from the ignition and ripped the microphone from the radio.

"You make a noise," Kit said, "and I'll kill you." She glowered at Jansson as she closed the door.

Chen was running to the nearest stopped car. "CIA," he shouted, pulling out his identification card. The driver was out of the vehicle, running toward them, his cell phone against his ear. "We need your car!" Chen said, rushing past him and jumping in the driver's seat. Kit was right behind him, piling into the back seat as he took off.

"What do we do now?" Chen shouted as Kit closed the car door.

"Get back on the Interstate," Kit said, climbing over the front seat to the passenger side. "Head to Richmond!"

Carter was giddy listening to Bryce as they stepped off the elevator. Bryce had been talking nonstop since leaving the luncheon. He'd watched the tape repeatedly on the ride back to their hotel, had telephoned Morley with the scoop, and a courier was dispatched to pick up a copy of the tape. It would be aired during tonight's news, the eve before the inauguration. There was word it might even make the national news.

"I swear to God," Bryce was saying as they walked down the hall, "Stallworth has a hidden talent for stringing expletives together. Never seen anything like it!"

"Come on, now, you really think he was up there cursing in front of everybody?"

"Okay, so he didn't actually say it out loud. He whispered it. Maybe he mouthed it. I don't have the audio, but you can see it, you can see his mouth moving. You can't mistake what he's saying."

Carter chuckled as they stopped in front of his door and he searched for his key.

"So, do you have proof that he's taking bribes?" Bryce asked, leaning against the wall.

"Not exactly."

"What do you mean, 'not exactly'? You can't accuse somebody of something like that, unless you have proof. Carter—tell me you have something."

"I have something. But I don't know exactly what I've got—yet." He found the key and slid it into the card reader. "You coming in?"

"Naw. I've gotta make a copy of this tape. The courier will be here any minute."

Carter opened the door, his eyes still on Bryce. "Come over after you get the dup. We'll have a drink."

"Anything for a drink, huh, Carter?" Bryce said, moving away from Carter's room and toward his own.

Carter smiled with a bit more confidence than he felt. His butt was on the line now. Stallworth knew he was on to him; that would make it more difficult to investigate any information that might come his way. They were adversaries now, and it was out in the open for the world—and God forbid, the press—to see.

He started to open the door, but it was stuck, as if something was wedged behind it. He reached his arm inside and flipped the light on. "What the…?"

"What is it?" Bryce called from next door, where he'd just begun to open his own door.

Carter didn't answer. He could feel the sweat breaking out across his forehead. For a split second, he debated whether to call security; then just as quickly, he became more determined to get in on his own. Finally, he wedged himself between the door and the wall and slid sideways into the vestibule.

The desk was turned over and was pushed against the door, completely blocking the entrance. His suitcases were open, its contents spilled on the floor. He didn't have the best of clothes and he wasn't a stickler for taking care of them, but it galled him to see his underwear and shirts strewn all over the room. The bed had been torn apart; even the mattress was off the frame and tilting against some of the furniture, as if someone had searched between the covers and even under the bed. All the drawers had been pulled out of the desk and dresser and scattered helter-skelter.

He flipped on the bathroom light. Everything he owned had been turned upside down. Even his shaving kit and toiletries had been wiped off the counter and splattered around.

He reached down and picked up a large piece of glass that had once been part of a cologne bottle. The cologne was seeping across the floor and into the carpet in the bedroom. There were shards everywhere.

"Geez, what happened in here?" Bryce said, poking his head inside.

"Hell of a maid service, isn't it?"

"Your room's been ransacked."

"Ya think?"

Bryce pulled out his camera and started filming. "Do you think this has anything to do with the luncheon?"

"Turn that thing off," Carter said, pushing past him.

Bryce kept filming, moving further into the room.

Carter managed to move the desk out of the doorway and bolted down the hall.

"Where are you going?" Bryce called.

Carter moved faster with every second, his blood pounding in his throat. He reached Tim's room and banged on the door.

"What are you doing?" Bryce called, rushing after him.

"Tim, it's me, Carter! Open the door!"

Carter strained to hear some sign of life inside. There was nothing, not even the sound of the television. "Open the door, Tim!"

Bryce was at the door now. "Who's Tim?"

"Stand back," Carter said as he leaned back and kicked the door. "Christ," he said after the third kick. The fifth kick broke the door, and Carter half fell, half climbed into the room.

The bed was still made, although it appeared as if someone had been lying on it. The television was turned off. Tim's backpack was gone.

Carter marched through the room, opening the closet, looking under the bed, and checking the bathroom.

He jerked toward the window. The curtains were moving ever so slightly. He inched his way toward them, motioning for Bryce to remain quiet, and then he yanked the curtains away from the wall.

No one was there. It was only the wind.

The window was open. Carter could feel the adrenaline pumping as he peered outside. Three floors directly below the window was a trim row of bushes. One was standing out oddly, broken and squashed.

Chen maneuvered the vehicle into a parking space in the Embassy Suites garage in Alexandria.

"You go first," Kit instructed. "Get a ticket to Richmond. I'll follow in a couple of minutes. We're not to acknowledge each other until we get on the train. If you see anything suspicious, split up… we'll meet at nine o'clock tonight at the bar at Uno's on Jeff Davis Highway in Chester. It's right outside of Richmond. Got that?"

"I don't know why we're going to Richmond," Chen said, "when we ought to be going to Washington."

"And see who? You said the Director's left for the Middle East."

"I don't know… the President."

"Are you going to march right up to the White House and demand to see him?"

"I don't know. But we can't do anything from Richmond."

"Chen, you can get on the train and go to Union Station. But once you're in DC, you're vulnerable. They could be anywhere. You can't go home. You can't go to Langley—you don't know who's with us and who's out to kill us—"

"I don't think anybody is out to *kill* us," he groaned. "Let's not get carried away here."

"Oh, maybe those were Bernard's or Joan's last words."

Chen sighed. "What are you going to do?"

"I don't know—yet. They won't think we've headed out of the area, that's for sure. They'd be thinking like you; they'd figure on us trying to get to the feds somehow. At least, that's what I'm banking on."

"Okay." He took a deep breath. "I'll see you on the train."

Kit watched as he walked through the parking garage toward the entrance. Then she headed for the elevator and the hotel lobby. Once there, she pretended to look at the events calendar while she peered over it to the street beyond. Directly across the street was the King Street Metro Station, and beyond it was the train—and her ticket out of here.

She couldn't see Chen anywhere. After a few moments, she left the hotel, crossed the street, and headed to the station.

The train had been en route for almost fifteen minutes before Chen slid into the seat beside her.

"Thank God," she breathed. "I thought something had happened to you."

"I couldn't find you," he said. "Do you know how many cars are on this thing?"

They sat in silence for a moment. There was a group at the other end of the car, laughing and joking, obviously employees on their commute home. Kit glanced at her watch. Unbelievable. It was five past three.

"I know this is a minor point," she said, "but when you took the car, you showed your CIA identification. I don't even have ID; aren't we supposed to be undercover?"

Chen smiled sheepishly and pulled his ID from his pocket. "Supermarket check-cashing card," he said.

Kit burst into laughter.

"Everything happened so fast—" he started, before becoming somber. "I hope those officers are okay."

"I'm sure we'll find out on the news tonight."

"I'm sure we won't."

"I don't know about the driver, but Jansson's wound wasn't life threatening." She avoided looking at Chen, wondering who she was trying to convince.

Her cell phone rang, startling both of them. She quickly yanked it out of her purse and stared at the caller ID as if it were a snake.

"Who is it?" Chen finally asked.

"My husband." She took a deep breath and answered the phone.

"Kit!" Frank's voice sounded anxious. "I've been worried sick about you."

She felt as if she was surrounded by a brick wall, and his voice was a million miles away. It didn't feel like she was on the phone with her husband of almost two decades.

"Where are you?"

"At work," she said. "Why?"

"I just tried your office; they said you weren't there."

"Frank, this isn't a good time, so just cut to the chase. What do you want?"

There was a pause on the other end of the phone. Then, "I made a mistake, Kit. I want to come home. I want us to be together again."

"You've got to be kidding!" she said.

"Kit, I'll make it up to you. I swear I will. I'm sorry I cheated on you. I'm sorry I hit you. I'll do anything— please, Kit, tell me where you are and I'll come to you. Please."

"What about *her*?"

"Lisa means nothing to me," he answered.

"I was talking about Miranda," she said icily.

There was silence on the other end of the phone. Kit felt as if her chest were being crushed. He started to backtrack, but she interrupted him. "Stop it, Frank. We're not going to have this conversation."

When he spoke again, his words were rapid and heated. "Where's Tim?"

Her mind was racing. "Call my attorney. We still have to work out visitation rights."

"Who went to his school this morning, claiming to be me?"

Her phone beeped, and she jumped. Startled, she clicked the phone off.

Chen took the phone. "It's just going into roaming," he said gently. "That's all it is." He handed the phone back to her.

"My nerves are shot," she said. She looked at the tiny screen, where the "roam" signal was flashing. Then the screen blinked and a page began to scroll across the screen.

"Oh, my God!" she exclaimed.

"What is it?" Chen leaned toward her.

Kit read the message: "Don't worry Mom. Was with 'Dad'. Now having coffee with the copperheads."

CHAPTER 37

三十七

Carter wasn't about to wait for the elevator; he dashed headlong into the stairwell as Bryce yelled after him. He stopped on the landing, momentarily glancing up at Bryce in the doorway.

"What are you doing?"

"Listen, Bryce, videotape my room and get it to Morley. You got that?"

"What are you gonna do?"

"I'll be back in an hour." With that, he rushed down the remaining two flights, his footsteps drowning out Bryce's objections.

He made it through the first set of doors before he spotted Detective Munski, approaching the hotel with another man. And from the look in his eyes, Munski had just spotted him. Carter hesitated, caught between the two sets of doors like a fish in a goldfish bowl.

"Going somewhere?" Munski asked.

"I can't talk now," he said.

"I'll walk with you to your car. You've met Agent Davidson, haven't you, Carter?"

"Don't think I have."

"FBI," the man said, extending his hand. "You must be Carter Leigh."

Carter shook his hand briefly before pushing through the second set of doors. "I'm in a hurry."

"I can see that."

A torrent of rain hit Carter full in the face, and for the first time, he realized that Munski and Davidson were soaked. The temperature had also risen to what felt like a balmy sixty degrees.

"Listen, Carter, there's something you need to know..." Munski was saying.

They reached the Expedition and Carter fumbled with the keys. His hands were shaking so badly that he was certain they would notice.

"Just say it, Ski. I don't have all day."

Munski took the keys and unlocked the door.

Carter climbed into the vehicle and started to close the door, but Munski grabbed it and held it open while he peered inside.

"Carter," he said, "what's going on?"

Carter glanced at Davidson. "Bryce is upstairs. He's got a videotape of a luncheon from this afternoon; the station's sending a courier for it now—"

"Well, isn't that interesting? I guess this afternoon, there'll be all sorts of couriers up and down I-95."

"What?"

"A courier dropped off a videotape at my office less than an hour ago. I haven't seen it yet, but some guys in my office have. They're en route here with it now."

"What kind of videotape?"

"Listen, Carter, I know you're sweet on this Olsen woman—"

"Christ. Not this again."

"You need to know she's been implicated in both the murders."

"Ski, I can guarantee you—"

"Save it, Carter. This tape is proof positive she's a spy."

Carter glanced at Davidson, standing a few inches away, listening intently. "You already told me you thought she was CIA—" he said to Munski.

"No! She's spying for the enemy," Davidson interjected, shaking his head. "She's spying for China."

The train ride to Richmond took two hours. As the minutes ticked by, Kit became increasingly warmer, unzipping her parka and finally abandoning it altogether. Outside, rain was coming down in sheets, obscuring the countryside. It was doing its best to melt the deep snow, bringing with it a mood of late March instead of early January. The group at the other end of the car discussed the rainfall and debated the date the rivers would crest. Southeastern Virginia had already experienced massive flooding, displacing thousands, and the general consensus was that things would only get worse.

Chen was staring out the window. Kit leaned back and closed her eyes, dozing off and on and then jerking awake as if her life depended on her ability to stay alert. It was difficult trying to prevent her mood from becoming as gray as the weather. When they finally pulled into the station, she thought the train ride had to have been the longest of her life.

"What now?" Chen asked when they exited the station. "Do we catch a subway?"

Kit chuckled. "You don't leave DC much, do you?"

"What do you mean?"

"There is no subway here. I don't even know if they have buses."

"Then how—?"

"We walk. There's a car rental not too far from here." Kit neglected to tell him that it was almost a two-mile hike, and she wondered how long it would take for him to ask.

They were both silent, Chen with a decidedly I-am-not-amused expression as he walked along in shoes more fitting for sitting at a desk than for walking.

"You haven't said much since getting that page," Chen said quietly.

"My son said he was drinking coffee with copperheads," she said.

"That's kind of weird, isn't it?"

"It's a code."

"Oh?" His face brightened. "What kind of code?"

Kit took a deep breath, her eyes on the passing traffic. "Tim doesn't drink coffee. So his message means he's at a coffee house."

"With snakes?"

She half-chuckled. "Chesterfield County used to be known as 'Copperhead County' because they had so many copperheads…at one time, not any more," she added hastily. "So it means he's in Chesterfield County at a coffee house."

"Great," Chen said wryly. "So how many hundreds of coffee houses do we check?"

"Like I said, you don't get out of DC much," she said. "This isn't exactly Starbucks country… there might be a dozen—if that."

They walked on in silence. Then Chen spoke again. "Did you know he was here? Is that why you wanted to come to Richmond?"

She hesitated. "I thought he might be. But that's only one reason I wanted to come here. Anyway, his page has me worried."

"Why?"

"Remember when he was kidnapped at that ski resort, when you helped me write the program?"

Chen nodded. "How could I forget?"

"When the kidnappers called me, they put Tim on the phone. He said he should have gone skiing in Copperhead County."

Chen stopped and leaned against a telephone pole while he emptied his shoe of a pebble. When they continued walking, he said, "So?"

"So, what he meant was, he should have gone skiing in Chesterfield County."

Chen looked at her quizzically. "So?"

"You can't go skiing in Chesterfield. It isn't cold enough, and there aren't any mountains. I didn't realize it at the time, but he was trying to tell me something."

"In code."

"Yeah, in code."

Kit could see the sign now for the car rental.

"What do you think he was trying to tell you?"

"I don't know… that they were planning on taking him to Chesterfield? Or they had a hideout in Chesterfield, maybe?"

"He didn't tell you when you got him back?"

She shook her head. "No. He didn't talk much about what happened…" her voice faded.

Chen was walking slower now. "You said there was another reason for coming here. Did you just want to get out of Washington?"

"It's more than that. You know Stallworth's inauguration is tomorrow?"

Chen nodded.

"His election was rigged."

He looked at her, his eyes widening.

"We can't let him take office."

"The election can be invalidated," Chen said. "He could be removed."

"You think so? When was the last time a governor was removed from office? For that matter, can you remember when *any* elected official was removed?"

He shrugged. "There was Riekner..."

She snorted. "Yeah, Riekner. His shenanigans were in the newspaper for more than a year before they ousted him. And now he's contesting that—from prison."

"What are you saying?"

"I'm saying, it's easier to prevent his inauguration than to oust him after he's in."

Chen stopped again and leaned against a traffic light pole. He wiped perspiration from his brow, and seemed to be searching for their destination.

"We're almost there," Kit said.

"How can you be so sure his election was rigged? I mean, I know the software—"

"It was rigged." She told him about the interview with Carter, finishing up as they walked into the car rental office.

A short time later, they were pulling onto Broad Street in a white Ford Focus.

"You know, they can track us here through your credit card," Chen said.

She nodded. "I know. But in less than twenty-four hours, it won't matter anymore."

"Oh?"

"If things go according to plan," she said, "this will all be over in twenty-four hours."

By the time Kit and Chen crossed into Chesterfield County, the sky had turned a dark, wintry blue-gray that cast a gloom over the landscape. The windshield wipers were moving at their highest speed, but Kit was still leaned forward in the seat, trying to see the road. In the narrow swath where the headlights hit the pavement, it looked so slick she felt as if she were driving directly into a barrel of oil.

She pulled into a parking lot on Midlothian Turnpike, and sandwiched the car between two parked vehicles. She'd spent the last half hour filling in Chen on Carter's involvement. Now she dialed Carter's cell phone number; he answered on the first ring.

"Where are you?" he said.

"Chesterfield. Where are you?"

"I just left the hotel. Kit, things aren't going too good here…"

"Did you take Tim to a hotel?"

"Yes, but—"

"Which one?"

"Homewood Suites in Chester. Now, stop interrupting me—"

"Did you lose him?"

He groaned. "Yeah."

"Don't worry about it; I can find him. Are you in Chester now?"

"Yeah."

"I need you to do something."

"Kit, we need to talk."

"And we will. We'll meet up in about an hour—"

"I can't. Things are getting hectic around here."

"What's going on?"

"I have to be at a dinner tonight, for Stallworth. And Munski's here, with an FBI agent; he tells me—"

"Are they looking for me?"

"If they aren't now, they will be."

"Carter, listen. I found the program, the one the kidnappers wanted. I know what it does now." She ignored the disapproving frown on Chen's face, and continued, "Stallworth's election was rigged."

"Rigged! How—?"

"The new elections program. The Chinese have operatives here. They were able to get into the program and change the election results. I think Bernard did it, but Joan knew about it, too. And my boss Jack and some guy named Toy—"

"Wait a minute. You're going way too fast for me. Are you telling me that Stallworth is a spy?"

"I don't know if he's a spy, or if he's a Chinese sympathizer. In any event, they're putting him in a position where he can push through legislation favorable to them—"

"I don't get it. He'll just be a governor. It isn't like he's been elected President—" He stopped. "Wait a minute. Are they setting him up for the presidency?"

"They're setting somebody up for it. I'm sure of it. That program was used all over the country. I don't have all the information on who was elected, but think about it, Carter, if they get enough people in positions of power, they can change the course of history. They can set people up for all sorts of positions—Senators, Congressmen, the President—they can get Supreme Court judges put in, people in charge of Defense and Commerce…"

"The possibilities are endless."

"Exactly."

"What do you want me to do?"

"I need you to get to my parents. I need them to check into a hotel or something, just for tonight. Jack and Toy know I'm gone, and they might come after them."

"Where do they live?"

Kit gave him the address and directions. "You're ten minutes from their house, tops."

"What about Tim?"

"I'll get Tim. I'll call you back in an hour."

"If I don't answer my phone, do not come to the Homewood Suites. Got that?"

"Got it."

"Listen, Kit, we've got to tell somebody about this— the FBI or…"

"Not yet. Wait until I call you back." She clicked the phone off and handed it to Chen. "Now we've got to find a coffee shop."

CHAPTER 38

三十八

Carter pulled onto what appeared to be an old logging trail and slowed the car to a stop. He was hopelessly lost on country roads that snaked past fields and woods, with an occasional mailbox the only sign he was anywhere close to civilization. In the rain, it was impossible to see street signs and house numbers. He turned the overhead light on and dug out his map from the glove compartment.

Kit's directions might have been good if there hadn't been so much flooding. He'd been turned around three times by streets closed due to rising water; in the dark, it appeared as though lakes or creeks had overflowed and were quickly claiming the surrounding land.

He found her parent's street, and spent some time trying to figure out how to get there from his current location. Then he turned the vehicle around, almost getting bogged down in the mud in the process, and headed back to the road.

He'd almost pulled onto the road when a vehicle zipped around a curve at a breakneck speed, drifting across the narrow lane, and straddling the double yellow line. His heart almost stopped as they drifted toward him before jerking the steering wheel and guiding their vehicle away from his. Somebody was in an awful hurry.

He pulled behind them, consciously repeating the new directions to the O'Reilly's house while keeping a wary eye on the other vehicle. They turned onto a cross street; after he slowed to read the sign, he took the same turn.

As he crept along, he peered at each mailbox. The houses were set so far back from the road he was unable to see them through the trees, and he wondered how anyone could live so far from everything.

The vehicle ahead of him turned into a gravel driveway so fast they went into a skid. Recovering, they continued until he lost sight of their taillights.

As he neared the driveway, he brightened his lights, and then did a double take. It was the O'Reilly's house.

There were times when a little voice inside him begged him not to do something, and he went right ahead and did it anyway. And then there were times when the little voice boomed and echoed and was so insistent he just couldn't ignore it. As he sat there in the middle of the deserted road, the voice became so overwhelming he finally drove past the driveway altogether. It might have been five minutes or ten when he spied a church parking lot and pulled in.

He thought about calling Kit. He thought about asking her what kind of vehicle her folks drove. And he thought about telling her he was in the middle of God-knows-where. But he didn't. He turned the vehicle around and headed back down the road.

He passed the driveway two more times before he'd formed his game plan. He finally pulled into a driveway almost a quarter of a mile away, and backed into the trees. He sat there for a minute, unable to see anything except masses of pine trees, towering oaks and the skeletal remains of underbrush.

He reached into the glove compartment and pulled out a pair of binoculars. Okay, so maybe it wasn't kosher for mainstream media to use them, but it wouldn't be the first time he'd stooped to paparazzi level. He turned off the vehicle and climbed out.

He was soaked by the time he'd walked far enough down the driveway to see their house. Several lights were on downstairs, but the upper level was completely dark. The vehicle he'd followed was parked out front.

He couldn't see any movement inside the house so he made his way along the tree line toward the back. Inside, he could see a fireplace's red and orange glow, and the warm light from scattered lamps.

Something near the edge of the room caught his attention, and he raised the binoculars. There were two elderly people sitting there, a woman in a chair and a man in a wheelchair. The man wore some sort of necklace with a large white object on the end of it. As Carter watched, he seemed to be pressing something on it.

On the other side of the room were two burly men. One was waving a gun and appeared to be shouting, but with the wind and the rain, Carter couldn't hear a thing. As he watched, he approached the man in the wheelchair and backhanded him with the pistol.

The woman on the couch was off her chair and on top of the gun-toting man like a wildcat.

It took both men to subdue her, but from the looks of things, both of them were going to be nursing some serious scratches. *That's got to be Kit's mother,* Carter grinned.

The man in the wheelchair wasn't moving; his head was bowed over the side, and as the woman tended to him, Carter realized he was bleeding. She was arguing with the men, and finally, one of them knocked her backward onto the floor.

Carter crouched down and studied them through the binoculars. He figured each man was close to six feet, and weighed at least two hundred pounds. What's more, he could see now they were both armed. Even with his Sig Sauer, he didn't stand a chance. And neither did Kit's parents.

He crept back to the front of the house, moving stealthily through the shadows of the trees, until he'd reached their vehicle. Then he slipped his knife out of his pocket and jabbed the tires on the side opposite the house, until they were visibly going flat.

He crept back to the safety of the tree line, where he blocked his cell phone number and dialed the police. While he was waiting to be connected to the dispatchers, he heard the crunch of a vehicle's tires on the gravel. As remote as the area had seemed just a few minutes earlier, it was now teeming with excitement.

As he hung up the phone and made his way across the driveway and back toward his vehicle, it sounded like there were police cruisers coming from all directions. It hit him as he hung up his phone—the white necklace had been an alarm of some type. He reached the Expedition, slipped inside, and waited.

He counted six squad cars speeding past him. Through the woods, the area was lit up like it was daylight. He started up the vehicle and slowly made his way down to the road, where he slipped away in the opposite direction.

Carter finished off a chicken leg and tossed the bone in an overflowing cardboard bucket. While he was driving around rural Chesterfield, Bryce had been busy getting the NBC courier registered in a room across from Carter's. Now the courier was gone, back en route to Washington with the duplicate video, and Bryce and Carter were situated in the courier's room with a clear view through the peephole of Carter's hotel door.

They'd missed Stallworth's dinner, but both knew now that they were sitting on a bigger story. Carter had come clean with Bryce. It was as much for self-preservation as to quell Bryce's anxiety; Carter had reached the point where he wanted someone else, anyone else, to know the entire story. If something happened to him—and he was beginning to think it would only be a matter of time before it did—he needed a trail. But what was more disturbing to them both was the CIA's involvement. He was beginning to give more thought to Agent Davidson and the FBI.

But their ace in the hole was the media.

They'd spent the last two hours reconstructing the story, beginning with the election program and Bernard's subsequent disappearance and murder, and ending with Kit's parents taken hostage this evening. But as they went back over everything, Carter realized much of it was pure conjecture. He didn't have the evidence.

They'd been on the phone with Morley off and on all evening. True to his nature, Morley had refrained from showing an ounce of excitement. Carter knew they were walking a thin line where they had to be both hard charging and cautious. They could be sitting on the biggest story since Watergate.

But the fact remained they didn't have any evidence.

He hadn't heard from Kit, and was reluctant to call her. She'd been so sure she knew where Tim was. The kid must have friends in the area, and they were probably at somebody's house right now, maybe finishing up dinner. Then why hadn't she called?

Bryce rewound the video from the luncheon and played it back, frame by frame. They'd watched it a dozen times by now; Bryce had been correct. Stallworth appeared to be muttering expletives under his breath, his eyes filled with venom, as Carter's shouts filled the air.

Carter himself had made the nightly news, but the local stations portrayed him as a nut who'd crashed the luncheon—an extremist of some sort who hurled accusations that were thought too preposterous to be correct. And now that Morley knew as much of the story as Carter, they were going to sit on the tape of Stallworth. When the story blew, he wanted the whole shebang.

What eclipsed Carter's run-in with Stallworth on the local news were the men at the O'Reilly residence. Attempted armed robbery. He didn't believe that the crime he witnessed unfolding had anything to do with robbery; but at least for now, the men were behind bars and Kit's parents were being checked—and hopefully protected—at an area hospital.

Carter leaned his chair against the wall, his eyes wandering from Stallworth's lips to his expression and finally to the people surrounding him.

"Wait a minute," he said, leaning forward. "Go back."

Bryce backed up the tape. "What do you see?"

"There. Stop it there."

Bryce complied.

"Can you blow it up? Zoom in?"

"Sure." Bryce began zooming in on Stallworth's face.

"No—go a little to the left, to the guy at the end of the table. The guy standing."

"This guy?" Bryce said, panning the spectators. "He's just standing there."

"Who is he?" Carter mused.

"I don't know; look at his posture. He looks like a Secret Service agent or something."

"Secret Service doesn't protect the Governor," Carter said. "Private security, maybe?"

"I guess. Why?"

"Go forward, but stay on him."

Bryce followed Carter's instructions. As Carter's voice could be heard in the background and others near the podium reacted in shock, this man stood completely still. Only his eyes moved; cold gray eyes that must have been following Carter's every move.

"He's not security," Bryce said. "He'd either have acted to protect Stallworth, or he'd been all over you."

"I know that man."

"What?"

"I mean, I've seen him before. But I don't know who he is."

"When—?"

"When Kit and I were returning from Ski Top Mountain. That's the guy who pulled the Expedition back onto the road."

"Are you serious?" Bryce now peered intently at the man.

"Dead serious."

"Poor choice of words."

There was a knock on the door, and both men froze.

"It's across the hall," Bryce whispered.

Carter nodded, slowly rose to his feet and slipped quietly to the door. He peered through the peephole, and then breathed a sigh of relief. "It's Ski." He opened the door. "Over here."

Munski turned around. It was then that Carter noticed Agent Davidson.

"Sorry, the desk told me—"

"Yeah, I know," Carter said. "Get in here."

As they entered the room, Carter stuck his head into the hallway and peered up and down the hall. Satisfied, he closed the door and locked it.

"Carter, can we talk?"

"Yeah. Whatever you want to say, you can say in front of him," Carter said, nodding toward Bryce.

"You sure about that?" Munski said.

"Yeah."

Munski sat down and picked up a piece of chicken. "You mind?"

"Help yourself."

"I haven't eaten since breakfast."

Carter motioned for Davidson to help himself, but the agent declined.

After he took a bite, Munski continued, "I know you don't like to talk about that Olsen woman."

"Go on."

"Like I told you, I'm back on the case. Not by myself, mind you." He nodded toward Davidson. "The feds are the primaries in the murder investigations."

"What have you got?"

"I shouldn't be here, you know. Shouldn't be telling you this." He grabbed a can of Pepsi and popped it open. "But Agent Davidson here and I discussed it and… well, I don't think you're involved in all this, but I think this woman that you're sweet on, is. And we're hoping you can shed some light on a few things."

"Oh?" Carter stole a quick look at Bryce.

"Emerson was shot twice in the head, killed instantly. Looks like a double tap."

"A what?"

"Two quick shots, one right after the other. Something a trained assassin would do."

"So it was a professional hit?"

"That's what it looks like. And if there hadn't been that snowmobile accident at Ski Top Mountain, his body probably wouldn't have been found until spring."

Carter opened the refrigerator in the small suite's kitchen and pulled out a beer. He took a long swig before turning back around.

Munski was busy with a second piece of chicken. "Joan Newcomb—that's a different story. They wanted us to find her. Tortured to death. It didn't come fast."

"What do you think that means?" Carter said before taking another swig.

"We were hoping you'd tell us," Davidson said. When Carter didn't respond, he added, " We've had Mrs. Olsen under surveillance, and a wiretap on her telephone. She's been acting suspiciously."

"Wiretapping's illegal," Carter said.

Davidson smiled conspiratorially. "Not anymore, it isn't."

"Oh, yeah," Carter said. "Homeland Security and the aftermath of 9-11. So, you think Kit Olsen is affiliated with terrorists?"

Munski cleared his throat. "Mrs. Olsen visited Emerson's widow. Shortly afterward, a hundred grand was deposited in Mrs. Emerson's account—the same amount withdrawn from the Olsen account."

"This is all circumstantial," Carter said.

Munski reached into his overcoat. "This isn't." He plopped a videotape on the table.

"What's that?"

"It was delivered early this evening. It offers conclusive evidence that Kathryn Olsen is a spy for the Chinese."

Carter picked it up and crossed the room. He removed the tape of Stallworth's luncheon and slid the new tape in. "So, you gonna charge Kit with spying?"

"The feds are. They're looking for her now. What's more, they're going to charge her with being an accessory to the Emerson and Newcomb murders. And something tells me, you know where she is."

Carter's cell phone rang, and he jumped, and then chuckled self-consciously. He pulled the phone off his belt and looked at the caller ID. It was Kit. "Morley calling again," Carter said to Bryce. He hit the *end* key, sending the caller to his voice mail, and put the phone to his ear. "Hello… not yet, we're still working on it… yeah, we'll have it soon." He clicked the *end* key again and nodded to Munski. "You were saying?"

"We wanted you to see this tape for yourself," Munski said. "I know you like this woman, but you need to know, she's gonna suck you into this, and if you stick with her, you're going down with her… So, watch the tape, and if you want to talk, we'll talk."

Carter hit the *play* button. They were quiet as they watched Kit handing over the disk to Toy. When they discussed her laptop, Carter and Munski exchanged glances. Bryce was conspicuously quiet. When the tape was finished, Carter popped it out and handed it back to Munski. "You're right," he said. "We need to talk."

CHAPTER 39

三十九

Kit knew she'd found Tim as soon as she entered the coffee shop on Iron Bridge Road in Chesterfield. There was a small group gathered around one table while a young voice wafted through the crowd, expounding on the virtues of staying connected through wireless communication. She firmly but politely pushed her way between the spectators until she was face to face with her son.

"Mom!" Tim said. "Gotta go, guys. It's been fun!"

The people around the table let out a simultaneous groan as Tim stood and packed up his laptop.

"What took you so long?" he asked as the crowd dispersed.

"Long story. How long have you been here?"

"Long enough to get real hungry," Tim said, slinging his laptop case over his shoulder.

As they headed out the door, Tim waved good-bye to the folks he'd met, and Kit tried Carter on his cell phone. After the second ring, it went to voice mail, and she hung up. They met up with Chen at the car.

"What now?" Chen asked.

"Carter didn't answer," Kit said. Then in a lighter voice she hoped masked her mounting feelings of anxiety, she said, "Let's grab a bite to eat, and I'll try him again in awhile."

A few minutes later, they were seated at Applebee's and eating as if none of them had encountered food for a week. When they'd started on desserts, Kit carefully surveyed the other diners around her. It appeared to be just another day in Chesterfield, with couples and families enjoying their meals.

"Tim," Kit said, "when you were kidnapped, you told me you should have gone skiing in Copperhead County. What were you trying to tell me?"

Tim took a bite of vanilla ice cream before answering. "This one guy was talking about a hotel room they had in Chesterfield County, over on Jeff Davis Highway. Sounded like a real winner; they rent the room by the month." He pointedly raised one eyebrow.

"Did they take you there?"

"No. After we talked, they decided it was too far from Ski Top Mountain… Anyway, I was trying to let you know which direction we were headed in."

"That was pretty smart of you," she said.

Tim beamed.

"So, what happened to you today?" she asked.

He shrugged. "That reporter guy, Carter, pulled me out of school, checked me into a hotel room."

"Did he tell you to leave? Or did you do that on your own?"

"I was watching TV in the room, and Carter said he had to leave but he'd be back. Then a little while later, I heard the elevator and I looked out the peephole. These people walked right past my door, going to his."

"Then what?"

"They knocked first. Then they used a key and just walked in."

"How many were there?"

"Three."

"Did you recognize them?"

"I recognized two of 'em. Mom, do you remember the Christmas party you had a year ago? The one where everybody from your office and Dad's was invited?"

"Well, not exactly everybody was invited, but I know what party you're talking about," Kit stole a glance at Chen. "I didn't know you then."

"No problem," he answered, sipping his coffee and watching Tim devour his dessert.

"So, two of the people had been at the party," Tim continued. "One was your boss..."

"Jack?"

"Yeah."

"Who was the other guy?"

"I don't know. But I did recognize the woman who was with them. It was Dad's secretary."

"What?!"

Chen kicked her. "Not so loud," he hissed.

Kit leaned across the table. "Are you telling me Dad's secretary and my boss were together—at Carter's room?"

Tim looked her square in the eyes. "That's what I'm tellin' you, Mom."

She leaned back in her chair. The server deposited their check on the table. As she left, Kit asked, "What did you do then?"

"I didn't do anything until I heard them tearing the room apart. It sounded like they were hurling furniture or something. So I got the hell out of there. I climbed out the window. And then I ran."

"Where'd you go?"

He shrugged. "I took the back way to Bermuda Square and hung around there… Then I made my way down here, and I paged you."

Kit put money on the table. "Let's get out of here."

They were in the car before Chen spoke. "What time did you see Jack?"

"Before noon, probably late morning."

Kit and Chen traded sidelong glances. "Are you thinking what I'm thinking?" Kit said.

"If Tim saw Jack before noon—"

"—then he couldn't have been at Langley when you called Ralston's office."

Kit pulled out of the parking lot and headed west on Iron Bridge Road. "Could he have rewired the phone? Programmed it to ring on his cell phone, and not in Ralston's office?"

"Anything is possible," Chen said. "He's high enough up the ladder, he could have ordered it done."

"Then the Director might not be headed to the Middle East."

"There's only one way to find out." Chen pulled out his cell phone.

Both Kit and Tim stopped him before he could dial the number. Both spoke simultaneously. "They can trace our calls."

"But—you just called Carter."

"It was a mistake. I didn't think about them being here." She turned left off of Iron Bridge Road.

"Where are we going?" Chen asked.

"South. Maybe to the North Carolina border, I don't know. We'll stop along the way and get a calling card. The calls are routed all over the country; by the time they trace it, we'll be long gone."

A half an hour later, they pulled into a small shopping center in Colonial Heights, where Chen ran inside and bought two calling cards. Once he was back in the car, they headed south on Route 1.

"There's something else we need to know," Kit said.

"What's that?" Chen asked.

"How long was the office in lockdown? How long were the incoming calls blocked?"

"Why is that important?"

She shrugged. "Maybe it isn't. I'd just like to know if Frank really tried calling my office today."

They made their way to Interstate 95. Once they'd crossed the North Carolina border, Kit pulled into the Welcome Center.

Chen was at the pay phone before Kit had the engine turned off. The call to Ralston's office took less than two minutes. Ralston was out of his office, but he wasn't headed to the Middle East. He was at UCT, along with a host of others from Langley. The facility was still in lockdown.

"But, listen to this," Chen added. "They don't know anything about a guy named Jansson—or Bonelli. They don't even have a record of their employment."

"What are you saying?"

"I'm saying if we were headed for Langley, we definitely weren't headed for Ralston's office."

Kit was silent as they doubled back and crossed over to Interstate 85. Just south of Petersburg, they checked into a Hampton Inn, opting for a two-bedroom suite.

Chen chose to sleep on the sofa bed in the living room, where he could hear anyone at the door. Tim took one of the bedrooms, and Kit took the other. But within minutes, they'd all found their way back to the living room, where they brainstormed about their options.

"There's only one thing we can do," Kit said. "We have to leak the information to the press."

"That would blow our cover, and everybody else's at UCT," Chen argued.

"We won't mention UCT. We won't even mention that we're CIA."

"You're CIA?" Tim exclaimed.

"Duh," Chen answered.

"It's a long story—and no, I'm not an agent," Kit said. "I just write programs. Anyway, I'll print out the part of the program that rigged the elections, and we'll distribute it to the press. We'll tell them what we know about Stallworth's election."

"Or we could use the proper channels within the agency," Chen said.

"Oh, yeah, that's a better idea," Kit said. "Let's see, that means I'll call my boss, Jack, and let him know what I've found out."

Chen groaned.

"We can't use the proper channels," Kit said. "They don't exist any more."

"The agency has a fallback plan."

"I know; I've been briefed on it as well as you. But how do I know that the one person I call and confide in isn't part of this conspiracy? They could tell us they're arranging to bring us in, and instead, we could be walking right into a trap."

Chen was silent as he rubbed his forehead. "How do you plan to notify the press without giving away our location?"

Tim spoke up. "We could give the information to Carter."

Kit agreed. "He already has most of it. All I need to do is get him the translated version of the program. He can let it leak to his colleagues."

"And just how do you propose getting him the program?" Chen asked.

Kit smiled and walked to the coat closet. A moment later, she was back, pulling the hard drive out of the pocket.

"You had that, all this time?" Chen asked.

Kit nodded as Tim grabbed the drive and proceeded to set up his laptop.

"I have my printer, too," he said proudly.

Kit looked at Chen. "We can do it. We won't be giving away any secrets—that is, any that would negatively impact America. And once the press gets hold of this, they won't let it die. It can't be swept under the rug."

Reluctantly, Chen agreed. Chen and Tim would stay at the hotel while Chen translated the code to English. Meanwhile, Kit would telephone Carter and let him know of their plan.

She drove almost sixty miles southeast, well into North Carolina, before stopping at a McDonald's and placing the call. Carter answered on the first ring.

"It's Kit," she said breathlessly. "Can you talk?"

There was a brief hesitation. "Are you in Georgia?"

"It's just the calling card," she said. "It routes all over the country."

"Where are you?"

"I can't tell you, in case someone is listening."

"Kit, we have to talk."

"I know. Carter, I have the program that rigs the election results. We're printing it out and we're going to make copies. We need to leak this to the press."

"How do you propose we get it to them?"

"I'm not sure… can you make a few calls?"

"I have a better idea," Carter said. "We'll call a press conference. We'll do it tomorrow morning, eight o'clock sharp. That'll give me all evening to call everybody I know. We'll get reporters from all the major networks, all the big newspapers. We'll put you in front of the microphone and you can explain to them what you've got."

"That's beautiful," Kit said excitedly. "They can't go through with the inauguration once we've shown proof that Stallworth didn't win. The results will have to be set aside."

"And you'll be safe. You'll have the press following you everywhere you go; there's no way anyone's going to try anything."

"Where do we do this?"

"Hold on." There was a moment of silence before he continued, "In front of the Police Department at the intersection of Iron Bridge Road and Lori Road—you know where that is?"

"Of course I do."

"I'll get everything set up. Pull up in front, and I'll take care of the rest."

"Eight o'clock sharp, at the police station."

"Kit?"

"Yes?"

"Leave Tim behind. Just in case. He is with you, isn't he?"

"Yes. But he won't be tomorrow."

"Are you two okay? Do you have a place to stay?"

"Don't worry about us. We're fine. I'll see you in the morning. And…Carter? Thanks for everything. I don't know what I would have done without you."

Carter pressed the *Off* button on his cell phone and turned to Munski. "God forgive me," he muttered.

CHAPTER 40

四十

When the morning sun peeked through the windows of the Hampton Inn, Kit, Chen, and Tim were finishing up breakfast. Room service had arrived promptly at seven; from the looks of Tim's plate, he'd ordered everything on the menu while Kit was having trouble motivating herself to eat a few bites of fruit. She hadn't slept well. Every time the heater kicked on or off, it had awakened her and she imagined someone was breaking in. Then once she'd drifted off to sleep, she'd had a nightmare. She dreamt that Lisa was sitting in the corner of her living room, calmly smoking while Frank, Miranda, and Jack planned how to kill her. When she was startled into wakefulness by room service, the dream had felt more real than the hotel room.

Chen had finished translating the program late into the night, and Tim printed out fifty copies. Kit figured that would be more than enough.

The television was tuned to the news. The headlines weren't about Stallworth or the inauguration, as she'd anticipated, but about widespread flooding. Ever since

Thanksgiving, Virginia had been buffeted by one snowstorm after another, heaping four feet of snow in some areas. Then a warm front came through with heavy rains and high temperatures, melting the snow and adding four inches of rain. Now the water had nowhere to go. Rivers and streams, including the James River that ran through the heart of Richmond, were unable to handle it all.

The media was expecting Stallworth's first order of business would be to ask the federal government to declare Virginia a disaster area.

The inauguration was to be at noon. High noon, Kit thought. Then she glanced at her watch. "We've got to get going."

Chen stood up. "I'm ready."

They'd agreed the night before that Chen would return to Washington. Kit would drop him off at the train station in Petersburg, and by the time she held her press conference, he would be well on his way. By late morning, he'd be at Langley. Just in case, she gave him her Glock. She would soon have Carter and the press surrounding her, while he would be completely alone, and on his way into a lion's den.

Tim would remain at the hotel. They put the "Do Not Disturb" sign on the door, and Tim was under strict orders not to open the door to anyone except Kit or Carter. She would call him as soon as the press conference ended, to let him know she was on her way to get him.

And if, God forbid, something unexpected occurred and he didn't hear from her, he was to remain in the room until nightfall. Then he was to take the hotel shuttle to the Richmond Airport, where he was to buy a ticket to Kit's brother Steven's home in Raleigh. He'd already researched the flights and seat availability online, and with any luck, he would be in North Carolina by late evening. Under no circumstances was he to try and contact his father. The dream was still fresh in Kit's mind, and she went with her gut that Tim would be safer on his own.

Kit kissed Tim on the forehead. For once, he didn't shy away.

"Be careful, Mom," he said as she put on her coat.

"Don't worry about me," she said light-heartedly. "I'll be back before you've finished watching your favorite shows. Hey, don't ring up a big bill here, ordering movies," she added, tussling his hair. She opened the door. "Remember to keep the door locked."

She and Chen stepped into the hallway and waited until they heard the deadbolt latch and the chain glide into place. She had a sinking sensation, as if her heart was dropping into her shoes, but she smiled and waved at the peephole. "See ya," she said.

He didn't answer.

Kit and Chen continued to the lobby and out to the car, each remaining silent on their way to the train station. Kit was turning onto Iron Bridge Road when she realized that she had no recollection of anything she and Chen said as he departed.

The police station was part of a small county complex that had been there for as long as Kit could remember. Long before Iron Bridge Road had four lanes, when the shopping centers and banks that lined this stretch of road were figments of the imagination, the plain square buildings kept watch over the county and its residents. Two of the boys Joan had dated in high school had joined the department, and the last Kit heard, they were still there.

If a passerby happened upon the station around mid-afternoon when the shift change occurred, the parking lot was filled with police cars. The rest of the time, it was almost vacant; on weekends, it was a sleepy reminder of a bygone era when Chesterfield was agricultural and everybody around these parts knew everybody else.

Things happened in Richmond, just ten minutes or so to the north, and in Petersburg, about the same distance to the south, but nothing much ever occurred in Chesterfield, which is exactly how the police department and its citizens liked it.

But now the police station was abuzz. As she rounded the corner at Lori Road, she recognized the white vans with the media emblems plastered on their sides, some of them with satellite dishes mounted on top, parked across the side street from the police department. The crowd surged toward her, a mass of bodies with cameras mounted on shoulders or microphones in hand, everyone speaking at once in voices that seemed to melt into one.

She spotted Carter pulling ahead of the pack, and she slowed as he neared the car. He motioned for her to park along the side of the building.

He was at her door before she turned off the ignition, opening it and offering his assistance.

"I'm impressed," she said as she got out of the car. "You must know a lot of people."

"I used a few contacts," he said, "and a few favors. What have you got?"

She held up the stack of papers. "The program. I thought I had enough copies to distribute, but now I'm not so sure…"

"I'll take them," Carter said, pulling them out of her hand. He pushed passed the horde, pulling Kit with

him, as they made their way to the side door of the
police station.

She spotted a man approaching her in a dark blue
suit, his starched white shirt collar and deep red tie almost
too formal below short-cropped silver hair and piercing
blue eyes. He fixed her with his steady gaze as if willing
her to look only at him. As they grew closer, her eyes
drifted just beyond his shoulder, and she grabbed Carter's
hand. "It's Munski," she whispered as she saw the
detective.

"I know," he said, squeezing her hand. "Everything's
gonna be okay. Just trust me."

The man with the silver hair reached them and
slipped his arm around Kit's shoulders as if he were
protecting her. Her first impulse was to shrug him off
and demand an introduction, but with the video cameras
rolling and bulbs popping, she managed to stay
composed. She felt Carter's hand slip away from her,
and when she turned in his direction, he was gone,
replaced by the mob that pressed ever closer.

"Why'd you do it?" shouted one person.

"Was it your idea to torture your boss?" shouted
another.

The shouts were drowned out by each other, the air
filled with a rising buzz of voices and clicking cameras
and people jockeying for position. And then she was
standing in front of Munski and flanked by two officers
in crisp green uniforms.

"Kathryn Olsen," Munski said in a booming voice
that silenced the crowd, "I am placing you under arrest
for the first degree murders of Bernard Gordon Emerson
and Barbara Joan Newcomb."

CHAPTER 41

四十一

There were moments in Kit's life when the world took on a surreal quality and events seemed to move forward in slow motion. During those times, she would feel as if she were outside herself looking in, seeing and feeling details that otherwise would have passed her by during a normal day's course.

In the moments following her arrest, the press surged forward, their voices filling her ears yet seeming miles away, like the distant roll of thunder on an otherwise peaceful morning. She tried to speak, but her voice was drowned out by someone at a microphone, and as she turned in that direction, she saw the man who had, only a few seconds earlier, wrapped his arm around her shoulder. Somehow in the crush of voices, she heard his introduction as her attorney, and as the officers handcuffed her wrists behind her back, he proclaimed her innocence.

She tried to move toward the microphone, tried to insist that she be heard, but her voice was swept away, the faces surrounding her turning simultaneously toward the man with the silver hair—all but one face, the eyes

locked on her, the outer edges turned downward in
sadness, the jaw rigid. As she stared into Carter's face,
every muscle in her body cried out, asking why he had
betrayed her, but the words froze on her lips.

Firm hands were upon her shoulders, turning her
away from the crowd. Then they were on her back,
seeming to both push and pull her down the sidewalk
away from the press and toward a waiting police car.
The throngs surrounded the vehicle as she was placed
into the back seat; in the front were two officers, one
male and one female.

It felt like an eternity before the car began to move,
before the flashbulbs ceased and the press' questions
stopped. But much to Kit's dismay, the throng followed
the slow-moving vehicle down Lori Road, past the police
department, past her car still parked along the side, past
a parking lot.

They turned right on Lori Lane and an immediate
right into a short driveway to the county jail. Two sets
of chain link fences topped with Constantine wire
awaited them. A sheriff's deputy cleared them through
the first gate.

While she waited for the second gate to open, Kit
found herself staring into a courtyard of male prisoners
in bright orange uniforms playing basketball, as if they
were on a school playground. Then the second gate was
opened, and they were inside.

They parked in a tiny lot opposite the courtyard,
and the female officer climbed out of the front seat and
opened Kit's door. As Kit exited the vehicle, she spotted
a black robe to her right. Turning, she came face to face
with a young nun. Kit's eyes were riveted on the large
cross that fell from her neck. The nun reached out and
squeezed her shoulder, nodding in silence as if to say
that everything would be all right. But her reassurance

wasn't enough. Kit knew now that if she couldn't convince Carter of her innocence, she had no hope of persuading anyone else.

They crossed the parking lot to the gawks of the male inmates, passed a dark brown building with barred windows, another area filled with female prisoners, and finally passed a temporary trailer to a doorway beyond.

Once inside, Kit found herself in a windowless waiting room with the strong odor of disinfectant mixed with sweat and bodies. At least it afforded her with some semblance of privacy. One of the officers spoke into a wall-mounted telephone, and they were buzzed into a hallway.

To her right, she glimpsed a set of offices. At the far end were windows looking out on Lori Road—where the press was looking in. A tall, thin man with a no-nonsense attitude stepped briskly through the offices and directed them down the hall, informing them that the magistrates' offices would provide no privacy from the press.

The officers were silent as they led Kit down a short hallway, taking her further into the bowels of the county jail and away from the public eye. They'd removed their hands from her back, and she was now propelled forward simply by the movement of the officers beside her.

They stopped inside a booking room filled with computers, a computerized fingerprint-electronic scan, and other equipment that Kit couldn't identify. The female officer, a stout young woman with pale blond hair pulled into a loose bun, removed her handcuffs. As Kit rubbed her wrists where the cold metal had been, she realized the officers had started back down the hallway away from her.

She heard a movement behind her and turned as a man in a dark navy suit stepped through another doorway and extended his hand. He looked to be in his forties with short, neatly combed brown hair, a starched white collar, his navy tie perfectly matching the shade of his suit. As she mechanically reached out, she glanced down. He was holding a card.

She recognized the emblem before she took the card.

"Special Agent Allen Davidson," he said. "FBI."

Before she could respond, a young woman with a slight build and shoulder-length hair followed Davidson into the room. "I'm Sheila Carpenter," she said. "FBI."

"I want a lawyer present," Kit said.

As if in response, the man with the silver hair slipped inside with Munski close behind.

"And he," Kit said, "is *not* my lawyer."

The man stepped forward. "Bill Vogel," he said. "CIA."

Kit froze.

"We're on the same side," he said.

"What side is that?" she said.

"Let's all have a seat," Agent Davidson said.

It took awhile for the five people to get situated in the small room. Kit was seated in the center, with Davidson perched on the edge of the desk. Sheila pulled up a chair in the corner, and Munski and Vogel seated themselves on either side of Kit.

"First of all," Munski said, "you're not under arrest."

"Then what was all that—?"

Vogel said, "You're under protective custody."

"Carter told us everything last night," Munski added. "Agent Davidson and I have been working the Newcomb investigation. We called Vogel after Carter told us what you'd found."

"Obviously, there are parties who want you to take the rap for your coworkers' murders," Davidson said. "But we were concerned they might not stop at that."

"What are you saying?" Kit said. She hadn't removed her parka, and now her flesh was so hot it was beginning to feel scorched.

"Your life is in danger," Agent Davidson said. "If those people are able to reach you, they'll kill you."

"So you arrested me?!"

"Precisely." Vogel moved forward. "With the FBI and police involved, they can't come in here waving their CIA identification, and demand that you be released into their custody. They'd have to go through the courts to get to you."

"So what do you plan to do?" Kit asked. "Keep me here indefinitely?"

"That's where I come in," Sheila said. The group turned to look at her as she continued, "I'm the decoy. We'll switch clothes and I'll be taken on the perp walk, as if I'm being extradited to Arlington. That'll take the heat off you."

"Not to be insulting," Kit said, "but you look too young for this. You're putting yourself into a dangerous situation here."

"Trust me," Sheila said, "I could write a book on the situations I've been in."

The door opened and a female Chesterfield County police officer stepped inside. "Everything's in place."

"Thanks, Sergeant Egges," Munski said. "And thanks for calling in the media. I hope this doesn't create a credibility problem for you."

"With the press? Not a problem," she answered briskly. "You guys just do what you've gotta do."

They were huddled around a closed circuit television set. Kit was in the center with Bill Vogel on her right and Agent Davidson on her left. On either side and behind them were various Chesterfield County sheriff's deputies and police officers, their attention riveted on the small screen.

They watched as a door opened behind the jail and a petite woman dressed in brown slacks and a long-sleeved tan shirt was led outside. Her hands were cuffed in front of her, but both were raised as she held a parka in front of her face, shielding her from the glare of the media cameras stationed outside the fence. The only thing visible from her neck up was a bit of light brown hair.

Detective Munski led her to a waiting Arlington County squad car, where he placed her into the back seat. He then walked slowly around the car to the passenger side, where he slid beside a uniformed police officer. They sat there for a minute or two, the woman in back still shielding her face.

In front of the Arlington County cruiser was a Virginia State Police vehicle. Behind it was an unmarked dark blue car with a forest of antennae that shouted FBI.

As they watched, the convoy slowly pulled out.

"Don't you understand?" Kit said, exasperated. They were back in the booking room: Kit again in the center seat between Davidson and Vogel. They'd both heard her story the previous night from Carter and now they wanted to hear it from her—the events surrounding Tim's disappearance, the program she and Chen created, how she met with Toy at the gristmill, and finally, to the discovery of the embedded program.

"If we don't stop the inauguration, we can't stop what China has put into motion," she was saying. "It could take years to remove elected officials from office, and in the meantime, they can push through legislation that affects every aspect of American life. Our country could end up looking the other way while China builds up a reserve of nuclear warheads in countries all over the world—some of which could even reach the continent U.S. Why, they could even control the warheads we have here."

"She's right," Vogel said. "They took a program we developed for covert operations in other countries, and they're using it against us."

"You mean—?" Davidson started.

"That's precisely what he means," Kit said. "We've propped up governments for years, staged coups, ousted leaders—the CIA's skilled at making people think they've elected their own leaders while we're really the puppeteers."

"Only now China controls the puppets," Vogel finished.

"And if we don't stop that inauguration," Kit said, "we've handed the puppet strings to them ourselves. Don't you see? We can't let Stallworth—or any of the others—take office."

"How many elections used this program?" Agent Davidson asked.

Vogel shrugged. "We're working on that now."

"We might not be able to stop them all," Davidson said, "but we're close enough to stop Stallworth." He rose. "You'll be safe here," he said to Kit.

"I'm going with you!"

"Oh, no, you're not. I can't let you do that," Vogel said.

"Listen to me," Kit said. "Jack and Toy are here; I know that. I think Frank is involved in this, too, as well as Miranda Wade and maybe others from my office. I can identify them; you can't."

The two men exchanged glances but said nothing.

"What do you plan to do? Just drive up the interstate to the State Capitol? You won't be able to get within a mile of that place, even with your FBI credentials."

"We've got that worked out—"

"And once you're there, how do you know the person standing directly beside Stallworth isn't one of the co-conspirators? I can identify them. You can't."

When neither man responded, Kit continued, "There's flooding all over. There's a reason for FEMA to have helicopters in the air, even during the inauguration. If we can arrange for a helicopter, we can fly right onto the Capitol grounds…"

"That would be pretty tricky, with the security they're bound to have."

"Get State or Capitol Police involved, have them clear us onto the Capitol grounds—by the time the conspirators know what's happened, we'll be there."

Davidson looked across the room at Vogel. "Okay, Bill," he said. "Let's get this show on the road."

CHAPTER 42
四十二

Before the Bureau car pulled through the parking lot to the waiting helicopter, Kit was shedding the nun's habit she'd been given to get her out unnoticed; but by the time they exited, the press was long gone. However, their nervous glances were reminders that it wasn't the press they were concerned about.

While Davidson, Kit, and Vogel jumped out of the car, a pilot held the door of the aircraft open for them. Kit climbed onto the boarding step and blindly clutched at a handhold. From inside the helicopter came a strong, firm hand that grasped her and hoisted her inside.

"Thank you," she muttered automatically, moving to the far end of the helicopter.

"You're welcome."

Kit's head jerked toward the sound of Carter's voice. Her mind was filled with all the things she wanted to say to him, to tell him how much it meant to her that he believed her, that he took care of Tim, that he spoke to Davidson—but all that managed to escape her lips was, "Thank you."

He nodded, his eyes not wavering from hers. "You're welcome."

"While you guys are stuck in an endless loop," Davidson said, seating himself across from Kit, "we need to brief you on what's happening. We've informed the press that FEMA will be assessing the flood damage from the air. We're not concerned about the general public, but we do want to get the word out there in case these guys get antsy with a helicopter flying over their heads."

An officer stuck his head into the cabin and handed a box to Carter. "Five thousand copies," he said. "The best we could do on short notice."

"That'll work," Carter said.

Vogel pulled the door shut and secured it while Carter reached into the box and pulled out a fistful of papers. He handed one to Kit.

"It's the program," she mused.

"We'll drop them over the crowd as we approach the Capitol," Davidson said.

The helicopter lifted off from the Chesterfield County Airport and turned northeast. They sat in silence as they watched the ground below them grow ever smaller. Then Kit feverishly pulled out her cell phone.

"What are you doing?" Vogel asked.

"Calling my son. He's got to be terrified by now. I didn't want to call him before, in case—well, just in case."

"Where is he?"

Kit responded while the phone was ringing. By the time Tim answered, Vogel was on his cell phone, issuing directives.

"Mom," Tim said. "What's going on? I saw you arrested on TV…"

Kit hurriedly explained, adding, "Don't be scared, Tim. Someone's on their way to get you now."

"I'm not scared," he answered. "But you'd better tell me what they look like and when they'll be here, or they won't find me."

She handed the phone to Vogel and listened while he described the agents en route to the Hampton Inn, a wry smile breaking out across her face. Tim had come a long way from barricading himself in his bedroom.

As Vogel finished the call, Davidson's phone rang. A moment later, he clicked it off and announced, "The warrants have been issued."

"Oh my God," she breathed a few short minutes later as they approached downtown Richmond. In contrast to the snow and rain the area had suffered through in recent weeks, the sun was shining high and bright in the winter sky, lending a spring-like quality to the day. The light cast the stark white Capitol in a diamond-bright brilliance that was only enhanced by the colorful spectators surrounding the south portico and lawn.

"How many people are down there?" she said as they peered outside.

"I heard they were expecting about seven thousand," Carter said.

"It looks like a coup…" Kit exclaimed. "Look, what are the military—?"

"It doesn't have anything to do with us," Vogel replied, calmly surveying the aircraft below. "They're fighter jets from the Virginia Air National Guard; they're scheduled to do a flyover after the inauguration."

"And the cannons?"

"Howitzers, for a 19-gun salute to the new governor."

"My God," she said again.

"Get ready," the pilot said. "We've been cleared for one pass directly over the Capitol before landing."

As they neared Capitol Square, Carter divided the copies among them, and they opened the windows to the helicopter. The aircraft, though it remained a fair distance above the building, was close enough for Kit to see the upturned faces of the crowd below, the starched uniforms of the marching bands, and the throngs of dark suits on the steps behind the podium.

"He's being sworn in!" Kit cried out.

They jockeyed for position at the windows. "Not yet," Vogel said, sweat breaking out across his upper lip. "It's the lieutenant governor; Stallworth won't be far behind. We're running out of time."

"Now!" Carter said, throwing a handful of programs out the window.

Kit, Davidson, and Vogel followed suit. The rotor blades caught some of the papers and hurled them far from the crowds below, while others found their way onto the steps and into the surrounding stands. As the helicopter turned toward the north lawn, Kit saw several reaching curiously for the papers.

"They won't understand it," Kit said.

"It doesn't matter," Carter said. "We just have to get it out there."

"We have FBI and Capitol Police meeting us as soon as we touch down," the pilot announced.

As the helicopter approached the landing site, a clearing on the Capitol grounds, Kit's cell phone rang. All four looked at it as if it were a loaded gun. "It's Frank's cell phone," she mused.

She answered tentatively.

"Kit," Frank said in a voice that seemed odd, as if his vocal cords were pinched, "please stop what you're doing."

"What are you talking about?" she said, while Vogel leaned toward the phone to listen in.

"If you go through with this, they'll kill me. It was all a trap—Miranda included—to get to you through me. I didn't know, Kit, I swear I didn't know…"

Kit's eyes met Vogel's. Whatever Frank did to her and to their marriage, he was still Tim's father. She hesitated before responding, "You got yourself in this situation. You get yourself out of it." Then she clicked the phone off.

The helicopter touched down on the north lawn. Carter had the door open before the blades stopped turning. Kit saw a swarm of officers running toward them.

They were out of the aircraft in seconds, racing around the building, heading for the south portico. Stallworth was standing now, to thunderous applause.

He was at the podium when they pushed their way past the spectators. He raised his right hand, and his voice boomed over the microphones. "I, Theodore Jeffries Stallworth…"

Kit arrived at the podium first, nearly knocking over Judge Sulley.

"Stop!" she cried out, her voice echoing over the microphones and across the grounds.

"What is the meaning of this?" Judge Sulley exclaimed. He looked around him as if searching for the police.

"Carry on," Stallworth directed, his right hand still raised. While the judge struggled to regain his composure, the governor-elect began reciting the oath without him.

Davidson pushed his way to the podium. "Theodore Stallworth," he said, his voice booming over the PA system, "a warrant has been issued for your arrest on charges of espionage and acting as a nonregistered agent of a foreign power to fraudulently control the outcome of a federally monitored election to the benefit of that foreign nation."

A collective gasp moved through the audience. Kit was facing Stallworth with her back to the crowd. Her eyes moved away from his face and to the spectators behind the podium, to the outgoing governor who was obviously perplexed, to the members of the State Senate and House and their families, all carrying expressions of total shock... and to Jack.

The blood felt as if it had drained from her face, and her heart froze in her chest. She watched as he rose from his chair, his back ramrod straight, his hand moving to his belt—and then she saw the glint of the gun.

She turned to Carter, a cry on her lips, her arms reaching toward him to push him out of the line of fire, but he was looking over her shoulder to something beyond her, his own face drained of all color, his lips parted as if he were struggling for words.

And then his hand crashed against her chest, catapulting her onto the steps as shots rang out. He fell on top of her like a lead weight, knocking the breath out of her; she struggled to shove him off so she could breathe, but she was unable to move. There was blood everywhere—all over his hair and his clothes, all over her, her hands streaked with it as she fought to rouse him.

And then he groaned and struggled to get up. All around her, she heard screams and the sound of running; over his shoulder, she saw a herd of feet dashing in every direction, legs in stockings and heels, dark pants with polished black shoes—and then she saw Stallworth's face.

She realized then that Stallworth was lying across them both and Carter was fighting to push him off, until there were hands that appeared out of nowhere, grasping the man who would be governor and hauling him off of them like a bag of mulch.

"Are you okay?" Carter yelled.

"Yes," she said breathlessly as he rolled off of her.

She managed to sit up, gasping for air as she searched the stands for Jack and Toy—and then she realized that the back of Carter's jacket was covered with blood. "Are you all right?" she screamed.

"I'm fine," he said.

"You've been shot!"

"I don't think so," he said as if in a daze.

Their eyes fell on Stallworth at exactly the same moment. He lay beside them, his eyes staring straight ahead, his black suit covered in blood, a gaping wound in the center of his chest. Carter turned him over. His back looked like bloody hamburger.

She realized then that silence had set in, that the steps were empty, that the front row of chairs where Stallworth had been seated only a few moments before rising to take the oath of office was pockmarked with blood and flesh. She rose shakily to her feet and peered around.

Jack lay on the Capitol steps, his head in a pool of blood, his eyes unseeing, his arms stretched outward and his feet resting several steps above his head, one foot strangely without a shoe. Vogel was leaning against an overturned row of chairs, struggling to tear his clothes away from a wound to his arm, and Davidson was rushing across the south lawn even as uniformed officers dashed in every direction.

Kit rushed to Vogel's aid and tore his jacket off of him, then ripped his shirtsleeve into shreds to apply a tourniquet to his arm. Somewhere behind her, she heard Carter's voice but it seemed far away and she couldn't make out the words. Her eyes drifted upward to men standing along the rooflines, men in uniform with rifles raised to their shoulders, peering through scopes at the surrounding terrain.

Then she saw the commotion in an open window across the street. It struck her what Carter had been looking at when he pushed her to the ground; as she had struggled to tell him of Jack's pistol, he had spotted a sniper trained on her.

Carter came to Vogel's side, helping to tighten the tourniquet, and her eyes fell again on Stallworth. Had the sniper's bullet reached its intended destination, she would be lying there now in a pool of *her* blood, and Stallworth would be preparing to assume power.

And then Stallworth gasped.

CHAPTER 43

四十三

Kit had just finished packing the last box when the telephone rang with the receptionist's announcement that she was escorting a visitor to her office.

She was taping the box shut when Carter poked his head into her office.

"Going somewhere?" he asked.

"They're shutting down UCT."

"Where does that leave you?"

"Off the record?" she gave him a quick smile. "I'm going to Langley. I'll be the key programmer assigned to figure out which elections were rigged."

Carter pulled up a chair and sat down.

"I caught your segment this morning," Kit continued. "You said Stallworth died at the scene."

"Yeah."

"You know he died en route to the hospital."

"Are you telling me I reported the facts wrong?" he said with feigned surprise. "That's going to come as a shock to Morley, especially since he gave me that raise."

"Congratulations, by the way."

"Same to you. Anyway, I thought you'd be more interested in China's official response."

Kit chuckled. "They did exactly what I expected. Deny involvement, and blame everything on a radical group that has no connection whatsoever to the Chinese government."

There was a moment of silence before Carter asked, "So what happens now? We stopped Stallworth's inauguration, but how many more have already been put into office? What happens with them?"

Kit perched atop her desk. "It's up to the Supreme Court, I guess. Every politician that didn't win is claiming the other party was part of the China conspiracy. We'll go through all the programs, locate the ones that were rigged, charges will undoubtedly be filed, there'll be a witch hunt in Congress—"

"I hope this doesn't usher in another McCarthy era."

Kit shrugged. "Everyone's pointing fingers at everyone else right now."

Carter rose and stepped toward the desk. "And how about you? How are you doing?"

"I'm okay, thanks to you."

"Something tells me, you'd have done fine without me," he said. "How's Tim and your parents?"

"They're all okay. Thanks for everything you did for them."

"I didn't do anything for your parents," Carter said. "They can take care of themselves."

Kit grinned. "Yeah, I guess they can, at that. Mom bought that combination medic alert and alarm for Dad when he became confined to a wheelchair. All these years, he complained it was a waste of money."

"Guess he doesn't think that now."

"Got that right. Anyway, my parents are in town for a few days. They took Tim to visit his dad today."

"Oh?"

"Well, he is still his dad, you know, even if he is behind bars."

"From what I hear, he'll be there for quite awhile."

"He was denied bail, but he's cooperating with the authorities…which is more than we can say about Toy."

"What are the charges?" Carter said.

"Frank's been charged with espionage; so has Miranda. From what I've been told, they used Miranda to get to me through Frank, when I was assigned to work with Chen. Toy's been charged with a lot more, including kidnapping and murder. But the guy who stopped to help us when we left Ski Top Mountain—they haven't located him yet."

"I heard they've identified him, though. He's a professional hit man—guy named Voorhees—"

"That's right. Johan Voorhees." She rubbed her chin. "He might have slipped out of the country by now. From what I hear, he's wanted all over the world. It's only a matter of time before they get him."

"It might take them awhile," Carter said. "I guess the guy is pretty skilled at masquerading—"

"Yeah, including masquerading as a security guard at a ski resort."

"Munski tells me that all the money going into your accounts were payoffs to Frank."

"Well, not all the money," Kit said. "Some of it was a payoff to me, to buy my silence." She smiled. "Which was obviously a waste. But Frank had opened a series of accounts I knew nothing about. They're still sorting things out, but it appears Miranda may have impersonated me on those accounts. They've frozen all of them in the States, but some of the money was transferred to Swiss accounts; they're working through the Swiss government to get those funds frozen or returned. It remains to be seen, whether they'll seize our house and other assets."

"Who decides that?"

"The courts; maybe the prosecuting attorneys. There's no doubt I didn't know what was going on, and half the house belongs to me…" her voice trailed off.

"So, what will you do now?"

She hopped off the desk. "Take things one day at a time. With Bernard, Joan, and Jack dead and Frank, Miranda and Toy in prison, it's all I can do."

There was a knock at the door and Chen stuck his head inside. After exchanging pleasantries, he announced he was leaving for vacation. For some reason that Kit couldn't quite put her finger on, she didn't really believe it was a vacation but rather an assignment. As Chen left her office, she wondered how long it would be before she saw him again. Just as quickly, she thought of Jansson and Bonelli. Both men had disappeared without a trace; no one was even sure of their true identities. She wondered what would have happened to Chen and her if they hadn't overpowered them on that fateful morning, and hoped that Chen would never encounter them again.

"Do you have any plans for tonight?" Carter asked, pulling her back to the present.

"Hadn't thought about it. Are you asking me out?"

"What if I did?"

She rolled her eyes. "I would probably say yes, but *only* if you were to take me to the new Italian restaurant that just opened up in Crystal City—"

"The fancy one, where I'd have to wear a tie? You mean, I might see you in a dress for a change—?"

She threw the roll of tape at him. "Fat chance. Now get out of here before I change my mind."

He caught the tape in midair. "Pick you up at seven."

"Don't be late."

He juggled the tape on his way out the door, and then tossed it over his shoulder. A few seconds later, Kit heard him whistling on his way to the elevator.

Then she grabbed the box and her purse. She had a new assignment waiting for her at Langley, one the country wouldn't want delayed.

A Note from the Author

While the characters in this book are fictitious, the statements made by both Carter and Stallworth regarding China, Tibet, and the United States were the result of exhaustive research.

Stallworth's statements in Chapter 24 regarding China's peaceful takeover of Tibet, the progress made in Tibet under Chinese rule, and the freedoms, luxuries and civil rights both the Tibetans and the Chinese populace enjoy, reflect the Chinese government's official position. Many of Stallworth's "facts" were taken directly from official government documents and newspapers owned by the Chinese government.

Carter's statements in Chapters 24 and 35, (except for the shoe factories in Virginia), regarding the brutal takeover of Tibet, the civil rights violations, the uneven ratio of imports versus exports, and the slavery conditions he alleges exist today in China and Tibet, were the result of research involving United States government transcripts, including some that were compiled as official reports to Congress.

Both the United States and Chinese government acknowledge other statements, such as the Sister Cities cited within.

I leave it up to the reader to form his or her own opinions.

About the Author

p.m.terrell is the internationally acclaimed author of the suspense/thriller *Kickback*, published by Drake Valley Press. She is also the author of several nonfiction computer books, including *Creating the Perfect Database*, (Scott-Foresman), *The Dynamics of WordPerfect* and *The Dynamics of Reflex*, (Dow Jones-Irwin), and *Memento WordPerfect*, (Edimicro, Paris).

Ms. Terrell is the founder of McClelland Enterprises, Inc., one of the first companies in the Washington, DC area devoted to PC training, and Continental Software Development Corporation, which provides programming, applications development, website design, and computer consulting services. Her clients have included the U.S. Secret Service, CIA and Department of Defense, as well as various local law enforcement agencies.

Ms. Terrell is a staunch supporter of Crime Stoppers, Crime Solvers, and Crime Lines, which offer rewards and anonymity to individuals reporting information on criminal activity, resulting in arrests, recovery of stolen property, and seizure of illegal drugs. She is proud to serve on the Chesterfield County/Colonial Heights Crime Solvers Board of Directors.

Visit her website at www.pmterrell.com.